A Blazing Bond

Book two of
The Heart Pyre

Audrey Martin

A BLAZING BOND

Paperback edition ISBN: 9789998797260

EBook edition ISBN: 9789998797253

Book Cover Design by Audrey Martin

Book Cover Illustration by Mona May

1st edition 2026

Daishegian Empire
Kano-Raeki Federation
Kingdom of Kal-Hemma
Mashod
High-Foshe
FaeHosh
River Kal
Menakala
Jodash
Hemmakem
River Hemmahes
Northern Jodan
Kefo's Pike
River Hemma
Namesh
Red Hill
Southern Jodan
Mohregi
Rosham
Meshohrem
Napahrit
Baedan
Historical Academy
Military Academy
Mellahen
Hrevim
Paeri-Boerite
Vellashta
Oceansthrow
Maevian Archipelago
Boeritian Islands
MaeVashot
The Grey Isles

Meshöhrem
Baedan
Nappahrit
Hrevim
Military Academy
City of Rancor
Vellashta
Oceansthrow

Chapter One

Rena

Rena stared at Logan's motionless body on the bed, the exhaustion of the last few days settling in her bones like a deep void. Asha and Rena had somehow managed to drag Logan's unconscious body back to Halvint after they were attacked by guards and luckily Darian, the innkeeper, had agreed to shelter them and helped them clean the long cut that ran over Logan's stomach. The wound wasn't deep enough to be deadly, but he'd lost a lot of blood on their way to safety and Rena wasn't sure they could grant him the rest that he needed. Darian and his wife had done their best to help — cleaning and bandaging Logan's wound, mixing a salve for it, letting him sleep in a quiet room — but how much could that truly help if they needed to leave town again as quickly as possible? Rena didn't want to stay in Darian's inn for longer than necessary, not with the possibility that the guards were still looking for them. She couldn't bear the thought of putting another person in danger.

Logan had been hurt, Kalani and Rodrick had been captured, Finn had gone missing, and it was all because she'd asked them for help. None of them had any connection to the Crow; they would have never crossed paths if it weren't for Rena and her stupid search for a sister who might not even be alive anymore.

Her throat tightened until she could barely breathe, her vision went blurry and the events of the previous day played out in her mind on repeat. She didn't quite understand what had happened, no matter how much she racked her brain. They'd learned that some of the Crow's acolytes had been hiding in Halvint and Logan couldn't help himself from trying to figure out why, so of course Rena had had to follow him. They'd snuck through the house until they inexplicably found her sister's dress in between the Crow's laundry.

Rena curled up on herself, sitting on the floor next to Logan's bed, the life of the tavern below faintly breaking the silence of the room. She buried her face in the dress in her lap and breathed in, pretending she could still smell Maya and her parents' bakery. No matter how much she replayed the events in her mind, she couldn't figure out why the Crow would have her sister's dress. Surely it had to mean that Maya was still alive, surely the Crow was keeping her somewhere. But why? What could they possibly want with Maya?

One of the Crow had told them where Maya might have been taken, although he hadn't sounded too sure about it. In all honesty, he hadn't sounded sure about Maya still being alive either but why else would the Crow have had her dress? Not wanting to lose any time, Rena and her companions had set out to cross the border, still unsure of where Finn might be, but had been attacked by guards just outside Halvint. Guards who had strangely been accompanied by Inkra, one of the Crow Logan had locked up in the basement of their hideout.

Rena wasn't naïve. She realised that not everyone who joined the guard corps had perfect intentions, but she couldn't believe that an entire troop had so willingly helped Inkra. There had been at least five riders circling their caravan as they'd left Halvint, potentially more. Had they been members of the Crow pretending to be guards? Had the Crow infiltrated the guard corps? Were the Crow sitting on a mountain of gold and that's how Inkra had convinced the guards to help her? Could the Crow offer them something else that would make them betray their kingdom? Her head hurt with all these possibilities, one more unthinkable than the other.

Her entire body was buzzing. All she wanted to do was run ahead and find Maya, but she knew she'd never succeed on her own. She didn't actually want to abandon her new companions, not after having dragged them into this mess, but her throat tightened whenever she thought of reasons the Crow might have taken Maya and she didn't know what to do with all those feelings.

Her eyes started to burn, tears welling up and spreading across the dress pressed against her face. She wanted her sister back. Wanted to hold her, run a hand over her hair, kiss her cheek, laugh with her, scold her, talk until the small hours of the morning. It hurt so much. The memories and the longing and the uncertainty and the hope that maybe, just maybe, she was still alive and Rena could see her once more. If she couldn't ever see her parents or brothers or uncle and aunt and cousins or even her friends ever again, at least she might be able to reunite with Maya. If only her luck held steady. If only the universe willed it so. She would never wish for anything else ever again. Her hand slipped to her necklace where Maya's ring hung next to the leaf-shaped pendant, the metal cold on the burn scar it had created just a few days ago.

"Fuck," Logan muttered as his body finally came back to life, and the utterance dragged Rena back to reality with a jolt.

"Logan?" she asked, her voice hoarse and hesitant.

She pushed herself up, her fingers and legs tingling all over, and came to sit on the bed next to Logan. She had never seen him this pale, his usual tan skin now the colour of wheat grains. His breathing was laboured and his brown curls were damp with sweat.

"How are you feeling?"

He raised a hand into the air and vaguely waved it around before letting it fall back down onto the bed, looking at her with half-closed eyes.

"Yeah," Rena breathed out.

Her gaze drifted down to her sister's dress in her lap, her fingers worrying nervously at the fabric.

"Everything hurts," Logan replied.

"I could ask Darian's wife if she has anything against the pain. She's the one who dressed your wound." Rena looked back at Logan and winced. "It really doesn't look great. I'm sorry."

"You know what would help? Like a whole bottle of wine. The really deep red one from up north. The one that tastes like berries."

Rena chuckled, her feelings tugging painfully at her heart.

"I don't think that would be wise."

"I never claimed to be a wise man."

Rena looked out over the room, her eyes idly fixed on the door. She felt an unusual reluctance to leave, as if she were afraid. She didn't know when Asha would be back from going to talk to Ocassian in the city of Rancor so until then, she was the one who had to keep Logan safe and as long as they stayed inside this room, it felt like no one was going to find them. Rationally, she knew that wasn't the case — Darian had simply brought them to the most remote room in his inn and if the guards wanted, they could very easily storm the building and find them — but she couldn't shake the feeling that if she stepped even just one foot out the door, calamity would strike at once.

"How are *you* feeling?" Logan asked, looking at her with concern.

"I'm okay," she replied automatically.

He didn't respond right away but then quietly said, "Liar."

She thought about telling him all about the chaos inside her mind but before any words could leave her lips, footsteps broke through the silence. Rena shot up, her eyes fixed on the door, her entire body tense. She barely had the time to think of what she could use to defend themselves before the door swung open and Asha stepped in.

"Oh, thank the stars," Rena sighed and sat back down.

"You're both awake," Asha stated and stepped to the foot of Logan's bed, closing the door behind her. "Good."

Logan tried to push himself up, but a cry of pain escaped him not even halfway through.

"Nope, bad idea. Very bad idea."

He lowered himself back down and draped both arms over his eyes.

"Don't force it," Asha told him.

She unbuckled her scabbard and placed it next to Logan's legs, then stretched her arms above her head.

"Did you run into any trouble?" Rena looked up at Asha whose exhaustion was plainly written on her face.

She shook her head and leaned against the wall, crossing her arms in front of her. "There was barely anyone on the roads. If someone's looking for us, it's definitely not the entire guard corps. I don't know which town the ones who attacked us belong to, but they seem to have crawled back into the hole they came from, at least for now." She tilted her head back and closed her eyes, sighing heavily before glancing at Rena and Logan. "You remember that they yelled something at us, right? That they were stopping us under someone's authority. Under whose?"

Rena frowned in concentration, her eyes drifting down as she remembered the previous night. She'd sat at the front of the caravan with Rodrick when the guards had ridden up to them from behind. They'd tried to get them to halt, claiming something about having to inspect their vehicle on the authority of some captain.

"Slanac?" Rena hesitated, only half remembering it. "Sarad... Sirac?"

"Silac," Logan replied sombrely. "Head of the guard in Hollowtooth. Strange fellow."

"Right." Asha ran a hand over her short-cropped, black hair, not having had any opportunity to shave it over the last week. "That fucker."

"Do you know him?" Rena asked.

"Heard of him," Logan replied. "A lot. Nothing good though. The whole family's got a bad reputation. Ran into him once or twice before but never for long."

"He's got a reputation for playing by his own rules," Asha added.

"What does that mean for us?" Rena glanced from Asha to Logan in concern. "Do you think he's working with the Crow? I mean, Inkra was with the guards when they attacked us."

"Wouldn't surprise me," Asha grumbled. "Nothing much's been done to stop the Crow until now. They probably run this stupid kingdom."

"That would be horrible," Rena murmured, her eyes drifting to the ground again.

She'd learned by now that Asha tended towards the dramatic and fatalistic but what if she was right after all? That this murderous group had taken control of their kingdom and no one knew about it. Rena was too exhausted to know whether the idea made any sense or not. She felt like she had a million angry bees in her head and none of them let her think rationally.

"I'm not convinced all of the guards are working with the Crow." Carefully Logan pushed himself up to lean back on his elbows, the pain distorting his face. "They'd be swarming the streets and barging into the inn if they were. If you didn't see anyone roaming the streets looking for us, then they probably don't have enough guards available to conduct a widespread search, which means only Silac's small group knows about the attack."

"I wouldn't call Hollowtooth's entire guard corps a small group," Asha muttered.

"We don't know if all of them are helping the Crow. Let's not assume the worst."

"Assuming the worst keeps us alive."

"But what do we do now?" Rena butted in. "Do we know where they've taken Rodrick and Kalani? Did they take them to Hollowtooth or the Crow's hideout? How can we even find out?"

"I spoke to Ocassian about it." Asha shifted uncomfortably, a shadow falling over her face. "We can't know for certain where they are but it's more likely they were brought to Hollowtooth than the Crow's hideout. Hollowtooth is closer than Baedan and crossing a border has its difficulties as a guard. They'd have to justify why they left their own province, especially when they're transporting prisoners. They could maybe try to sneak their way to the hideout but they'll probably think it too risky."

"Is Cass joining us?" Logan asked.

Asha shook her head. "Rancor is moving. They have to focus on that, especially with everything going on at the moment."

The city of Rancor where Asha, Logan, and Kalani were from was a marvel of a place. The kingdom had a few of these so-called cities of outlaws that welcomed anyone, whether they wanted to stay for a day or the rest of their lives. They were built in such a way that they could move at any moment as the buildings were mostly tents. With the help of all inhabitants, they could be dismantled whenever deemed necessary.

"What about your tent, Logan? Asha, and your uncle?" A sudden fear for her friends' homes overcame Rena.

In a regular town they would have been able to just lock the doors to keep their belongings safe — even if there was always the possibility of someone breaking in — but in a city made of tents, especially once all the other tents had left, how could any of it be safe? She felt guilty for keeping them from moving with the rest of Rancor. She wouldn't have been angry if they'd decided to go back to the city, even though she desperately needed their help.

"I've got friends who'll take care of it," Logan replied with a shrug. "Wouldn't be the first time. And I'm certainly not the only one who isn't home when the city moves. Can't really wait for everyone to come back before moving."

"And there are enough people looking after my uncle," Asha added.

"But Cass really trusts us to save their wife on our own?" Logan asked with a hint of disbelief. "Even after knowing who we are?"

"Wife?" Rena looked from Asha to Logan in confusion. "Are we... talking about Kalani? Ocassian and Kalani are married?"

"Yeah, I suppose that's never come up before," Logan murmured in contemplation.

"They've been married for a while," Asha replied. "Since before I met either of them. But to get back to Logan's question, I think Cass trusts Kalani to save herself if we fuck up. Which we're not gonna do."

"All right, but what's our plan?" Rena nervously played with her necklace, her stomach twisting at the thought of running into the guards a second time. "Are the roads safe enough to travel on? I know you said you didn't see anyone on your way to Rancor but getting to Hollowtooth might be a bit more dangerous, right?"

She glanced over at Logan, who seemed fine for now, but she knew what his stomach looked like under his shirt and bandages.

"We can ask Darian for some help," Asha replied, although she didn't look happy about the prospect. "Maybe he can drive us there by cart and hide us underneath something."

The idea didn't thrill Renna either — they'd already involved Darian too much, and she didn't want to endanger him any further — but she had to admit it might be the fastest and safest way to get to Hollowtooth.

"And once we're there?" Logan shifted position although he didn't seem to find one that was comfortable. "We just wait for Kalani to drop from the sky into our arms? Getting to Hollowtooth is the easy part; we can find a million ways to get there without dying. I'm worried about any steps after. Either the guards are keeping Kalani and Rodrick in a secret hideout or they're being treated like any other regular prisoner and neither of those options seem like something we can solve in an afternoon."

Asha sighed and ran a hand over her face.

"I'm not sure yet." She groaned and pushed herself away from the wall, nervously pacing the room. "There are a few people we can contact in Hollowtooth — Cass told me some names — but I don't know how much I trust them. The only one I've met before probably won't be any help. She doesn't have much sway in the city, especially if we're going against the guard corps or the Crow. Everyone else... we simply have to trust Cass' judgement."

She stopped and ran a hand over her face once more, standing in the middle of the room for a few heartbeats, unmoving, until she let her hand fall to her side again.

"We'll figure it out once we're in Hollowtooth. There's no point in wasting any more time here when all it's doing is giving us a headache."

Chapter Two

Rena

As Asha predicted, Darian was willing to help them get out of Halvint. His wife claimed she needed to drive to Hollowtooth anyway, and Rena wondered whether that was true or whether she simply wanted them out of her town. She assured them that if she hid them underneath a canvas covering the back of the cart and she took the slow roads to avoid patrolling guards, they'd arrive safely. Rena wasn't sure she liked the plan — they didn't really have anything to defend themselves with if anyone did decide to inspect the cart — but she also hadn't come up with any alternatives.

Darian and his wife also gave Rena, Asha and Logan new clothing. Logan and Rena's clothes were covered in blood, unsalvageable, and although Asha's tunic had been miraculously spared from any major stains, its shade of blue and specific cut were too recognisable to blend into any crowd. She had, however, refused to take off her golden jewellery and instead opted to hide them underneath the hood of a short cape.

Their journey to Hollowtooth was oppressive, the heat building up underneath the canvas, Rena's muscles hurting from the little space she had. Sweat stuck her hair to her skin and she could smell the others' acrid odour beside her. She closed her eyes and thought of her sister, how all the pain and hardship would lead to her safety, that it wasn't all in vain. They just needed to get Rodrick and Kalani out, just needed to find their way over the border, just needed to follow the Crow's trail. It wouldn't be easy, but it would all be worth it. She had to believe in it — she couldn't falter now. Vivid images of what her life could be like in ten years flashed before her eyes, how she would live in a modest house with her sister and they would operate a small bakery together. Her new friends could come visit them at any moment, stay with them for however long they wanted. Maybe Rodrick and Vincent would permanently live with them. Perhaps Maya wasn't even the only other survivor from Oceansthrow; maybe they'd find more people and rebuild their town as best as they could. Rena could even reopen their school and help the younger children learn to read and write.

The cart stopped and Rena's eyes shot open, the visions of a better life dissipating. Darian's wife had dropped them off at the edge of the fisher's district, not far from the ocean, between old buildings that had seen better days. The group unfolded from beneath the canvas, the fresh salty air filling Rena's lungs, her head spinning from her blood rushing back into her body. Rena and Asha didn't take their eyes off Logan as he got off the cart, making sure he wouldn't collapse after their long journey. He tried to wave them off, but it was plain to see that he was struggling. His skin tone didn't look much better under the bright sunlight and thick drops of sweat ran down his temples. Even though he smiled at them and joked around, his knuckles were white where he was holding on to the cart, his legs struggling to hold him up.

Rena looked around, trying to figure out where they could find a bed for him to rest, but she already knew how he would react if she proposed they take a break. Was arguing with him worth it? He clearly needed the rest but there was no time to waste if they wanted to guarantee Kalani and Rodrick's safety. She hated that resting had become synonymous with wasting time. It should never be considered a waste, especially when someone was hurt as bad as Logan was, but they had no money, no place to stay, and they still knew nothing about Kalani and Rodrick's whereabouts.

The group said their goodbyes, thanking Darian's wife profusely for her help, then set out towards the centre of town. Rena's daydreaming had affected her more than she wanted to admit, her emotions in a bigger turmoil than before. Reality didn't seem solid anymore, as if a veil had been draped over the people and buildings surrounding her, as if it had all been plunged deep under the ocean. She desperately wanted to snap out of it, knowing that this hope would only hurt her in the end, but she couldn't get herself to focus on what was right in front of them, on what was important.

Hollowtooth was a busy place, somewhere people came to do business and rest near the sea. The houses looked grander than what Rena was used to from Oceansthrow or even Halvint, but they couldn't compare to the splendour of the Plains' inner sections. The roads were less busy than during the height of summer when people from all over the kingdom came to enjoy the heat and the cool water, but plenty of people still whizzed past them as they left the fisher's district.

Hollowtooth was an old city that had tried to keep the charm it acquired centuries ago, and as much as they'd managed to not let it fall into disrepair, some things just couldn't survive the test of time. The cobblestones had deep grooves in them, created by years of carts traversing town. Some streets were even too narrow for carts to pass through, built long before the kingdom had formed, forcing vendors to get their wares delivered on foot. The air had a lingering sour smell, a faint whiff of fish that it could never get rid of, perpetually mixing with the saltiness of the ocean.

Logan led them through the crowd on the main road, weaving between the mass of people. He was standing upright as if nothing was wrong, but Rena could still see the pain in how tense his shoulders were. She wished he could be more honest with them, that he could admit that he wasn't feeling well, but she supposed that a lifetime on the road had taught him to ignore any discomforts.

Rena felt tense herself. Her eyes kept wandering from side to side, scanning people's faces, dreading the moment when she would recognise someone. She couldn't remember what any of their attackers had looked like — not truly — but she thought that if she saw them, alarm bells would go off in her mind. But what if the guards recognised them first? They were wearing different clothes but there wasn't much they could do about their faces. If the wrong person recognised them, it could doom them all.

Rena had wrapped the shawl she'd received around her head, the way her mother used to wear them. She pulled it lower over her forehead and kept her gaze low, hoping no one would be able to see her face. Her heart was racing, her hands trembling. If someone were to recognise them, what could they do? They certainly wouldn't be able to fight, so running away was the only option, but where to? They were in Captain

Silac's city now; if one guard recognised them, how likely were they to send all of the city's guards looking for them? Now that she thought about it, it felt wild that they would be going towards the people who were looking for them instead of far away from them.

Rena shook her head, knowing she couldn't let those thoughts run rampant in her mind. They had to focus on saving Rodrick and Kalani. The faster they could regroup, the faster they could rescue Maya. Rena didn't have the time nor the luxury of panicking, no matter how much her body wanted to.

They followed the crowd to a busy market where merchants were selling all kinds of things, but worst of all, food that made Rena's stomach grumble and turn until the pain made her dizzy. She'd barely even noticed how little she'd eaten over the last day until all those smells hit her.

"I'm so hungry," she murmured as they passed a stall selling cheeses, her eyes glued to the variety on display.

A moment later, Logan was holding out two fist-sized balls of fried dough covered in almonds.

"Here you go," he whispered as he bit into a third one.

She stared at them, her steps faltering.

"Where..." she started, then thought better of it.

Clearly, Logan didn't have the same concerns about not attracting any attention as she had. She waited for someone to yell after them, to come running and demand their payment, but as no one did, Rena carefully took one of the dough balls and bit into it. The crunch of the almonds gave way to the sweet softness of the honey cake. She closed her eyes for a second, letting the taste of the pastry flood her senses, feeling the dough pass down her throat to her stomach, alleviating the dull pain of hunger.

"You better not get us into trouble," Asha grumbled as she took the last dough ball.

"Would be the easiest way to get into the holding cells though." Logan looked back with a grin and winked at Asha.

"It would also be the stupidest."

"Yeah, I know." Logan rolled his eyes and continued walking, keeping his voice low so only Asha and Rena could hear him. "But we haven't exactly come up with a better plan yet either. It's not a place we can just walk into without getting noticed. I've been inside the guard station before. They really put a lot of money into that building. Renovated all of it about five years ago after some guy blew up the back walls. It's not a big building but the cells don't touch the outer walls anymore. Makes it harder to escape."

He paused and looked at the stall they were walking past, then pointed at some colourful headscarves, glancing at Rena as if to ask if she might be interested. Rena barely had time to process and react before he had already shrugged and turned back around. She looked back at the scarves in confusion as they continued on their way, wondering if there was something she had missed. Maybe he wanted her to try them on as a disguise, maybe they held a specific significance that could be a clue, or maybe he simply thought she might like the way they looked.

"There's this spot in the entrance hall," Logan continued murmuring as if he'd never stopped, his eyes wandering from stall to stall, "where you can look into the room in the back where the cells are. If Kalani and Rodrick are actually being held here and we're lucky enough for them to be in the right cells, we would be able to see them. That would be the easiest way to verify if they're here or not. Otherwise, we'll have to somehow find our way into the cells which honestly isn't that difficult — it's more the getting out that's a bit of a headache. The spot to look into the other room is a bit weird though. Might make you look suspicious if you stay for too long. You kind of have to stand to the very left against the wall and hope someone walks through the door to the back so you can look through."

"I could try," Rena whispered, hoping they could get this first step over with as quickly as possible. "I could pretend to be lost if they start talking to me."

"You're probably our best shot," Logan admitted, although the grimace on his face showed how unhappy he was with the idea. "If you act all young and sweet, they won't get mad at you, at least not to the point where they'd arrest you. Asha and I don't have that privilege."

Before them, the market parted to reveal a big, rectangular building that had clearly been renovated recently — the façade's white stucco glowed in the sunlight while the trim of the door and windows had been painted a deep blue that hadn't had time to fade yet. Iron bars encased the windows all around, which made it difficult to look inside.

They strolled to the edge of the market, to the left of the guard station, huddling together as if they were waiting for someone. They kept one eye on the station to observe it, the other on the market crowd, but nothing much seemed out of the ordinary. Guards and civilians walked in and out with varying degrees of urgency, sometimes together, more often alone.

Logan started to get impatient, unable to stand still to the point that Rena feared he might burst into the station on his own. She took a deep breath, collected all her courage and calmly walked in, clutching her hands tightly together so they wouldn't tremble.

The station wasn't much different from the one in Halvint. A handful of tables were strewn across the rather small front room with people sitting or standing around them. The wall to her left was covered in wanted posters showing the faces of supposed criminals. Her eyes flew over them, scared she might recognise any of the faces, that she might find herself on one, but luck seemed to be on her side.

Rena steel herself and walked further, pulling her scarf over her face as much as possible without it looking strange. She told herself over and over that the guards who had attacked them were, in all likelihood, out looking for them and therefore no one in the room would be able to recognise her. But no matter how often she repeated the words in her mind, she couldn't make herself believe them.

She slowly approached the left wall, feigning interest in the posters. She hoped that if she didn't look at any of the guards, they wouldn't notice her presence, but deep down she was deathly afraid she might recognise one of them and they in turn would recognise her. She kept her eyes fixed on the wall until she stood right in front of it; only then did she dare glance towards the back of the room. Behind the desks, to the very left, was a door, as Logan had mentioned. Rena angled herself with her back facing most of the room so that she could see whenever someone walked through the door. Soon, the door opened as a guard entered the front room, slow enough for Rena to see the metal bars that made up the holding cells but too fast for her to recognise any of the prisoners inside.

She grew increasingly nervous with every passing second. She slowly paced the length of the wall, letting her eyes trail the posters. She couldn't keep her mind from imagining what her own face would look like on one of these posters, what Logan's or Asha's or Rodrick's would look like. What would their charges be? What might their punishments be?

A cold shiver ran down her back. She knelt down and untied the bow holding up her canvas shoes. She couldn't look at these posters anymore. They filled her with too much dread, reminding her of everything she had gone through. Her throat tightened, making it hard to breathe. She couldn't let herself get caught, not if there was no one else left to save her sister. She had to be the one to get Maya back, to free her from whatever the Crow had planned for her.

She retied her shoes, taking her time to flatten the ribbon perfectly to her ankle. She glanced towards the door, but no matter how often it opened, she could never get a good look into the other room.

"Can I help you, miss?"

Rena shot up and found herself face to face with an older, heavyset woman, maybe in her late forties, with a weathered guard's uniform and a bored expression.

"Excuse me, yes, I need help," Rena stammered, forcing her eyes to stay on the woman. "I'm lost, actually. I was trying to get to the harbour, but I couldn't find it."

She winced. She'd wanted to sound more confident, but the guard had taken her by surprise. She inspected the guard's face in case she'd run into her before but nothing clicked. The guard clearly didn't recognise Rena either as her expression stayed confused and annoyed instead of turning to realisation.

"I'm truly sorry," Rena continued with a nervous giggle, hoping to somehow remedy the situation, the words tumbling out of her before she could think better of it. "I suppose seeing all of these 'hoodlums' has shaken me more than I thought it would. I've never been to Hollowtooth before. My father asked me to meet him at the harbour to help him with his stock, but the city is so much bigger than my hometown and I'm not used to streets that are so full of people and I suppose it confused and scared me a bit too much. I'm so sorry, I know you have more important things to do, but I didn't know where else to go, and my father always said if I were in any trouble I should ask the guards for help, so here I am! Would you mind telling me how to get there? I would very much appreciate your help, and I promise I won't bother you any further if you could just point me in the right direction."

Rena wasn't proud that this was the character she'd chosen to play. She could see on the woman's face that she was judging Rena for being so ignorant and uncultured, but if the performance was convincing enough to keep the guard from being suspicious of her, then that was all Rena needed.

The door in the back opened once more and this time it stayed open just a fraction longer. Rena didn't want to look at the opening for too long, worried the guard would notice her inattention, but something caught her eye. Her heart leapt into her throat as she noticed one of the people pacing inside the cells. A tall woman with long braids, black skin and lighter spots peppered over her face and hands. She couldn't see the woman's face before the door closed again, but the glimpse was enough to make Rena's breath hitch.

"You just have to follow the main road south and you'll stumble upon it," the guard said with a deadpan expression, the tone of her voice indicating just how little she cared about Rena's explanation.

Rena forced her eyes back to the guard and smiled, her heart beating loudly in her ears. She was sure the guard would soon become suspicious of her and keep her from leaving the station. Her excitement had to be written plainly across her face, no matter how much Rena tried to hide it.

"Head south through the market and follow the smell of the ocean," the woman continued. "It's a giant body of water; you can't miss it. I really don't know how you couldn't find it on your own."

"Thank you so much!" Rena replied and bowed deeply, enunciating each word with overdramatic gratitude. "You're right, I should have been able to find it on my own." She chuckled nervously. "I just got so overwhelmed with this big city. I've never really left my town before, but you're right. I'm not a child anymore. I should not be so scared by silly things like this."

"Just ask someone at the market next time. We aren't map vendors, you know."

"Yes, I know, I cannot apologise enough!" Rena slowly stepped back, her eyes darting once more to the now closed door. "Thank you so much. I won't bother you any further!"

Rena turned around and hurried out of the station. She wanted to get out of that building as quickly as possible, even if she couldn't be certain that the person she'd seen was truly Kalani. She tried to reassure herself that the likelihood of it being a different person who looked so similar to Kalani had to be minuscule, but deep down she knew that it wasn't zero. She'd seen into the room for such a short instant, she couldn't be certain that her brain hadn't been playing tricks on her out of hope.

But what stood before them now was the difficult part — finding a way to get Rodrick and Kalani out. They couldn't storm the guard station, so they'd need to infiltrate it somehow. Maybe with the help of one of Cass' contacts, they could convince the guards to release Rodrick and Kalani or sneak them out at night, but either option felt like an impossible task to Rena.

As Rena reached the station's door, she had to step aside for a larger group, which pulled her out of her deep thoughts. Her eyes landed on a very familiar face — piercing blue eyes above sharp cheekbones. Finn only glanced at her for an instant, looking away as if he hadn't recognised her. His eyes were bloodshot and his skin looked paler than usual, almost translucent, with a bruise underneath his right eye. What astonished her more was that he wasn't being escorted like a prisoner. He walked in, surrounded by guards, as if he belonged there and they were under his authority.

Rena stood frozen for a moment, staring at the empty spot Finn had just walked through, her blood pulsing in her ears. Mechanically, she opened the door and stepped out, heading south like the guard had told her to.

Had Asha been right about him all along? Had Finn been the one to help Inkra and betray them? Asha had said from the start that they couldn't trust someone who was part of the guard corps, but he had guaranteed their escape from the archives, even jeopardizing his own life by running away with them. Didn't that mean he was on their side? And if he truly worked with the Crow, why had he just walked past her? He could have easily signalled for her to be arrested and thrown into the cell with Rodrick and Kalani. Maybe that would have made her arrest too public? What if he was waiting for a better time with fewer eyes on them? Had Rena just endangered Asha and Logan by indicating to Finn that they were in the city?

A million questions swirled through her mind as she left the station and aimlessly drifted through the market, not paying attention to anything happening in front of her.

Chapter Three

Finn

He had just passed Rena, he was sure of it. Even if she'd had her scarf partway over her face, even if there was no reason for her to be in Hollowtooth, he had recognised her right away. Finn hadn't known how to react, so he hadn't. He let her leave the building and continued on his path as if she'd simply been any random person. The guards accompanying him guided him through the station's front room and up the stairs, leading him to the office of the captain of the guard.

He felt out of his depth. The environment certainly wasn't an unfamiliar one, but it wasn't where he wanted to be and he couldn't quite figure out how to get back to Rena's group without drawing the ire of those who had apprehended him. He had been biding his time, trying to convince the guards that he wasn't a threat and they didn't need to keep a constant eye on him. Finn didn't want to rush anything; he needed to analyse the situation from every angle, but he hadn't anticipated that he'd run into any of his companions in Hollowtooth. If he wanted them to all reunite, he needed to act.

His face hurt, the bruise around his eye throbbing, and he hadn't slept since the guards had found him outside of Oceansthrow. He couldn't let himself sleep, not while he didn't know the people around him. They had first tried to capture him as a prisoner until Captain Silac had recognised him. For some reason, Silac was elated to have found Finn alone stumbling out of a forest far away from the Plains. He hadn't asked Finn any questions about how he'd gotten there, hadn't asked him why he was on his own, hadn't said anything about Finn having no business so far away from the archives. There was something in Silac's eyes that was just waiting to figure out how he could hold it over Finn's head and the waiting crushed all the air out of Finn's lungs.

He didn't know much about Captain Silac. Rumours about the man had floated through the province for decades but Finn had never bothered memorising any of them, especially if no two people repeated the same thing twice. He vaguely remembered that Captain Silac came from an old family who used to have influence in the region but had somehow fallen from grace. That also made him distant family with other influential people in the province, but the distance was great enough that the connection didn't really matter.

Finn had never had the opportunity to interact with the man face-to-face and that made Finn extremely nervous. He didn't know what to think of Captain Silac, couldn't quite tell what lay behind his façade. There was something unnerving about him, something that bothered Finn more than usual.

"Ah, Captain Liberic, welcome!"

Silac stood up from behind his desk as the guards led Finn into his office. It was an opulent room, decorated in various rich shades of red and orange, with satins and jewels and painted mirrors. It was like an attack on Finn's senses, the sheer quantity of decorative objects tearing at

Finn's already frayed patience. Even the cupboards had mother-of-pearl detailing as if they'd been imported from the royal palace.

"I hope you had enough time to rest," Silac said as he gestured Finn towards a chair. "I do so apologise about your eye — the guards in question have been thoroughly reprimanded."

Captain Silac was a tall man, with black hair and a neatly trimmed beard. He had an aquiline nose and sharp, green eyes, and his clothing reflected the room around them. He smiled at Finn expectantly, but Finn had never been good at reading others' faces and knowing how they wanted him to react, especially not when he was sleep-deprived.

Finn sat down on a red-cushioned chair on the other side of Silac's desk. Even the armrests were made of intricately carved wood, as if every centimetre of the room had to reflect Silac's status.

"Thank you for welcoming me into your city," Finn said, his eyes drifting over the furniture around him.

He cringed at the mess on the desk. Documents that should have been stored with great care were lying open, with objects placed on top of them and cutting folds into them. A cold shudder ran down Finn's back as he realised what kind of documents were lying in front of him for all the world to see — arrest records, communications with other guard stations and the military academy, files about the guards working in Hollowtooth. Any of these should have been stored in cupboards that could be locked and only taken out when needed, but by the dates on some of these, Finn doubted that Silac ever bothered to put them away. He dared not think about the documents that did make their way into a cupboard. A man who cared so little about his desk surely did not bother with categorising his cupboard correctly.

"Fetch us some tea," Silac ordered one of the guards as he sat back down, a hint of green flashing over his eyes for just a second.

Finn paused, unsure of what he had just seen. His mind told him that rationally, it had just been the reflection of one of the thousand objects in the room that reflected light, but he couldn't be sure, and it triggered a strange tension in his body that didn't want to leave. He hated trusting a feeling more than his mind, but the last few days had been exhausting and his mind wasn't as sharp as he was used to. His hands balled into tight fists, and he felt like he should tread ever so carefully in Captain Silac's presence.

"Have you ever been to Hollowtooth before?" Silac asked him, leaning back in his chair and interlocking his fingers.

He stared at Finn with such intensity that Finn didn't dare look away. He knew what people thought of him when he averted his gaze, had been told often enough in his childhood that it made him look weak, and he could tell that Silac was only waiting to find his weakness.

"I've visited the city before, yes," Finn replied, choosing every word carefully. "But I sadly haven't had much opportunity to travel in recent years."

"Of course. You must be very busy." Silac smiled at him and Finn stopped breathing. "I do hope you'll find the time to see the changes this city has gone through over the last few years. Not that I would take sole credit for it. My predecessors did a fine job and, of course, the city council are responsible for some of it. We've had quite the increased influx of visitors from all corners of the kingdom, which can only be attributed to how well this city is run and how little danger can be found on its streets."

Finn wasn't sure what the point of this conversation was. Silac didn't seem like someone who conversed simply to be pleasant, so what did he want? He was already the captain of the guard; there wasn't much else Finn could help him achieve. Did he need a favour from the archive's administrator in Mellahen? Finn had lived there for many years, had climbed the ranks in the archive's own guard corps, but that didn't mean he held much sway when it came to the administrator's decisions. She was a strict woman, only bending to the will of those above her, and she'd certainly never developed a soft spot for Finn.

He felt restless. This conversation was just a waste of time, taking up too much of his attention. He needed to find a way to escape, to find out why Rena was in town. He considered the possibility that she'd come to the city on her own. She might have changed her mind and decided to let the guards deal with the problem of the Crow after all, but he doubted that was the case. But then where were the others? Had they sent her into the guard station alone as she was the least likely to be recognised? That was a possibility but it didn't explain what they were doing in Hollowtooth.

Finn wondered if they were looking for him, but he didn't dare linger on the thought. He was sure Rena had recognised him but just like him, she hadn't reacted. She might have simply been surprised, as he had, unsure how to react surrounded by so many guards. Or maybe she simply didn't care.

He steeled himself from those thoughts, taking himself out of the equation. It didn't matter why Rena and the others were in Hollowtooth if Finn couldn't find a way to slip away from Silac.

"It is a wonderful city," Finn replied after noticing that Silac was waiting for a response. "Quite charming."

"Yes, indeed, a true asset to our kingdom."

The guard came back in with the tea, placing it on the desk between Finn and Silac and poured them both a cup. The smell of anise and chamomile spread through the room.

"Leave us," Silac said, waving the guard away, the hint of green flashing over his eyes again.

Finn stopped breathing, his gaze fixed on Silac's eyes, waiting for the shimmer to reappear. He was certain he hadn't imagined it, not the second time. It couldn't have just been a reflection. The room was decorated mostly in reds, there wasn't anything bright green that could have caught in the man's eyes.

"Of course, Hollowtooth could be even greater," Silac continued, as if nothing was amiss. "With how many visitors we get each summer, we're rapidly reaching our capacities."

"I can imagine."

Finn pressed his nails into the palms of his hands. He wanted to crawl out of his skin, wanted to escape Silac and this conversation. He'd never understood why humans spent so much time talking around a subject, why every word had to be a mystery.

"But, of course, that is not a problem that can be easily solved," Silac continued. "As prosperous as the city has been over the last decade, our funds are, sadly, still not expansive enough to develop Hollowtooth into the city it deserves to be. However, if the province saw the potential, I'm sure we could create something wonderful that would benefit us all. And, of course, I'm sure such an expansion would benefit more than our small province. It would benefit the entire kingdom."

Finn stayed silent, hoping Silac would give up and switch subjects on his own — the strategy had worked before. Finn just needed to withstand Silac's gaze.

"You have family in the capital, if I'm not mistaken," Silac pushed forth.

"I have," Finn reluctantly forced out.

"Family who could recognise the benefit this development could have for our kingdom, if only they knew of it."

"Potentially."

They stared at each other, in a stalemate as long as Silac didn't want to admit *why* he had invited Finn to his office. Silac's smile grew sour, his anger showing in the small twitch of an eye, in the flare of his nostrils, but it wasn't the first time Finn brought forth such a reaction from people trying to talk to him. He was well aware of the way others discussed politics. So much of it was discussed through implications, through words never said out loud, and Finn had no interest in participating in it.

"Maybe a visit is in order," Silac said and got up in one swift motion. "To show you the renovations we underwent recently. Sadly, the space we have to keep prisoners is quite limited, but the expansion of the city would of course also involve a new guard station, someplace we could keep our prisoners longer instead of having to send them west. I think that would also greatly benefit the province as a whole."

Captain Silac led Finn through every room of the guard station, introducing him to anyone they stumbled upon. Finn had developed a headache the moment they'd stepped out of the office and every further step had made it worse. Silac had not been able to bear the silence between them, telling Finn all about the renovations, his future plans for the city, and all that could be achieved with funds from the Royal Council. Finn had tried to explain that he had no influence over these things, that he had never met the people who allocated funds to the provinces, that the kingdom was busy with other projects in the North. There was, after all, the development of the train network to think about. Of course, the mention of the train only led Silac into another monologue about the benefits of building a train line from the capital to Hollowtooth to facilitate travel during the summer months for any visitors, especially from their neighbouring countries.

Finn eyed the door to the outside warily as they passed through the front room, weighing the benefits and downsides of simply running out. He knew that he didn't have enough energy to get away from the guards, so he kept following Silac, politely nodding in greeting at the next people he was introduced to.

"And this way leads us to the most important part of the station," Silac said, opening a door at the back of the room and beckoning Finn to enter.

Finn stepped into the room. It was bigger than any other in the station but also much dimmer. It held no decorations and barely any furniture and the sun only filtered in through small windows high up on the outer walls. Four guards were stationed in the four corners of the room, following Silac and Finn with their eyes. The middle of the room held eight cells in two rows made of thick iron bars, each keeping a handful of prisoners.

"As you can tell," Silac said, locking the door behind them, "we are in desperate need of a bigger facility."

He waved for Finn to follow him, leading him along the passage around the cells. Finn barely dared to look at the people inside, even though he could feel their eyes on him. He wasn't used to walking through such facilities, didn't know how to behave in them. They only had a small holding cell in the archives. Any person caught stealing or damaging the documents was held at the archives for no more than a day before they were transferred either to the Plains' guard station or directly to the military academy.

"It would be a benefit to all if we could build a second facility outside of the city centre," Silac continued, hands clasped behind his back as he looked at each prisoner. "Quite frankly, considering the size of Hollowtooth, a new facility should have been built years ago. I suppose that is one unfortunate oversight from my predecessors. You understand why I would appreciate any help from the province of the Royal Council."

And then, Finn's eyes fell on a person he recognised. Instantly it clicked why he had seen Rena. Rodrick looked back at him, his eyes growing wide with recognition. He opened his mouth to say something, but Finn quickly shook his head. There was a second person in the cell next to Rodrick, a dark-skinned woman with vitiligo and long braids, someone he had never seen before. By the way Rodrick and the woman stood close to each other, Finn supposed that they somehow knew each other.

Silac's chatter faded into the background, Finn's thoughts racing with every possibility of what might have happened. Silac kept walking, not having noticed anything, and Finn had to keep following to not raise any suspicions. How had Rodrick ended up in a cell in Hollowtooth? It had barely been a day since they'd all parted ways, but their goal had been to investigate Oceansthrow and its surroundings. How had they ended up in Hollowtooth of all places? Did the Crow have a presence in the city that the others had tried to investigate? Finn hadn't noticed anything that would point towards it. The only oddity he'd come across had been Silac and the strange green reflection in his eyes, and Finn wasn't even sure it hadn't simply been his exhausted mind making things up.

Silac kept talking and talking, repeating the same points with different words, hoping that some of them would entice Finn to help him, until he finally understood that Finn had no interest in doing so and the air between them soured. Silac brought them back up to his office and regarded Finn in silence, fingers tapping rhythmically on his desk. Finn met his gaze with unfocused eyes, his headache making his perception hazy. His breathing was laboured and he needed all his attention to keep his breakfast in his stomach.

"Liberic, you have a sister in the capital, if I'm not mistaken," Silac finally said.

"I do, yes."

The bruise around his eye pulsed. Out of all the people Silac could have mentioned, this was the worst choice. Finn wasn't of a mind to talk about his sister, not with someone like Silac.

"How often do you see her?"

"Not often."

"And the rest of your family?"

Finn stayed silent for a moment, partially to keep himself from vomiting and partially because he really didn't like the direction this conversation had taken.

"I don't see how that has anything to do with Hollowtooth."

"You don't," Silac replied, more a statement than a question. "I think it is quite obvious. I help you, you help me. That's how the world works. I could have asked you why you were stumbling through a forest alone so far away from your home, close to the place where a guard had recently been assaulted, but I didn't. I could have reported it all to the administrator, asked if there was a reason for you to cross these lands on your own, but I didn't. I sheltered and fed you, asking nothing in return except for you to hear me out."

"And I thank you profusely for all those things," Finn said automatically, knowing there was nothing he could say that would stop Silac.

"It isn't easy to achieve one's goals, no matter how convinced one is of their merits," Silac continued, idly playing with the edge of a paper on his desk. "So much depends on the opinions of others, how they see you, how they see your family. It is all just luck. A fate predetermined by birth. I had no influence on my family's downfall, just as you had no influence on your family's rise."

He paused, looking out into nothingness past Finn's shoulder.

"I feel like we all used to have our own individual fate, before our kingdom changed so drastically, before the Royal Council became what it is today. People could still rise above what had come before them, could still determine their own lives through hard work and wit. So many people achieved greatness from nothing back then. Now it all depends on who you know, who you've had the luck to be introduced to at some dull feast, which lord or margrave or countess you happen to be related to who likes you well enough to still speak to you. No matter how great your idea is, you will get nowhere without shaking the right person's hands."

Finn kept his breathing slow and steady as his eyes drifted down to the papers lying across Silac's desk. If he didn't move, Silac would be too distracted to notice what he was trying to do.

"We have lost our way, Liberic," Silac continued, speaking more to the room than to Finn, "too concerned with the opinions of our neighbours. The Royal Council seems to think that we cannot be strong on our own, that our foundation is too weak to stand upon, but it seems to me that they know nothing of what made us who we are."

Finn's gaze glided over the documents as he tried to identify what each of them talked about. He blinked repeatedly, willing his eyes to focus again. His hope was that Silac hadn't bothered putting away Rodrick's arrest records — if he had ever written any. His headache didn't make reading the documents easy, especially as they were upside down and covered with Silac's overly intricate handwriting, but soon he noticed a document partially covered by another that looked like an arrest form.

"They're looking in the wrong places, I say. Imitating the Kano-Raeki Federation isn't going to be what propels us into the future and kissing the Daishegian Empire's ass will only lead to us losing our border territories again. We should have never given them half of the High-Foshe island! It used to be all ours, but no, the Council doesn't care about what used to be."

Every few seconds, Finn glanced up at Silac, but the captain was so enraptured by his own words that Finn could have melted off his chair and the other man wouldn't have noticed. He strained his eyes to read the document sideways while forcing his head to stay straight.

"There is so much we can learn from our own history, so much strength we can gain from it. Our nation turned its back on the old faith and, in my opinion, that was the worst mistake we ever made. So much pain, so much strife, so much agony has settled over our lands since we abandoned it."

The form spoke of an arrest made outside of Halvint and how the subjects were to be transported to the military academy to be imprisoned. Finn frowned, unsure if he was reading it right. If the prisoners were to be transferred to the academy, Silac had used the wrong form. And anyway, that decision was not his to make. He scanned the table for correspondence between Silac and the academy that would confirm such a decision from the correct party but couldn't find any. Then he noticed the date of the supposed transfer and winced before quickly looking up at Silac to make sure he hadn't noticed, but Silac had started retelling a story about a god Finn couldn't care less about.

Finn tuned the noise out and focused his attention on the document again. The transfer was supposedly planned for the next day, which was not only highly unorthodox but also impossible in the framework of their legal system. He tried to wrap his head around how Silac could have gotten the approval for the transfer in such a short timeframe, but the only valid reason would have been if Silac had caught a highly dangerous and high-profile individual, which Rodrick clearly was not.

A strange feeling settled in Finn's stomach as he started to think about *why* Silac would have chosen to forgo standard proceedings for Rodrick and the other woman's arrest, and he very much didn't like any of the possibilities.

Chapter Four

Rena

"Rena! Hey, Rena! Where are you going?"

Rena turned around in a daze, not having noticed how far she'd walked. Logan jogged up to her, looking around nervously at the market surrounding them.

"What happened?" he whispered as he reached her. "Are they not in there?"

Rena's mouth felt dry, her vision blurry. She had to blink a few times before she recognised Logan's face. Drops of sweat had collected at his hairline but his eyes looked as sharp as ever.

His frown deepened with every second she stayed silent.

"Are you all right?" he asked, his gaze darting to the side as he held her by the shoulders.

Asha calmly walked up beside them, the bag with their belongings slung over her shoulder.

"Yes, I'm fine," Rena hesitated, her mind refusing to clear.

Finn's reappearance had completely destabilised her. How had he found his way to Hollowtooth? Her first thought was that he'd also been captured the way Kalani and Rodrick had, but he hadn't been handcuffed and no one had been holding on to him. Had she been wrong to trust him? Was he secretly working with the guards? Asha had been suspicious of him from the start, what if she'd been right all along?

But then, why did he have that big bruise on his face? Why did he look so miserable? Why hadn't he reacted when she'd walked past him? She tried to analyse all the times they'd spoken and interacted with each other over the past few days in the hopes of finding something that would explain it all, that would show that he'd planned to betray them from the start, but she couldn't find anything that fit.

Her head hurt from all the back and forth. It would be so easy to simply hate him and condemn him, but she couldn't bring herself to do it, not without having talked to him first.

"What happened?!" Logan looked at her with utter confusion, desperation flooding his voice. "Are Kalani and Rodrick not in the cells? Are they hurt? Talk to us!"

He pulled Rena away from the crowd and towards the edge of the market — close enough to still blend in but not so close that anyone could hear their conversation.

"Sorry, sorry, yes, they are." She shook her head, trying to clear it.

She couldn't decide whether she should tell Logan and Asha about her encounter with Finn. She knew exactly how Asha would react and she wanted to avoid being influenced by it. She had to form her own opinion of the situation, one way or another.

They had other things to focus on anyway. They needed to get Kalani and Rodrick out of that cell as fast as possible so they could find the Crow and save Maya. Rena wasn't sure she had the time to unravel Finn's mystery.

"Sorry, I guess I'm a bit shook up," Rena continued. "One of the guards came to talk to me but I managed to talk my way out of it. I don't think she'll send anyone after me, she just looked annoyed. But yes, I think I saw Kalani. Or at least someone who very much looks like her."

"Good." Logan sighed in relief and let go of her, taking a step back. "At least one thing."

"Let's get away from the market," Asha murmured and waved for them to follow.

She led them down a side street towards a small square with a well at its centre where they could be alone. Logan sat down on the edge of the well, his breathing laboured, hands clasping the wall tightly. He let his head hang, his hair covering his face — he had tied it up into his usual bun in the morning, but it had unravelled over the course of their journey. Rena glanced around, keeping an eye on the street behind them to make sure no one had followed them. She was quite sure that no guard had recognised her — they certainly wouldn't have let her leave if they had — but who knew if Finn hadn't changed his mind and decided to rat her out after all.

"I've been thinking," Asha said, standing in front of Logan with her arms crossed, a grave expression on her face. "There really aren't any easy solutions here. We don't know what the guards are planning with Kalani and Rodrick. If it were a proper arrest, they would only keep them here for a couple of days before they'd be transferred to the military academy in the West, but they'd need to go through a whole lot of stupid bureaucracy to make it happen."

"And it's not that easy to fake those documents," Logan added between heavy breaths. "At least if you want to fake them well enough that no one notices. But we don't know if that's what they want or need. They might have someone inside the academy who helps them and just ignores any inaccuracies."

"Oh stars, do you think even the academy is on the Crow's side?" Rena asked in disbelief.

"I don't think so," Logan answered, but his face revealed his uncertainty. "Arrest documents pass through multiple hands. The academy might not notice that the documents are fake in the beginning and accept the transfer, but every arrest gets checked for validity and reevaluated by some internal committee to avoid overcrowding and keep the province's guard stations in check. They'd notice that things aren't right. It's too risky of a move. And I highly doubt that everyone at the academy got corrupted by the Crow."

"You never know," Asha grumbled.

"Yeah, but the positions in the academy change so often, you really can't tell who'll be the one looking at the documents. Especially if some fucker from the North decides to send their kid to the academy to learn some discipline. It's just too volatile for the Crow to have control over it. What could the Crow offer those rich pricks that they don't already have? Or that someone else has already offered them?"

"Right, I'd forgotten about all the rest of the corruption," Asha said.

"So you don't think they'll be sent to the academy?" Rena asked, unsure if she was following Logan's train of thought.

Logan sighed and let his head fall back, closing his eyes, his sweat-damp curls hanging over the well's void.

"It's always a possibility but I doubt it. Didn't think I'd ever say it, but for once all the bureaucracy might be our saviour."

Asha ran a hand over her face and groaned.

"Time to go find Cass' contacts and hope they aren't incompetent assholes."

Logan slid off the edge of the well and sat down on the ground. He let his head rest against the wall, closing his eyes, his breathing slower and heavier than ever. Rena observed him for a while, growing increasingly concerned about his well-being.

"I think we need to find somewhere to rest first," Rena suggested even though her own mind screamed at her that they had no time to waste.

"No, we don't," Logan insisted, although he didn't even bother looking at her. "I'll be fine, I just need to sit here for a moment."

"You better not be lying to us." Asha looked down at him, concern and annoyance mixing on her face.

"We can't waste our money on a bed. We already barely have any on us and we might need it to pay people off."

Rena glanced over at Asha, their eyes meeting, both clearly thinking the same and not knowing how to force Logan into it.

"Logan," Rena started carefully but before she could say anything else, his body slid to the side, limp and unconscious.

"For fuck's sake, not again." Asha swore under her breath as she leaned down and pulled him up.

Rena sighed, trying her best not to grow angry at Logan, and stepped forward to help Asha.

Chapter Five

Rena

They managed to drag Logan to an inn Asha knew without drawing too much attention to themselves. It wasn't easy not to resent Logan for not acknowledging that he needed to rest. He'd put them in unnecessary danger. Had the wrong person run into them, they wouldn't even have been able to get away quickly without leaving Logan behind.

Rena tried to see it from Logan's perspective. He'd pushed himself beyond his limits so they wouldn't need to take a break — his intentions had simply backfired. And after all, the real fault lay with the guards who had attacked them, not with Logan who had to deal with the injury, no matter how much Asha cursed him out. But they'd needed more than a bed to get him back on his feet, especially if they wanted to make sure his wound wouldn't get any worse.

While Asha remained at the inn, Rena hurried back to the market with some of their last remaining coins. Their weight in the pocket of the blue dress Darian's wife had given her was ever-present, making her more nervous than she already was. She kept her scarf tight around her head, her eyes darting to each person who stepped too close to her. She remembered seeing a stall selling salves and tinctures close to the guard station and as much as she dreaded approaching that building again, she didn't have the time to look through the city for another merchant. The quicker she could find an appropriate ointment, the quicker they could get back to rescuing Rodrick and Kalani and then finally head out to save Maya.

Rena weaved a way through the market's crowd but couldn't stop herself from glancing at the bright, white building at the edge of the market. She kept wondering about Finn's reappearance and the bruise on his face. She desperately wished she could talk to him and figure out what had happened since they'd been separated, but she knew she needed to focus on getting Logan back on his feet first.

She hurried through the market, making quick decisions about which sellers were trustworthy and which weren't — at last a skill she'd learned over her short life. There was a stall selling bandages and flasks of clean water with alleged healing properties. Rena wasn't sure if she really trusted the claim, but the water had to be cleaner than that found at the inn and that was good enough. She had just found another stall selling salves, when something caught her eye.

Finn stepped out with three other people — a man dressed in fine clothes with a brown cape slung over his left shoulder and two guards trailing behind. With utmost restraint, Rena managed not to whip her head around. She stared at the vendor's mouth as he explained the different salves on display although none of the words registered in her mind. She forced herself not to hurry through the interaction, knowing that picking the right salve was more important than keeping track of

Finn. In the end, she picked one that seemed best for the little money she had, thanked the vendor and turned around.

Her eyes darted from side to side, scanning the crowd in the hopes of finding Finn again but his group had already disappeared. She wanted to run forward but at the same time admonished herself for it. She needed to get back to Logan as quickly as possible. There was no time to waste.

She hurried through the crowd, her mind endlessly racing with all the questions she wanted to ask Finn, and then she caught a glimpse of his blond hair. Her body tensed. Maybe it wouldn't be so bad if she followed him for just a little while, just to see how he was doing, just to make sure the people with him were treating him right. He had been her friend, even for just the briefest of times, and she couldn't abandon him if the possibility existed that he was in danger.

The finely dressed man led Finn and the guards through the market, wildly gesticulating as he told them something Rena couldn't hear. She didn't recognise the man, but his clothing and the intricately decorated sword attached at his hip signalled that he was a higher-ranking member of the guard corps.

She made sure to always have people between her and the guards and observed Finn from afar. She hoped his body language would betray whether he was being held captive or not. His posture looked rigid, with his hands clasped tightly behind his back, but Rena didn't know how to interpret it. The knuckles of his right hand were bloody and scraped, so he clearly had been in a fight, but did the tension in his shoulders come from the pain, was he simply uncomfortable in a big crowd, or was he scared of the people escorting him? She'd never had to read the body language of someone she hadn't grown up with and she found it incredibly difficult. It had always been easy with her siblings — it almost came naturally to her — but she didn't know Finn well enough to understand how he carried stress and pain on his body.

Rena stayed close behind Finn's group, flowing with the market's crowd, always standing close enough to a group of visitors so that it looked like she belonged with them. The man in the fine clothes led his group through the market, talking to Finn with wide hand gestures, barely acknowledging the presence of the guards accompanying them. They didn't look at any stalls, which meant Rena had to follow them at a quicker pace than she was comfortable with.

She started to worry about how she'd follow them once they were out of the market. Maybe that would be the point where she had to admit it had all been a futile endeavour, that she had just been wasting her precious time for nothing. She started to panic, her mind circling back to the archives and Rodrick's hasty plan, how she'd almost ruined it all with her clumsiness. She needed to find an alternative, some way to signal to Finn that she wanted to speak to him alone, if only for a few seconds. She glanced around, thinking she might be able to lead him towards one of the side streets. She was deeply aware that she was gambling with her safety and that she'd begrudged Logan for doing the same just a few hours prior, but she knew just as well that if she left now, her encounter with Finn would nag at the back of her mind for the rest of her life. No matter how factual she tried to stay, she just couldn't believe Finn had been dishonest with them.

There were a few options to get Finn's attention but none of them seemed safe. She could simply throw something at him so he'd turn around but she might miss and hit one of the guards instead. She could take the extreme route and cause a ruckus by making a stall collapse or pushing someone over. But who was she kidding — she could never cause such chaos on purpose. What else was there? Pretend to faint and hope they would come to her aid? The risk of one of the guards recognising her was too great and even if they didn't, how would she communicate with Finn? No, she needed to find a way to only get Finn's attention, and for that, she would need to be in his field of vision.

Rena took a deep breath and picked up her pace, weaving through the crowd as if she had a particular stall she was trying to get to. She made sure not to bump into anyone and politely asked to pass between groups so she wouldn't draw anyone's ire. It cost her precious seconds but the last thing she wanted to deal with was drawing the guards' attention if someone shouted at her.

Relief flooded her chest as she noticed that the well-dressed man had stopped in front of a stall selling ornamental daggers and swords. If luck truly was on her side, they would stay there long enough for her to catch Finn's attention. She slowed down and crossed to the group's other side, her heart hammering loudly in her chest as she stopped at a stall to their left. She angled herself towards them, pretending she was also interested in the gem-encrusted sheaths, and dared a quick peek at Finn. His bloodshot eyes were cast to the ground, his expression blank. Now that she could see his face from up close, she recognised that the tension in his body was exhaustion. The bruise she'd glimpsed earlier was a shadow of yellow and purple under his right eye spreading over his too-pale skin. How had he gotten that bruise? *When* had he gotten it? If he'd gotten caught right after they'd visited the ruins of Oceansthrow, it might also explain why he hadn't found his way back to Halvint like the rest of them had. That possibility seemed likelier to Rena than the thought of Finn being the one to help the Crow and sending the guards after them.

Finn suddenly looked up and their eyes met. Rena froze, neither of them blinking for what felt like minutes. With her entire body rigid, she forced her head to nod slightly to the left, towards one of the side streets, before averting her gaze and turning away. She walked past the last few vendors, her stiff muscles aching with each step, then turned to the left and disappeared down the street, never looking back to see if anyone was following her.

Once she'd rounded the corner at the end of the side street, she let go of the tension in her body and took a deep, shaky breath. Her body was trembling, her fingers worrying at her necklace as she paced back and forth.

Why had she simply left? She'd acted on instinct, walking away before she could think better of it. Had it been enough for Finn to understand what she'd tried to tell him? Had her nod been clear enough? Had he even recognised her? Of course he had, why wouldn't he have, they'd only been separated for a day or so.

She needed to calm down or she would panic. She blocked every thought overanalysing her actions, every doubt that crept in at the back of her mind, every comment admonishing her choices, no matter how impulsive they had been. The deed had been done; there was nothing she could do to change it. All she needed to do was wait for Finn to show up.

Rena clutched Logan's salve tightly in her hands, the flask of water and bandages weighing down her dress. She counted her breaths, swearing that if she reached one thousand before Finn arrived, she would count her losses and go back to Logan and Asha like she should have done half an hour ago. As long as she didn't wait too long, no one would complain about how much time it had taken her to run some simple errands.

She crouched down with her arms wrapped around her legs. She let her head fall onto her knees, not caring anymore if she looked strange to anyone walking by. Her breaths slowed further and further, stretching the time until she reached one thousand.

"Rena?"

Her head snapped up and there he stood, in his blue coat that showed what he had lived through these past few days.

"Finn?"

She stood up slowly, her legs shaky, and stared at him until he looked away and stepped closer.

"What are you doing here?" His eyes scanned the street around them as he came to stand in front of her.

"Ehm... I... uh..." Rena stammered, unsure what to do now that he was finally right there. "Rodrick and Kalani are being held captive in the guard station. Did you not notice?"

"Yes, yes. I know," he muttered. "Of course you're here. That was a stupid question." He shook his head and continued with a steadier voice. "Are you alone? Where are the others?"

"No, Asha and Logan are with me, but Logan's hurt."

"That's suboptimal." He stayed quiet for a while, his gaze focused on the street he'd come from.

"What happened to you?" Rena asked, taking a careful step closer.

"It's fine," he replied, shaking his head. "It doesn't matter."

"It doesn't look like it doesn't matter."

Finn refused to look at her, his jaw set tight.

"Where did you get the bruise?" Rena insisted. "And why are you with the guards?"

Finn glanced at her, then looked away again, his reluctance plainly written on his face. He closed his eyes and breathed in deeply.

"They captured me," he finally admitted. "After Oceansthrow. I couldn't do much but play along for my own survival."

"Are they the ones who gave you that bruise?"

"Yes."

Rena observed him for a moment, knowing it would only make him more nervous. He finally met her gaze, his eyes fixed on hers by force, his body rigid and unmoving.

She tried to read whether he was lying to her or not, whether he was trying to lead her into a trap or was just too exhausted to explain the situation well. Her stomach twisted and turned at her indecision, scared any step she took was the wrong one, but she couldn't do nothing either.

"Do you know anything about Rodrick and Kalani?" Rena asked, wishing upon all the luck she still had that was the right direction to take.

"Kalani is the woman in the cell with Rodrick? I've seen them. They don't seem hurt beyond a few scratches. What happened? Why did they get arrested?"

"The guards attacked us outside Halvint when we were leaving the Crow's hideout." Rena paused for a second. It only really hit her then how quickly everything in her life had been changing. "There's a lot you've missed."

"The Crow's hideout," he repeated slowly, his eyes knitting together in confusion.

"In Halvint, yes. They were staying near a farm on the outskirts of town." She wanted to tell him all that had happened but knew it would have to wait for a more private setting. "When the guards attacked us, they mentioned someone. Captain Silac. Do you know him?"

He nodded slowly, his eyes drifting away from her again.

"Silac is a strange man. He was with me at the market when you found me."

"The one with the cape?"

"Yes. He's the head of the guard. He's taken a strange liking to me because of my family. It's been quite uncomfortable, if I'm being honest. I almost wish he'd sent me back to the archives."

"Wouldn't that be dangerous?" Rena hesitated. "With how you helped us escape and all the rest?"

"Possibly, but I'm sure I could have talked my way out of it with the administrator. At least I know what she's like."

"Can you help us free Rodrick and Kalani?" Rena asked hastily before she thought better of it.

He glanced at her for a moment, his jaw tightly clenched, before looking away again, his eyes darting over the ground and the buildings surrounding them as if he was searching for something that wasn't there. His eyebrows knit together, deep in conversation with himself. Dread that she shouldn't have asked him for help tried to claw its way into Rena's mind but she couldn't let it in. They didn't have any good alternatives and she'd rather trust Finn than people she didn't know whom Asha didn't have much confidence in either.

"I'm not sure," he murmured. "It'll be difficult, but there might be a way. I'll need to think about it. Things aren't the way they should be in this town."

"What do you mean?"

"There are rules and protocols that exist in this province that aren't being upheld," Finn replied, annoyance overtaking all other emotions in his voice.

"Okay?"

"Protocols that ensure the correct operation of towns and guard corps that shouldn't be able to be circumvented, even by any power-hungry captain going rogue. There are specific, impartial agencies to prevent these things. The kingdom's had enough problems with it in the past; it shouldn't be happening anymore. Even if the agency isn't always able to do a perfect job, it shouldn't happen to the level it is here."

"That bad?" Rena asked, unsure if she really understood what he was talking about.

"It's... strange." He paused again and Rena let him think. "I wish I could explain it better. There's something about Captain Silac that doesn't sit right with me. He's so blatantly violating these protocols and doesn't seem to care if anyone notices. It makes no sense to me. He should have been caught months ago."

"Is it gonna make rescuing Rodrick and Kalani difficult?"

"Potentially. At least it makes planning more difficult. I can't be sure procedures will unfold the way they do in other towns. But we shouldn't be discussing this out here and I need to get back before they come looking for me."

"Can we meet tonight?" Rena asked, throwing caution overboard.

"After sundown. I think I'll be able to sneak away then."

She almost suggested that they meet in the tavern Logan and Asha were waiting in but then thought better of it. She could already picture Asha's face if she brought Finn to their room.

"It might be best to meet near the docks," Finn continued, "It has been quite a while since I last visited the city but as far as I remember there are old hangars on the eastern side that aren't used anymore. The sea is much calmer on the western border, most of the industry moved there a few years ago. I'm quite sure I would have heard about it if they'd revitalised that part of the city, so as long as we're careful, it should be safe to meet there."

"Okay," she replied, unsure of herself but knowing they needed to find a solution fast. "I'll tell the others."

"Good. I'll try to think of a way to get Rodrick and Kalani out."

Before Rena could say anything more, Finn had turned around and walked down the street in a few hasty steps.

Rena clutched the salve to her chest, watching Finn disappear. She dreaded having to recount her encounter to Asha and Logan. Convincing Logan wouldn't be too difficult, she guessed, but getting Asha to trust Finn seemed almost impossible. The last hope that Rena had was that the other people who could help them free Kalani and Rodrick were even less trustworthy.

Maybe Rena was naïve, maybe she'd led too easy a life, maybe she'd even end up regretting her decision to trust Finn, but she'd much rather go through life trusting the people who had helped her than be cautious of every small step she took.

Chapter Six

Rena

When Rena got back to their room, Logan was sitting upright in bed, a bright smile forming on his lips when he saw Rena. Asha didn't look quite as amused. She was sitting on a chair next to Logan's bed, elbows propped up on her knees, her interlinked hands in front of her face.

"How are you feeling?" Rena asked Logan as she approached.

She had to keep her voice low to not bother the other guest in the room. They hadn't been able to afford a room to themselves, so they were sharing it with another person and two unoccupied beds.

Only then did Asha look up and straighten as if she hadn't noticed Rena come in.

"Never felt better," Logan replied with a grin.

"You are such a liar," Rena muttered and gestured for him to lie back down so she could take a look at his wound.

She placed the salve, fresh bandages and the vial of water next to his legs and helped him lift his shirt. They unwrapped the soiled bandage from his midriff to uncover the gash across his stomach. It looked red and bloodied but not much worse than the night before. Logan poked at it with a finger and Rena had to swat his hands away so he wouldn't make it worse. With relief, Rena saw that the wound had mostly stopped bleeding and all they had to do was make sure it wouldn't get infected.

She looked around the room, unsure how best to clean Logan's wound without making a mess. At home, she would have known how to properly take care of it, but here she didn't even know where to get a clean cloth from. She sighed and bunched up the old bandages, trying to find a fold that didn't look too dirty. She carefully trickled the water from the vial onto the wound, making sure it didn't spill onto the mattress, and wiped away the dried blood. She washed her hands with the remainder of the water, then applied the salve over the shallow cut before carefully wrapping the new bandage around Logan.

To his credit, Logan barely flinched during the process, only his sombre expression hinting at his discomfort.

"Any fever?" Rena asked.

"Don't think so," Logan replied, pulling his shirt over his bandaged midriff.

"Good." Relieved, Rena sat down at the foot of the bed.

From the corner of her eye, she observed the other person in the room. A man sat on the bed on the opposite side of the room, back turned to them, hunched over something Rena couldn't see. He hadn't paid them any mind since Rena had entered and she hoped he was too engrossed in his own affairs to care about them.

"What do we do now?" she said quietly, hoping her voice didn't carry to the other side of the room.

Asha pulled her chair closer until her knees bumped into Rena's and placed the knapsack with their belongings between her legs.

"I've been thinking," she said so quietly that Logan had to sit up again to hear her. "I want to get them out as quietly as possible, so barging in or blowing up a wall isn't going to be an option. Not that we have the resources for it anyway." She ran both hands over her face and her short, black coils and sighed heavily. "We definitely won't get them out without someone who works in the guard station. I know who we can talk to about it, I just hate the guy."

"The old guy with the thinning, black hair?" Logan asked. "Who drinks too much but pretends he doesn't have a problem?"

"Fazzar, yeah." Asha paused for a moment, her eyes unfocused. "He knows Ocassian and Kalani so he knows not to double-cross them, but that won't keep him from holding it over our heads for the rest of his meaningless life, more than he already does with his job in the guard corps."

"Yeah, but we can live with that," Logan murmured, "if you think he can actually get Kalani and Rodrick out."

"As far as I see it, he's our best shot," Asha replied, but her face conveyed just how little she liked the idea.

Rena had bunched her head scarf in her lap and was nervously fretting at it. That was the moment she had to tell them about Finn — he would be exactly what they were looking for, after all — she just needed to find the courage to broach the subject.

"I..." Rena started, choosing her words carefully. "... ran into someone. In the guard station."

Asha and Logan stared at her, waiting for her to continue, but Rena couldn't meet their gazes.

"Who?" Asha asked in a low, careful voice.

Rena pressed her lips into a thin line then took a deep breath.

"Finn."

"What?" Logan exclaimed, his eyes darting nervously to the other man in the room before he scooted closer and continued in a quieter voice. "How? Wh—Was he hurt? Was he in one of the cells?"

Rena shook her head. "He wasn't."

"He's working with them, isn't he?" Asha snarled. "That fucking bastard."

Rena shook her head again, more forcefully.

"They caught him outside of Oceansthrow," she hissed, making sure her voice wouldn't carry beyond their circle. "When we got separated in the forest. I'm not sure what happened to him since, but I don't think he's staying with them voluntarily."

"But they're not keeping him prisoner, hmm?" Asha replied, one eyebrow raised. "How convenient."

"Did you talk to him?" Logan asked.

"I..." Rena hesitated, afraid she'd get scolded. "I might have. When I was at the market. He was there with Captain Silac and some guards but he managed to slip away to talk to me."

"Rena," Asha said in a warning tone, letting her eyes convey the full force of her disappointment.

"I know." Rena turned her attention back to the scarf in her lap. "But I just had to talk to him." She gathered all her courage and met Asha's gaze. "I think we can trust him."

Asha opened her mouth to argue but Logan cut her off. "How is he doing? Did it look like he was doing okay?"

"He looked a bit rough but I think he's okay. Just had a few bruises but nothing major, mostly he just looked exhausted. But I think he could help us get Rodrick and Kalani out."

"We can trust him more than Fazzar," Logan murmured to Asha.

"We barely know the guy," Asha replied, looking at them as if she couldn't understand why they would ever dream of trusting him. "All we know is that he held a high position in the archives and he barely looks old enough to have abandoned his mother's tits more than a month ago. Something isn't adding up for just a random guard."

"Why do you hate him so much?" Logan glared at her in annoyance. "You know nothing about Rodrick either and I don't see you ready to stab him in the face every time the wind changes."

"Why do you like him so much, hmm?" Asha retorted but turned her attention back to Rena before Logan could reply. "What did he tell you? About Kalani and Rodrick?"

"He said they were unharmed. And something about the documents not having been filled out correctly — I didn't quite get that part, though — but he said he'll try to come up with a plan on how to best get Rodrick and Kalani out unharmed. We talked about maybe meeting up tonight at the docks. To the east near the abandoned buildings."

Asha stared at her, taking a deep breath then letting the air out slowly. Rena didn't dare avert her eyes, hoping that if she held the other woman's gaze it would show her determination. Asha's eyes were a dark brown, almost black in the low light of the room, and Rena could read all the thoughts passing through her mind — how the incredulity turned into anger then into consideration to finally land on a reluctant acceptance.

"Fine," she muttered between gritted teeth and looked away, clearly annoyed by her own decision. "He's probably not *working* for them, you're right, but that doesn't mean that I'm happy to stroll through the meadows with him."

"No one asked you to do that," Logan remarked with a hint of a smile.

"He's more trouble than he's worth, you'll see soon enough." She stood up and stretched. "It was a mistake to bring him along in the first place."

They waited for the sun to set, then headed out to the docks. They quickly found the abandoned buildings that Finn had talked about but had to wait at least another hour for him to show up, which didn't exactly help brighten Asha's sour mood. She glowered at him as he stood across from them, her arms crossed over her chest, her golden sword deliberately poking out of their knapsack. It all made the atmosphere between them denser than it had to be and Finn looked visibly uncomfortable. To Rena, he appeared worse than when she'd met him that afternoon, not because of any additional injuries, but his shoulders seemed tenser and his eyes looked heavy and bloodshot.

"So..." Logan said, drawing out the vowel as he rocked back and forth on his heels, no sign of the injury that had immobilised him just hours prior. "You're gonna help us escape a second time? Well, at least some of us. You're starting to become a real expert, huh?" He chuckled lightly but no one joined in, so he quickly stopped.

Finn looked back at the darkness at the end of the alley. "I might have a plan, but it could be risky."

"And why should we trust you?" Asha cocked her head so she'd look even taller than she already was.

"Because we don't have any other options," Logan dismissed her then addressed Finn. "What is it? And how risky are we talking?"

Finn paused before replying, his gaze still fixed on the end of the road, the muscles in his jaw working as he considered his words. The night air was cool and smelled of the ocean. The city had quieted down, only the faint noise of late-night work at the shipyard carrying over the ocean waves.

"Their transfer to the academy is planned for tomorrow morning."

"Tomorrow?" Rena asked, shock running through her as she thought they would have more time than that.

Finn nodded. "It's strange. According to the usual procedures, transfers should be organised at the earliest three days after the initial arrest, to ensure the correct paperwork can be filled out by all parties, but it's quite clear now that Silac doesn't care about any of that." He paused, a dark shadow settling over his face. "I don't know why Silac's trying to get them out of Hollowtooth this quickly but I've got a suspicion they might never arrive at the academy if we let them leave Hollowtooth."

"What do you mean?" A nervous feeling was settling in the pit of Rena's stomach.

"They'd make them disappear," Asha deadpanned, shifting her weight from foot to foot. "Make them vanish during the journey. Lose the paperwork with them. Make it seem like they never got arrested in the first place. Probably why they don't even bother with the papers."

Finn glanced at Asha for a second, then nodded.

"Doubt it's the first time they've done that," Logan sighed.

"We don't have evidence for it," Finn said reluctantly, "but if I consider everything else I found, it might be a possibility. I just don't understand how this has never been reported to the correct authorities before."

"You can't imagine all of them being corrupt?" Asha sneered. "I can."

"Not all of them," Finn answered, shaking his head. "Logistically, it just doesn't make sense. What would Silac be bribing them with? He doesn't have any particular influence or wealth. His family used to have power in the region, but not anymore. At least not enough to cover up something like this on a regular basis."

"Probably looks away whenever they want to do something," Asha said with a shrug.

"That might work for some of them, but all? The region is too interconnected for something like that to work. Others would notice. The academy would notice and they don't care about the influence of some old noble family who has fallen from grace."

"Or he's filled his station with people under his influence."

"He hasn't been head of the guard for that long; I would have heard if Hollowtooth's guard corps had been completely rearranged. And most people weren't all too happy about his appointment anyway. He can't have won all of them over in three years."

"So we think they plan on making Kalani and Rodrick disappear?" Rena asked, anxious to get back to their actual problem.

"We're not going to let it happen. Like I said, I've got a plan, even if it's a dangerous one. If we arrive before Silac when the transfer is planned, I should be able to convince the guards on duty that the procedure has been changed and that I'm taking over. I'll tell them you're my personal guards from Mellahen and you'll replace the ones who were scheduled to accompany the transfer. It will take them a while to notice we never arrived at the military academy. It would give us enough time to ditch the vehicle and continue on foot to safety."

He looked at each of them in turn, waiting for them to respond.

"I'm not sure they'll believe we're your personal guards if we're dressed like this?" Logan replied, gesturing towards his body.

"I'm fairly certain I can manage to find some uniforms for you if I arrive at the station early enough."

"Don't bother, we can get those ourselves," Asha remarked. "Pretty sure we can even get some from your precious archives."

"We don't exactly have a whole lot of money to pay for them, Asha," Logan noted with a grimace.

"But Cass does."

"Right, the privilege of being Cass' guard dog. Forgot about that."

"What bothers me most is the timeline of your plan," Asha said, pivoting her attention back to Finn. "I don't like that it hinges upon arriving before Silac."

"He has a habit of disregarding time."

"That doesn't give me any kind of guarantee."

"Could work though," Logan interjected. "If we're lucky."

Asha groaned and turned around in frustration, running a hand over her scalp.

"I hate this," she grumbled. "I hate it so much."

"Do we have any alternatives?" Rena asked carefully. "If they're being transferred tomorrow, we don't have time to go talk to the other guy you mentioned. And you said you didn't trust him much anyway."

"I know," Asha snapped. "That doesn't mean I have to be happy about this. And what do *you* gain from it, Finn? If we go through with this, they'll know you were involved. You'll fuck up your life more than you already have. Why give up your cushy life for people like us?"

Finn stayed silent for a while, meeting Asha's intense gaze without blinking.

"There's something rotten at the core of this kingdom," he finally said, his voice slow and sombre. "I don't know what it is, but I can't keep living my *cushy life*, as you put it, without at least trying to do something about it."

Asha snorted derisively and rolled her eyes.

"And you think you can save the kingdom. How fucking noble. Who are you, anyway? Why do you have so much authority that you think you can commandeer a prisoner transfer without anyone stopping you? You're what, twenty years old?"

Finn paused, then answered carefully, "Twenty-one."

"I doubt you've had time to climb the ranks through hard work, so what is it? Nepotism? Blackmail? You're just someone's puppet?"

Rena and Logan looked awkwardly from Asha to Finn and back, their eyes meeting in the middle, unsure what to do about the tension in the air.

"We don't really have time for this, Asha," Logan said carefully.

"If he's supposed to convince the guards to give him the reins of the operation, he has to have *some* sort of authority and one that is much higher than Silac's."

Asha approached Finn until she was towering over him and stared down at him. Finn held her gaze, his body unmoving, hands clenched tightly into fists. They stayed like this for a moment, the air between them growing heavy, before Asha continued.

"We'll go through with your plan for Kalani and Rodrick's sake but once they're both safe, I want the two of you" — she looked over at Logan and Rena — "to think about this whole situation very carefully. He's twenty-one and pushing his weight around as if he were a grand-general. That's just not adding up for a regular military career, is it?"

"Can we not fight?" Rena pleaded feebly. "He's here to help us, Asha. I don't see how his career is important right now. We don't have the time to argue over it."

"I just know he's putting a bigger target on our backs than we're realising. They'll want to get him back, whoever he is. Probably won't matter what the collateral damage will be."

"I will tell you later," Finn replied, carefully weighing every word. "But as Rena said, time isn't on our side."

Chapter Seven

Finn

Finn's hands had been trembling since he'd woken up. He'd once again not slept much, too afraid he wouldn't wake up early enough to execute their plan. He was staying in an inn only a few metres from the guard station, an arrangement that was clearly in place for any higher-ranking visitor. One of the guards was waiting for him at the inn's entrance, had been standing there the entire night, not because Finn was a prisoner but for his own safety, Silac had assured him. It had been a significant obstacle the night before, but Finn had managed to slip away by pretending to go out for a drink in the busy quarter of the city and losing the guard among the crowd of revellers. If Finn wasn't a prisoner, no one could fault him for enjoying his time in the city; the guard couldn't disagree with that, could he?

An additional advantage to waking up so early was that the guard tasked with keeping an eye on him hadn't been relieved of his duty yet and would hopefully be too tired to argue much with Finn or notice anything strange about his behaviour — like the fact that Finn was wearing his full getup including his rapier.

Finn had racked his brain all night trying to figure out how best to get the guards to play along with his plan once the transfer arrived. He wanted to avoid any of them fetching Silac before the vehicle arrived, so he knew he had to keep their suspicion to a minimum. He knew he couldn't ask them to look at any of the official documents. Even if they wouldn't dare deny his access to them, the likelihood of them waking Silac over it was much too high. What he'd landed on, in the end, was that he would simply ask for paper and ink to write a letter and pretend to look busy until he heard the transfer wagon approach.

The guards offered him one of their tables in the front room, brought him tea and then went back to their work, even if Finn was very aware that all of their attention was still focused on him. He scribbled something on the paper, pretending he was recounting the previous day's events to the administrator, omitting certain details in case anyone was looking over his shoulder. What he hadn't considered was how shaky his hand would be and how much of his concentration he would need to write. Too much hinged on uncertainties, too much could go wrong, and with the exhaustion coursing through his body, he hadn't been able to find any better solution on how to get Kalani and Rodrick out. He was also painfully aware that if he went through with this, he would never be able to go back to his old life. Helping Rena and the others escape the archives would mean sanctions, travelling with them for a week would mean scorn, but all of it could be forgiven. Commandeering a prisoner transfer to let the prisoners escape couldn't. Not that he much cared for his old life. There were more important things than how soft one's bed was or how few holes one's clothing had. He could live without it all if he knew he had done something of importance with his life.

Finn had reached the end of the page when he heard the faraway rumbling of the transfer vehicle. He placed the quill on the table and folded his letter, sliding it into the inner breast pocket of his coat, before he got up and thanked the guards for their hospitality. His hands were clenched tightly behind his back, his vision blurry, and the bruise on his face throbbed painfully. He longed for darkness, somewhere he could be completely alone and could forget about the physical world, but he had wished for that escape so often in his life and gotten it so seldomly that it wasn't all too difficult to ignore the feeling.

He headed straight for the door next to the wall of wanted posters that led out to the side street, ignoring the puzzled looks of the guards around him. Not long and one of them would rush to inform Captain Silac of what was going on, but if he had all planned it correctly, they would be long gone before Silac could arrive.

He knew that the guards accompanying the transfer would recognise him — his entire plan hinged on it. His role in the archives over the last few years had included overseeing any prisoner transfers. As long as the guards accompanying Rodrick and Kalani's transfer weren't new to the academy, they would know who he was and accept his word as truth.

The transfer wagon stopped next to the guard station, its engine rumbling as it idled. Its sheer magnitude distinguished it from Rodrick's now clearly homemade vehicle. It still had a few remnants of a horse-drawn carriage, but not many. It was wider and more angular, with a chimney sticking out next to the driver's cabin, which was only a small open space to one side of the wagon's front. The wheels were bigger and larger than the ones on Rodrick's, reinforced by steel to make them sturdier. The vehicle was painted red and silver, with thick metal bars running over the length of it, only leaving a small opening in the back for the door.

Said door swung open and four guards stepped out, lining up next to the vehicle with their hands clasped behind their backs. Without looking, Finn noticed that Asha, Logan and Rena were lined up opposite them, their backs to the station, just as he had told them to, wearing uniforms that looked worn but not out of place.

"Change of plan," Finn said as he approached the vehicle, projecting his voice as loudly as he could. "On orders of General Mirid and the Royal Council, I'm taking over the transfer." He turned to the guards behind him. "Go get the prisoners."

He made sure to look them in the eye, squaring his shoulders to imitate the authority the administrator exuded. For a second, he was scared that it wouldn't work. He recognised the confusion in the guard's face but then they nodded and stepped back into the station.

"You will be staying here," Finn continued as he turned back to the guards who had accompanied the transfer. "My troop will accompany me instead."

"Sir?" the driver of the vehicle asked as he came to stand with the other guards.

"I was not sent here by the archives but by my family." Finn hated having to invoke the influence of the Liberic name, but it was the one thing that would get them out of Hollowtooth as quickly as possible and with the fewest questions. No matter how strained Finn's relationship was with them, no guard would dare challenge their orders. "One of the prisoners is of great interest to the Royal Council."

The driver had a sour look on his face, his lips pressed tightly into a thin line. Finn held his breath, his gaze never wavering from the driver's eyes, waiting endlessly for the other's reaction.

"Captain Liberic," the driver finally said, "may I remind you that a special authorisation is needed to operate this vehicle, sir? Only I am allowed to drive it, sir."

The tension in Finn's muscles eased marginally. If that was all the driver disputed, Finn wouldn't argue against it. They could find a way to get rid of him once they were out of the city. It would take them several hours to travel across the province, after all.

Finn set out to reply but then Rodrick and Kalani were brought out in shackles. He simply nodded to the driver, then gestured for the wagon door to be opened. Asha and Logan stepped forward, Rena just behind, and guided the prisoners into the vehicle.

Rodrick anxiously looked around until he recognised his companions but was smart enough to school his features. Logan led him into the wagon, Rena holding on to his other arm, and Finn hoped that none of the guards were looking too closely at his supposed troop.

Kalani only had eyes for Finn, looking him up and down, her features growing grim with hatred. She spat at his feet before Asha jostled her into the wagon and for a moment Finn couldn't tell if her animosity was real or just played. He didn't know the woman, couldn't tell if they'd ever ran into each other before, if she'd somehow recognised who he was and held a grudge against his family, but her disgust at him certainly did help sell the illusion of their changing plans.

"We should leave swiftly," Finn said, turning back to the guards who had brought the prisoners out. "We have already wasted enough time. General Mirid is waiting."

He held out his hand for the keys to the shackles and it took the guard a beat to hand them over. The atmosphere felt like it might burst at any moment. They needed to leave before one of them grew the courage to second-guess him or ask for any official documentation.

"I will be back to discuss the transfer with Captain Silac by the evening," Finn told the guards, hoping it might reassure them.

Without any further words, he signalled for the driver to start the vehicle and climbed in after his companions, not giving anyone the opportunity to stop them.

Chapter Eight

Rena

Rena rushed up to the bars the second the wagon jumped into motion.

"How are you doing?" she asked, frantically looking from Rodrick to Kalani. "Did they hurt you? What happened? Did they feed you right?"

The back of the wagon was divided into two sections. The side towards the driver's cabin had been fashioned into a holding cell with bars separating it from the other side where simple benches had been built along the walls for the accompanying guards to sit on.

Rodrick stepped closer, holding tightly onto the bars as the wagon's movement made it difficult to stand.

"Do not worry, my child," he said, his voice wearier than usual. "We are quite all right. A few scratches and bruises, but nothing all too serious."

Kalani stepped closer and placed her hands atop Rena's on the bars, her thumb running over Rena's fingers in a comforting gesture. Her knuckles were bloody and scraped, deep red lines running over her brown-and-white skin — they would need a thorough cleaning to avoid infection, even a healing paste to be on the safe side — and the pair of shackles had irritated the skin at her wrists, but those were the only injuries Rena could see. Neither of them seemed to be in pain or have any trouble walking, and a huge relief washed over Rena.

"How are you, Rena?" Kalani asked, looking her up and down in great scrutiny. "You don't look hurt. That's good." She smiled. "Thank you for coming to our rescue."

Rena felt the warmth from where Kalani's hands were holding hers radiate through her body until it reached her cheeks. She smiled back, endlessly relieved that they were finally all back together.

"I'm not hurt, thank you," Rena replied, then turned to look back at the rest of their group. "Uhm, Logan got injured though, but we've been taking care of him as best we can."

"I'm fine," Logan dismissed with a wave of his hand. "It's really not that bad."

Asha stepped forward and unlocked the door to let Kalani and Rodrick out, Finn just a step behind her to unlock their shackles.

"Who's he?" Kalani eyed Finn curiously as she rubbed her wrist.

"Family with the Royal Council, apparently," Asha responded dryly as she unbuttoned the coat and trousers of her guard's uniform and threw them into the back of the cell, revealing her blue tunic underneath.

"What?! How do you know?" Rena asked nervously, her eyes darting from Asha to Finn in confusion.

"His name," Logan groaned as he carefully lowered himself onto the bench. Rodrick hurried over to help him down before Rena could get to him. Logan let his head fall against the wagon's wall and looked at Finn with a tired expression. "Isn't that right, Captain Liberic?"

Rena looked between her companions, her mouth slightly open in confusion. She hadn't recognised the name even though she'd had lessons about the Royal Council at school, but the kingdom's history had never been her favourite subject and she'd already forgotten most of what her teacher had taught them.

Finn's eyes were fixed on the wall beside Logan, the muscles in his jaw tight. He stood, unmoving, like a deer that knew it was in the presence of wolves.

"Maybe you haven't noticed yet," Logan continued, looking over at Rena, "but the nobles have these stupid naming conventions. The suffix at the end reveals their rank. And Captain *Liberic* here has the highest of them all." His head rolled to the side again as his gaze went back to Finn. "Is Finn just an abbreviation of your actual name or did you give us a fake one?"

"It is my name," Finn said tensely, his eyes never wavering from the spot to Logan's right.

"B-but... I've never heard of it," Rena stammered.

She pivoted around, searching for Rodrick, knowing that he would be able to confirm or deny what Asha and Logan were accusing Finn of being.

"Well," Rodrick replied pensively, "these patronymic or matronymic last names change depending on the parent. It's actually a very interesting tradition that is more recent than we might imagine. It only appeared in its current form about seventy years ago, although the highest level denoting the royal families was established at the same time as the creation of the Royal Council. But I digress. If my history serves me right, our friend's father must have been grand-general Liberic Orid, son of Orid Vassid, high counsellor to the court and sister to High Lord Ste—"

"Can we stop talking about it now?" Finn snapped.

No one moved, their eyes all fixed on Finn who was still staring straight ahead. His knuckles were white from how tightly he was clenching his fists, and his nose flared with each breath as the base of his jawline trembled.

Kalani finally stepped forward and held a hand out towards him.

"Thank you for helping us escape."

Finn barely moved, only his eyes shifting to stare at Kalani's hand. His back straightened slowly, his arm twitching as if he wanted to reciprocate the gesture but his body refused to play along.

"Really, Kalani?" Asha rolled her eyes as she leaned back against the wagon's door. "You also want to congratulate him for putting a giant target on our backs?"

"The target was there no matter what." Kalani let her hand drop and simply nodded at Finn before she shifted her gaze to Asha and Logan. "And I don't hold someone's past against them. The city of Rancor would be much smaller if we did."

"He made the target a million times bigger," Asha grumbled but then crossed her arms and looked down, scraping at something on the floor with her foot.

"Has anyone perchance found Vincent?" Rodrick butted in anxiously.

A knot twisted in the pit of Rena's stomach as she realised she hadn't thought of the dog all day.

"Oh stars, no, I'm truly sorry," she replied, horrified at herself.

She thought that, with some luck, the dog had found his way back to Halvint by now and Darian was taking care of him. She didn't dare imagine any other scenario.

"Maybe he's waiting near my old caravan," Rodrick muttered, his eyebrows drawing together in concern.

"Guards might be waiting near the vehicle," Finn remarked in a careful tone. "Once they notice we've commandeered this one, they'll know that your old caravan is the likeliest place we'll return to."

"I'm not abandoning my dog!" Rodrick snapped, offended by the mere idea of it.

"That's not what I said," Finn continued, an air of confusion washing over his face. "I meant that we'll need to be careful if we want to return there."

"Most of our stuff is still in that vehicle," Logan remarked. "Though I don't know if we absolutely need it. Might be better to travel light."

"Oh, but all the wonderful things I collected over the years," Rodrick said, defeated, then sighed. "I suppose they would only be a hindrance if we cannot continue our journey by caravan. I would appreciate it very much though if I could at least get my notebooks back."

"And the scrolls we found in the Crow's hideout are still in there," Rena added. "If no one has stolen them yet."

"Right, but let's figure all of that out after we've gotten out of *this* vehicle," Kalani said. "The longer we talk, the closer we get to the academy, which leads us to the question of how we can get back to

Halvint." She turned back to look at the wall that separated them from the driver's cabin. "I don't suppose the driver is also on our side, right?"

"I'm sure we can overwhelm him once he stops," Logan said. "... If he stops."

The group devolved into a loud discussion about how to get the vehicle to stop, everyone having a million wild ideas. Rena noticed that Finn had sat down on one of the benches and let his head hang between his legs, wrapping his arms over his head, his hands clenching and unclenching rhythmically. The tension in his shoulders relaxed with each exhale.

She walked over and sat down next to him, but when she saw that her presence caused his body to go rigid again, she decided to scoot to the right to leave more space between them.

"I'm sorry they've been so tough on you," she whispered, hoping he could still hear her above the noise in the room. "In all honesty, I didn't know what to think either when I saw you yesterday. I couldn't tell if we should trust you or not, but I want to believe you. I really do. I don't think you would do all that you've done just to betray us in the end. It doesn't really make sense to me. And why should I trust you any less than the others just because of your family? I've known you just as long as the others and that really hasn't been any time at all, if I'm being honest. So thank you for all your help. We couldn't have freed Rodrick and Kalani without you, and without everyone's help, I'd barely have a chance to save my sister."

Finn stayed silent for a moment, then murmured, "It's been a long day."

It was, in fact, still the early morning, but Rena understood what he meant.

"I don't know much about the Royal Council," she continued, looking down at her hands, "you know, beyond what they taught us in school but even then, I didn't truly pay attention, so I'm not sure why there's so much tension between Asha and you. I know bad stuff happened in the Grey Isles and I'm sure the Royal Council has to be implicated somehow — I just don't know what your family has to do with it. I'm honestly kind of annoyed with myself that I know so little about it; I know I should have paid better attention during lessons. But even if your family was involved in it, I don't think that should be held above your head, especially if it happened when you were still a kid or even before that. What I know is that you've helped us so far and that you've endangered yourself over it; I don't think that should be ignored."

Finn straightened, his hand carding through his blond hair as he took a deep breath.

"They conveniently leave out a lot in your schools," he muttered, then sighed and continued in a louder voice, "but Asha isn't wrong. My presence is putting you in more danger than you would be on your own."

"Your presence is also getting us out of situations we wouldn't have gotten out of on our own. And everyone's bringing their own past with them. If she can accept Logan, then there shouldn't be a problem with you either."

"No one on the Royal Council knows Logan by name and could send the entire kingdom's army after him."

Rena shot him a small smile and said, "Maybe not, but from what I've heard, he's making enemies on other fronts."

Logan detached himself from the other group and came over.

"What are you two gossiping about? I've heard my name."

He sat down on Finn's other side and tried to drape an arm over his shoulders, which Finn evaded with poise and precision.

"She's informed me that you're a menace to polite society," Finn said, scooting closer to Rena.

Logan grinned at him and winked.

"Oh, I'm so much more than that."

Kalani walked over, followed closely by Asha and Rodrick, their discussion seemingly having concluded.

"No time to chit chat," Kalani said as she came to a stop and crossed her arms. "The longer we wait, the closer we get to the academy. We need to stop the vehicle, so let's try to dismantle the benches. Maybe the noise alone will make the driver stop. Rodrick, do you think you can drive this wagon?"

"I-I haven't looked at its mechanics yet," he stammered, "but it shouldn't be too different from my own. I think."

"All right." Kalani nodded, seemingly satisfied with his answer, before she addressed the entire group. "Enough standing around — let's break some stuff and make that anchor."

At first, Asha tried to pry the benches off the floor as a whole but she quickly realised that was impossible and resorted instead to kicking the top of the benches until they broke in two. Together with Kalani and Finn, they dismantled most of the furnishings surrounding them, throwing it all together into one big pile in the middle of the room.

Rena's assigned job was to fashion a sort of rope out of the clothing they didn't need anymore, although the reality was that she spent most of her time trying to keep Logan from helping break the benches and inadvertently making his wound worse.

Even with all their ruckus, the driver never stopped or slowed down. In all likelihood, the walls were too thick and the device powering the vehicle drowned out any of the noise they were making.

They fastened one end of Rena's makeshift rope to the stumps still jutting out of the floor, using Rodrick and Kalani's shackles to hold everything tight, while the other end was tied around the pile of debris they'd gathered.

They threw their contraption overboard and although it didn't quite seem to work as an anchor as they'd hoped it would, the noise it made was so loud that even the driver couldn't ignore it, and the wagon soon stopped.

They all stood motionless, staring at the road beyond the open door. The sudden silence was deafening, and then, bit by bit, the sounds of the forest broke through. Rena breathed as shallowly as she could, waiting for any indication that the driver was coming their way.

"Captain Liberic," a voice called from afar, "is there a problem, sir?"

Rena grabbed Logan's arm and gently pulled him back, but she wasn't sure if it was to keep him or herself from running forward.

"Let me distract him," Finn whispered. "You can go around the vehicle and sneak up on him from behind to overwhelm him."

"I'm not letting you do anything," Asha muttered and before Finn could reply, she'd already drawn her sword, jumped out of the vehicle and rounded the corner.

"For fuck's sake," Kalani swore and rushed after her, grabbing a plank of wood from the pile they'd thrown out.

"Hey!" the driver called out. "What are you— Get back!"

Rena jolted the instant she heard Asha's sword strike something metallic. Finn didn't hesitate and jumped out, his rapier ready in his hand.

"Captain? What is th—" but the guard could not finish his sentence before a blow shut him up and his body hit the ground.

The moment the fight was over, Logan slipped out of Rena's grasp and hurried outside, Rena and Rodrick close behind.

"Why didn't you wait for us to come up with a plan?" Finn shouted, rushing towards Asha. "This could have gone wrong in so many ways!"

"I'm a better fighter than you'll ever be," she snarled, looking down at him.

"I never doubted that you were, but that doesn't mean he couldn't have hurt you!"

"What do you care if I get hurt or not?"

Asha closed the distance between them until their chests met, emphasising the height advantage she had over him by keeping her head held high. Finn rolled his eyes and simply walked past her towards the unconscious body on the ground, turning the driver over so he lay on his back.

"I care about how quickly we can get out of here," Finn said, a bitter note in his voice, "and having to take care of one more injured person would've been an unnecessary waste of time."

"He's right," Kalani said with thinly veiled anger. "Just because you don't like him doesn't mean you have to be reckless. I expect more of you."

Asha opened her mouth to reply, but one look from Kalani kept her silent, even if her displeasure was plainly written on her face.

"We should get the body away from the road," Logan said, looking towards both ends of the road. "Asha, if you're done throwing your tantrum, can you drag him into the forest?"

She stared at him for a second, her jaw tight as if she was ready to pounce on him, but then she sighed and stepped forward. She hooked her arms under the guard's armpits and dragged him over the ground deep into the forest without care for his well-being.

"Won't the wolves get him?" Rena asked, observing the scene with some discomfort.

"If they do, it was fated to be," Kalani said in such a tone that Rena didn't dare ask another question. "Rodrick, get into the driver's cabin and get the vehicle running. Everyone else, free up the road. I want to be out of here as quickly as possible. And find a way to disguise the vehicle. Throw some mud on it or something."

"I don't think that's necessary," Finn replied. "The shape alone tells you what it is. It's impossible to make it look like something else; there are only a handful of these coal-powered vehicles in the province. Throwing mud on it won't do anything."

"Well, at least they won't recognise us from afar," Kalani retorted, bending down to pick up some of the debris they'd thrown out. "Stop standing around like wilted flowers, everyone. Get moving!"

They all scattered in different directions, doing exactly what Kalani had told them to do. It didn't take long before the vehicle was covered in mud and had rumbled back to life. Rena wiped her mud-covered hands on her new trousers, hoping that it would make them less recognisable as part of a guard's uniform, though it made them quite uncomfortable.

What they hadn't considered as they'd dismantled the interior of the wagon was that they wouldn't have anywhere to sit on their journey back. Logan lay down in the middle of the floor while the others sat with their backs against the walls, Rena and Finn on one side, Kalani and Asha on the other. They didn't talk, most of them opting to close their eyes to seize the little rest they could get on their journey.

Chapter Nine

Rena

Their journey back to Halvint took longer than Rena was comfortable with. Rodrick purposefully drove across the less-travelled roads in the central parts of the province, far away from the busy coastline. Nature had taken back most of these paths and it was a miracle their wagon could advance at all, but the risk of getting stuck was preferable to running into guards on the southern roads.

The wagon's shaking and rattling didn't help lessen Rena's nerves. Now that they'd all found their way back together and were on their way to picking up Vincent, there was nothing stopping them from focusing all their attention on rescuing Maya. All they needed to do was cross the border into Baedan. They wouldn't have to comb through the entire province, only the parts close to the border. If they could trust Michael — the acolyte who'd tried to help them — the old monastery the Crow was staying in was somewhere in the hills near Vellashta. Rena closed her eyes and tried to picture a map of the region. She knew the border crossed somewhere through the forest between both provinces, but she couldn't remember just how much of it was in Vellashta. She also knew that two provinces bordered her own — Baedan to the east and Napahrit to the west — which meant Baedan didn't span the entirety of the kingdom's peninsula, but where it stopped, she couldn't visualise either.

She took deep breaths, trying to calculate how much of the area they could comb through in one day. They would have to leave Logan behind, probably also Rodrick, considering his age. It was unlikely that they'd be able to travel over the hills with a wagon, so they'd have to walk on foot. Maybe they could find horses somewhere — Kalani might have contacts who could lend them one or two — then they could find the monastery much faster. It would definitely take longer than a day, except if they got very lucky, but maybe it would only take them three or four days, a week at most.

"I think it's best we go back to Rancor once we've saved the dog," Kalani suggested, deep in thought as she stared at the floor of the wagon.

Rena looked up and frowned.

"The city's moving," Asha informed Kalani, head resting against the wall and eyes closed. "Cass thought it smart to get out of the region."

"They're probably right," Kalani mumbled. Her eyes narrowed in thought.

"Isn't it best if we try to find the Crow right away?" Rena suggested nervously. "I mean, Michael told us where they were keeping Maya, so we just have to find the right monastery and if we start looking for it right away, we'll get to them before they have the chance to move. Because if Inkra gets back to them, maybe she'll warn them about us and the more time we give them the likelier they are to come up with a plan to counter us or to just leave the region and I don't know if we'll be able to find them again if they decide to leave."

"*Just* find the right monastery?" Asha had opened one eye and was looking at Rena, her eyebrow raised.

"Maybe I shouldn't say it like that, but I'm sure we could find it if we just looked for it, and the earlier we start looking, the faster we'll find it, no?"

"I don't think you realise just how big Baedan is," Kalani replied and straightened her back, twisting from side to side to stretch. "And even if we were to randomly stumble upon it, we still wouldn't know what'll await us inside. Better not to go in completely unprepared."

"But—"

"I know you're scared for your sister, Rena, but there are a lot of abandoned structures carved into the hills of Baedan. The region is famous for it. Probably why the Crow decided to settle there, so they wouldn't be discovered as easily. It would take us days if not weeks to comb through the region, especially while injured and exhausted. Better to find a place where we can rest and maybe find someone who could help us locate them."

Kalani looked at Rena with a soft smile, which instantly killed any argument that was bubbling up inside her. Rena looked down at her lap, heat rising to her cheeks. She wished she had the heart to disagree with Kalani, but no plan she came up with could guarantee their safety and she didn't have the knowledge or connections to come up with anything better. She didn't even know who to ask or where to go to gain more knowledge about the situation. All she could do was trust her companions and simply do what they told her to do. It didn't feel right, especially since it was *her* sister they were trying to save. Rena had dragged them all into this mess and she couldn't even contribute to getting them out of it.

"What's the plan, then?" Logan asked, pushing himself up on his elbows.

"Hrevim, I think," Kalani replied, frowning slightly in thought. "It gets us closer to the hills and we know people there who could help us, or at least find us someone who can help. *Someone* has to have heard where the Crow is hiding."

Rena had heard of Hrevim before — a big city on the coast of Baedan, famous for its port — and had even dreamed of going with her family at some point. A pang of grief shot through her heart as she realised they would never get to experience the city together.

"One of the best libraries in the kingdom," Rodrick added. "Depending on what you're looking for, of course. But definitely the best in the province, much better than the one in Meshöhrem."

"Very important, of course," Kalani replied with an amused smirk. "But I also think we all deserve a night of rest. Some of us desperately need it. And the better rested we are, the better our outcome against the Crow will be."

Without truly looking, everyone's attention was on Logan, but Rena thought Finn might also fall apart if he didn't get a few hours of uninterrupted sleep soon.

They abandoned the stolen vehicle north of Halvint and tried to find their way back to Rodrick's caravan on foot. They walked through the forest as quietly as possible, always keeping an eye on the road so no one could surprise them. As they got closer to the site of their crash, they started hearing a commotion, a mixture of shouting and a dog barking. Kalani raised a hand and they all stopped, listening intently and straining to see anything between the trees.

Kalani looked at Asha and nodded towards the road, then gestured for the others to stay. Logan stepped forward to join them, but Rena and Rodrick grabbed his wrists at the same time to keep him back. He opened his mouth to complain, but Rena shushed him before he could utter a single word. He rolled his eyes and pressed his lips together, shaking his arms free and stepping back.

Rena picked up the knapsack Asha had left behind as she'd followed Kalani and placed it in front of her feet. She crossed her arms tightly and kept her breathing as shallow as possible, unfocusing her eyes as she put all her concentration on her hearing. It was highly likely that the barking dog was Vincent, but the shouting people could either be scavengers trying to get inside Rodrick's caravan or guards looking for Rena and her companions. She could hear at least four people, some closer than others. At first, she couldn't understand what they were saying, but then a jolt ran through her when she recognised Kalani and Rodrick's names.

Rena glanced at the others, a million questions in her eyes, but they seemed just as clueless about the best course of action. She scanned the forest for any signs of Asha or Kalani, but nothing seemed to move around them.

Finn stepped carefully towards the road, his rapier drawn. He seemed hesitant, as if he didn't want to leave the others behind. He stopped just at the edge of the forest and craned his neck. He didn't instantly recoil, which probably meant there weren't any guards in sight. Rena turned to ask Rodrick and Logan if they should move, but then froze.

"Oh, come on!" she hissed. "Logan's gone."

Rodrick looked around in confusion, blinking as if he had just been in a trance.

"But he was just here," he whispered. "I didn't even hear him leave."

Rena buried her face in her hands, desperately wanting to groan but suppressing the urge.

"Sometimes I really hate him," she muttered then looked back up at Rodrick. "Do we follow him?"

"No," Rodrick answered without hesitation, as if anything else would simply be madness.

Footsteps approached and Rena stilled, her mind desperately trying to figure out where they were coming from.

Before Rena had the time to consider what to do, Kalani appeared to their left and waved at them to follow, not waiting for them to move before she left again. Rena hurried to catch up, picking up their knapsack and frantically looking from side to side in the hopes of seeing Logan.

"Asha's distracting the guards," Kalani hissed over her shoulder. "We're gonna get to the wagon, pick up everything we need as quickly as possible, then head back, okay? A handful of minutes, no more."

Rena was about to tell her that Logan was missing but then the dog stopped barking. Her muscles tightened, scared that something might have happened to Vincent. Her eyes flicked to Rodrick, who looked just as concerned and confused, and they both picked up their pace.

They emerged onto the road next to Rodrick's caravan, which had crashed into a tree, debris strewn across the road, although most of Rodrick's possessions seemed to have stayed inside the vehicle. Logan was kneeling beside the wagon and was busy rubbing Vincent's belly as if they currently weren't in any danger. Kalani frowned and scanned their surroundings before turning back to Logan, only just then realising that he hadn't stayed with the others. He smiled up at them, then quickly grimaced when he saw Kalani's expression.

She elected not to say anything and instead turned to Rodrick. "Open the wagon."

"I was just trying to help," Logan murmured as he came to stand next to Rena, who sent him another look that shut him up.

She might have replied if Vincent hadn't jumped up to greet them all, even Finn, who jerked back the second the dog approached him. Vincent seemed unharmed, just a bit dirty from lying next to the caravan for more than a day. Emotions welled up in Rena as she knelt to pet the dog, so incredibly happy that he had waited for them to return and had tried to protect the caravan. She ran a hand through his fur, burying her face in it, and deeply inhaled, ignoring the fact that it wasn't actually that nice of a smell emanating from him.

"Finally," a voice boomed from behind them, and Rena froze. "I thought you'd never show up."

They all whirled around as a figure emerged from the forest behind them. Captain Silac still wore the brown cape from the day before, but now Rena saw the golden details woven across its edges, intertwining with shimmering pearls.

Rena slowly got up, her hand never leaving Vincent's head. Logan stepped forward and held an arm out in front of her, guiding her to stand behind him. Her eyes darted around, waiting for the guards to emerge. The forest moved to her left and her breath hitched for a moment before she recognised that it was Asha who had found her way back to them. Their eyes met and Asha opened her mouth as if she was about to say something, but then stopped and frowned when she saw Rena's expression. She stepped onto the road, only then noticing that they weren't alone.

"Just let us leave and nothing bad will happen to you," Kalani called back to him. "There's six of us and only one of you, and I'm not waiting for the rest of your troop to catch up."

"Captain Silac," Finn warned, his rapier ready at his side, "this is going against every protocol our kingdom has. You had no authority to imprison these people, let alone try to send them to the academy with faked documents. Let us go and I won't report you to the grand-general."

Silac approached slowly, his brown eyes filled with rage as he stared at Rena, ignoring both Finn and Kalani.

"You think I don't know who you are? Inkra told me all about you, you ungrateful brat. You could have had such an easy life — thank your luck for surviving and start anew. But no, instead, you're gathering all of these lowlifes just to be a pebble in our shoe. Because that's all you are.

Just a tiny pebble that we need to get rid of. You think you're important enough to stop this, but you're nothing!"

Dread and fear crept through Rena, tightening around her throat. She wanted to look away from Silac but couldn't.

"Clearly we're enough to get you riled up," Logan replied, pushing Rena further behind him.

"Silence!" Silac shouted before he turned to Rodrick, and then his voice grew strange, as if it came from everywhere and nowhere at once. "You! Old man! Bring me the girl!"

As he spoke, veins crept over his eyes, but instead of being blood red, they pulsed a yellowish green.

Rena turned to Rodrick, her eyes wide with fear. He stared back, the worry and panic slowly draining from his face until there was no expression left. Was he on Silac's side? But how could that be? Had Silac recruited him in the holding cells? Had he been lying to her since the beginning? No, something wasn't right.

He took a shaky step forward, and then another, his body advancing one part at a time. His eyes were glazed over, as if they weren't focusing on anything. His arm raised — first the shoulder, then the elbow, then the wrist — until his hand was reaching for her. Vincent came to stand in front of her, head bowed low as he growled at his master.

"Rodrick?"

Chapter Ten

Rena

Something wasn't right. Rodrick advanced towards Rena, slowly, as if his body was trying to resist its own movement. She stepped back, unsure of what to do, unsure whether she should run away or not.

"Rodrick?" she asked, her voice cracking midway. "What's happening?"

He didn't respond or react. He simply continued advancing, his hand reaching out towards her, his face blank.

Rena looked at her other companions, but they all stared at the scene in horror.

"Faster!" Silac's booming voice echoed over the road.

Rodrick's body jerked forward, his legs advancing first, his upper body having to catch up to the new speed. It overshot and he lost his balance, making him fall to the ground, his body never making an effort to catch itself as his right hand reached for Rena.

"Oh stars! Are you all right?" Rena cried out and instinctively leapt forward, wanting to help him up, but then quickly jumped back.

Rodrick's legs wriggled over the ground until they found a grip, pushing his body over the dirt. His face lifted up, emotionless and covered in mud, his eyes unfocused but locked on Rena all the same.

"What are you doing to him?!" Rena yelled at Silac as Logan reached for her arm to pull her away from Rodrick.

The yellow-green veins had completely covered Silac's eyes, his pupils barely visible anymore. The veins were creeping out onto his skin, slowly spreading over his face, pulsing like a heartbeat.

Asha was the first to move. Without hesitation, she leapt forward, swinging her sword at Silac.

"Stop!" he shouted, and as he spoke, the veins erupted over his skin, spreading further in one big surge.

Asha froze mid-movement, her sword hanging in the air as if time had stopped.

"What are you?!" Logan shouted, panic colouring his voice.

"What do you want?" Kalani said at the same time, calmer than Rena could have ever managed.

"I don't know why any of you are bothering to help this insolent child," Silac replied in his regular voice, gesturing towards Rena. "As if you have nothing better to do with your own lives. You are meddling in affairs that have absolutely nothing to do with you, that might even improve your poor excuses for lives if you let it happen. But what do I expect from people who have never lived through any hardship? Nothing bad ever happens in this lifeless province, engineered to stay the same year after year after year, devolving into nothingness for the amusement of others. Be glad you don't live in Red Hill or Jodan. They don't have luscious forests or a blue ocean to sell to those in power. All they have is what lies underneath their feet, and you can't even imagine what it's like to live off that."

"What does any of that have to do with us?" Logan asked, confusion washing over his face.

"No one recognises the true strengths of our homeland," Silac continued, head held high as the veins pulsed over his face. "This kingdom is destined for greatness! *I* am destined for greatness! We have always been — it has been foretold for centuries — we just lost our way when we created the Royal Council. They claim that anyone has a chance to help shape our kingdom's future, but have you ever seen anyone ascend to the throne who wasn't from the same three families? Oh, they might pretend that they've voted someone in that is not related but you don't have to look far to see the connection. They would never even entertain the idea of someone like me joining their ranks and none of it is due to my own failings.

"There is nothing I can achieve in life that would erase in their eyes what my family has done, and then they claim that their system is fair?! That we have improved our kingdom? That turning our backs on our gods was not the greatest mistake we could have made? They're worshipping steam now. Steam! Can you imagine that? A bit of water that lost all its form. They have turned their backs on our great and powerful gods for that? Of course our people are suffering if steam and coal and gas are their new masters. But you wouldn't know that, would you? Because they keep you ignorant and docile and you don't even question it."

Rena's cheeks ran red hot but not because of Silac's aggression or the strangeness of the situation. She felt embarrassed. She'd always been proud of their little school in Oceansthrow. It hadn't existed yet when her parents had been young, forcing them to travel long distances for school, and her grandparents had never had the opportunity to get an education at all. Hers was the first generation to learn how to read and calculate and about their kingdom's history in the comfort of her own town. But every day, it seemed, she learned of something new she had no knowledge of. Silac was talking about suffering, and Rena had no idea what he meant. She barely even knew where Red Hill or Jodan were or what life was like there. And even Finn had mentioned earlier that there was a lot their schools didn't teach them. She didn't even understand why Silac was talking about the old gods. They'd always just been stories people used to tell a long time ago. Why were the Crow and Silac so obsessed with these gods? What did they think these stories could bring them?

"You speak of the greatness of the kingdom," Finn said, choosing each word carefully, "and yet you ally yourself with an organisation that burns down villages and kills hundreds of people? How is that not treason to our so-called great kingdom?"

Silac turned to look at him and laughed derisively.

"Who are *you* to talk, Liberic? Is *this* not treason? The grandnephew of a High Lord running away from his duties to join a troupe of lowlifes? But who would have expected anything else from you? No matter how high you hold your head, you'll never be able to hide the fact that your family simply didn't want you."

Finn's jaw clenched tight, his whole body rigid, the knuckles of his fists turning white.

"At least I'm trying to achieve something with my life," Silac continued, "instead of rotting away surrounded by crumbling parchment just because your father didn't want the trouble of raising you. Look at your sister, what she has accomplished. Aren't you ashamed of yourself? I've had a fraction of your privilege growing up and I've still found a way to help my kingdom. Sure, some sacrifices had to be made, but it's nothing compared to the lives that will be lost if we don't stop the Royal Council!"

Rena's eyes darted from Silac to Rodrick, who was still crawling towards her, to Finn, who had completely frozen in place. Rena didn't know enough about his life to understand what Silac was talking about, but she didn't need to understand. She wished she had the courage to tell Silac to shut up. The words were on her tongue but her lips didn't want to part. She wanted to dissolve into the mud beneath her feet so Silac couldn't turn his attention back to her, too afraid that he'd make her body do something she didn't want to do.

Kalani stepped forward, standing in front of Finn, and commandeered Silac's attention to her.

"What do you want, Silac? Or are you simply here to insult our families?"

From the corner of her eye, Rena noticed that Logan had stepped back and was sneaking towards the left, keeping Asha's unmoving body between Silac and him. He advanced slowly, his eyes fixed on Silac, stopping any time the captain turned his way.

"Isn't it obvious?" Silac asked, throwing his arms out in exasperation. "I knew your lot was stupid, but I didn't know it was to such an extent." He stopped as if he was waiting for them to come to a conclusion themselves, then raised an eyebrow and continued. "I want you to stop your little quest and crawl back into the rotten holes you came from."

Kalani let silence settle between them before she replied, her anger barely concealed behind the steadiness of her voice.

"You want us to stop looking for people who had no qualms about burning down an entire village? More than one, actually. Do you know how many people have died because of your friends? Do you even care?"

Silac rolled his eyes and sighed heavily.

"None of you understand the sacrifices that have to be made," he groaned. "Our kingdom is dying from within and if we don't act now, there will be more deaths than your little villages. We should have never turned our backs on the gods and now we're all paying the price for it."

"Stop it!" Rena finally burst out, rage running red hot through her veins. "My entire family is dead because of you! I had siblings who had barely had a chance to live and you robbed them of a future because of this stupid plan of yours. Who cares about your stupid gods? What have they ever done for any of us?!"

Suddenly, something brushed against Rena's ankle and she cried out. She jerked back, realising that Rodrick had dragged himself all the way to her — mud and dirt covering his face and once-white beard. His hand was swiping at her, but the motion was so uncoordinated that she had no difficulty stepping out of his reach.

Rodrick's appearance was a nightmare to behold. His eyes were barely looking at her, or at anything at all for that matter, and no emotion crossed his face as he incessantly crawled closer. Even Vincent seemed conflicted about the situation. He snapped at the hand between barks but never close enough to hurt Rodrick, as if he recognised that something was very wrong with his master.

"Stop it!" Rena yelled at Silac, stumbling away from Rodrick. "Please, there has to be another way! I know nothing of the suffering you talk about or how the Royal Council could be responsible for it, but this can't be the solution, to take people's lives away! Would your gods really condone this?!"

She kept an eye on Rodrick as she stepped away — Vincent always positioned between the two of them — but from the corner of her eye she saw how Logan was slowly circling Silac.

She knew this was a risk. There was no guarantee that appealing to Silac's pride would distract him enough that Logan could overwhelm him — and even if Logan did, who knew if it would break the hold he had on Rodrick and Asha? — but Rena didn't know what else to do.

"We have tried other methods. They all failed." Silac kept his eyes on her, the green veins pulsing over his face. "The gods do not oppose their own resurrection so if this is the method we have to use, so be it. I do believe that we were too soft before, that we failed because we were too cowardly to do what had to be done, but no more! Look at me. Am I not proof that our methods are working?"

He grinned a wicked grin, the veins distorting his face. A cold shudder ran over Rena's back. Panic started rising in her as she looked up at Finn and Kalani who stood silently, fear rooting them in place. Rena wanted to yell, to cry, to run away, but she needed to keep his attention on her to give Logan the time to sneak behind him.

She stepped away from her group, pretending to be backing away from Rodrick.

"I don't know what you are," she stammered. "I really don't understand any of this. You speak of the evil deeds of the Royal Council and it makes me realise that I know so little about our kingdom."

"Of course you do," Silac snapped. "They only feed you that which makes them look best."

Rena flinched but then continued.

"Maybe. You're not the first to tell me so. But what you and the Crow are doing is just as wicked. You talk about sacrifices but none of them are your own."

Logan was now almost opposite Rena, long past the safety of Asha's shadow. If Silac were to turn around, he'd certainly realise what they were trying to do. The blood pounding in her ears made it almost impossible to hear what Silac was saying and although she was forcing herself to breathe normally, her head was spinning.

"Don't talk about things you know nothing about, child," Silac sneered. "You can't even imagine the things I've had to sacrifice, but if we want the ritual to succeed, we need to be fearless, our eyes focused on what truly matters."

Suddenly Logan tackled Silac to the ground and for a moment, Rena wished Logan had let Silac keep talking. He'd been so close to revealing something that might help them understand what was going on and she doubted they would get him to confess more if they subdued him.

Finn didn't miss a beat and leapt forward, leading the attack with his rapier but it missed and he got dragged into the pile of limbs. Rena barely had time to understand what was going on before the blade had pierced Silac's thigh and he cried out in pain, the yellowish-green veins bursting over his face before they vanished.

With a big inhale, Asha finally finished her motion, her sword swinging to the ground and her body stumbling right after. She crumpled in on herself as if strength had left her body, her breath coming in ragged and panicked, interrupted by constant coughing.

Rena turned to Rodrick, who had snapped out of his state, blinking wildly as he pushed himself off the ground.

"Rodrick!" She ran to help him up.

Kalani had rushed to Asha while Logan and Finn tried to pin a bleeding Silac to the ground, but then Logan faltered, his face contorted from pain as he wrapped an arm around his stomach.

Vincent was still apprehensive, not letting Rena get to Rodrick, but he soon seemed to realise that his master had regained control of his body and started sniffing him carefully.

"Are you hurt?" she asked frantically as she pulled him to his feet. "What happened to you?"

"Stop!" the same strange voice from before boomed out over the forest, and suddenly something gripped Rena tight as if her body had frozen like ice.

It enveloped her mind, jumbling her thoughts. Her chest didn't want to move anymore, forcing her lungs to expand into her stomach as they had nowhere else to go.

"Fight each other!" Silac commanded.

Rodrick slowly lifted his arm out of her grip as if he wasn't too sure of the motion. His trembling hands reached out towards her. Panic surged through Rena, ebbing and flowing as if the emotion wasn't too sure about itself either. A dull fog kept her from understanding what was going on around her, all sound drowned out by Vincent's constant barking. Her vision was blurry and bright as if she were staring into a flame, drenching Rodrick's face in a strange halo.

Rodrick's hands came closer, wrapping gently around her face, then sliding down to her throat. A strange energy tugged at Rena's limbs but it wasn't strong enough to actually lift her arms. With all her might, she pushed against it, forcing her hands to lay on top of Rodrick's instead of hurting him like the energy told her to.

The rest of her companions stumbled around like drunken puppets. Asha swung her sword towards Finn but only managed to hit his rapier out of his hand, the force of the movement making her stumble to the ground. Logan leapt on top of her and both rolled around in the dirt, grabbing each other tight, a multitude of limbs flailing around with no real purpose. Silac staggered back, blood dripping down his leg, and disappeared into the forest.

Chapter Eleven

Rena

The strange energy vanished from Rena's body just as Silac disappeared into the forest. She took a deep breath and let herself fall forward into Rodrick's embrace, wrapping her arms tightly around him. Relief and panic burst through her like a tidal wave. She didn't understand what had just happened, why she hadn't been able to move, what those strange thoughts of hurting her friends had been. How had Silac done that? How did a few simple words command another person's body and mind? His voice had become so strange, so unnatural. And those veins...

She had never felt so scared in her life, unsure if she could still trust the world around her. Reality had shifted and her mind didn't know how to accept it.

"Oh, my child. I am so sorry," Rodrick mumbled over and over again, a hand incessantly caressing her hair.

Tears streamed down Rena's face, dampening Rodrick's shirt. She had trouble breathing through her sobs but her body refused to stop. Never had she even considered something like this to be possible. Was this the Crow's grand plan? To change the world until it was unrecognisable? In all the chaos and confusion, Rena kept thinking of her sister and what she had to be going through. It was impossible to know anymore what the Crow wanted Maya for, but it didn't really matter if Rena could get her out of there fast enough.

Logan and Asha were still rolling around in the dirt, but at least Vincent had stopped barking, opting instead to anxiously pace between all humans to sniff them.

"Stop fighting!" Kalani shouted with a tremble in her voice as she walked over to them. "You look like toddlers quarrelling over the last almond ball."

Rena took one last deep, shaky breath and stepped away from Rodrick, drying her cheeks with the back of her hand.

Kalani helped Asha up but Logan stayed on the ground, arms and legs splayed out, mouth agape as he stared at the sky with wide-open eyes. His chest was rising slowly and his right hand came to lay above his wound, the expression on his face unreadable. A few meters away, Finn was hunched over his rapier, his arms wrapped over his head.

"What was that?" Rena asked, her voice just above a whisper.

Kalani looked at her for a moment, fear in her eyes, before she answered in a voice Rena had never heard before. "I don't know. I've never experienced anything like it. I-it shouldn't be possible. That's not something people should be able to do."

"That fucker took over our bodies!" Asha roared, stomping back and forth, a hand sliding over her scalp. "How is that possible? I almost choked to death because of him! I couldn't fucking breathe! And then he makes us fight each other?! How? What is he? What the fuck did the Crow do to him?!"

"It doesn't matter for now," Kalani replied, scanning the forest around them, "we need to get out of there as fast as possible. We can talk about this when we're safe. I'm sure we can still find some useful stuff in Rodrick's old caravan but pack light, we might have to walk. Finn?"

He hadn't moved since Silac had left, still crouching over his rapier with his hands over his head.

They waited for his response but he stayed still as a statue. Rena considered approaching but before she'd made up her mind, Logan had jogged over to him. He crouched next to Finn and said something in a low voice that Rena couldn't hear. Logan lifted his hand to put on Finn's shoulder, but then thought better of it, his hand coming to a halt just above Finn's back.

Slowly, Finn unwrapped his arms and stared straight ahead, eyes wide, his face blank. In one slow, rigid motion, he picked up his rapier and stood up. Logan got up with him, his hand still hovering, saying something none of the others could hear. Finn nodded and turned to the rest of the group. He looked at them for a moment, then walked closer, his eyes turned to the ground. He came to a stand between Kalani and Asha and nodded once.

"All right." Kalani looked at him for a moment, assessing his condition, then turned to head to the caravan.

The back door had jumped out of its lock and was standing ajar but not wide enough to indicate that anyone had been inside. As they all followed suit, Rodrick stepped up to the vehicle and carefully laid a hand on its side, tracing the details with his fingers.

Kalani stepped inside and handed anything she found essential to Asha who distributed it on the ground around them. They filled one knapsack with all the food they found. Another knapsack was filled with clothes, smaller items that might be useful on their journey, and Rodrick's notebooks that he refused to leave behind. The rest would have to be abandoned with the caravan, although Kalani agreed to take some of the fancier trinkets after Logan pointed out they could sell them in the next village, to Rodrick's dismay.

They had also found the dress with the red vest Rena had gotten from Darian's wife the first time she'd stayed in Halvint. She picked it up and clutched it tightly to her face, breathing it in. She couldn't wait to get out of the muddy guard's uniform, and she was certain the others felt the same.

Something moved in the corner of Rena's eye. She turned, panic spiking in her instantly, but it was only a fox. A fox that was sitting at the other end of the road and staring at her, unmoving.

She stopped and stared back, waiting for it to move first, but it never did.

"Hey!" she finally cried out, frustration rolling over her that the fox had decided to show up right at that moment.

It jumped into action and bounced over the road and disappeared into the forest. Rena ran after it but quickly lost it among the trees.

"Hey!" she cried out again, anger rising in her. "Stop! What do you want? Why are you following me?"

She craned her neck to see if she could still catch a glimpse of orange between the bushes, but even with the sunlight poking through the treetops, she couldn't see anything move.

"Rena?" Logan called out and jogged up to her. "What's going on? Did you see someone?"

"The fox!" she exclaimed, gesticulating wildly in frustration. "There's a fox that's following me around! It was in the Plains and the archives and the forest near Oceansthrow and it just stood right here!"

"What?" Logan chuckled nervously, his eyes scanning the road around them.

"I told you about it in the archives! When you were talking to those ladies. It just keeps sitting there and staring at me and then it runs away. I don't know what it wants. It just keeps showing up everywhere!"

Kalani joined them, the rest of their group still busy sorting the trinkets. "A fox, you say?"

"Yes!" Rena replied, her frustration rising.

"Do we think that's another ally of the Crow that can transform into animals and is spying on us?" Logan asked, trying to make a joke but they were all too on edge to laugh.

"Let's not go that far," Kalani said in a low voice, then paused and looked out at the forest. "Next time you see it, tell one of us, okay?"

"Sure," Rena sighed, defeated.

They safely found their way back to the guards' wagon. Rena kept waiting for the moment where Silac would stop them once more — this time accompanied by his guards — to drag them all back to Hollowtooth, but it never came. Even after Rodrick had started the vehicle and they were on their way out of Vellashta, she couldn't shake the feeling that someone was about to apprehend them. The group stayed silent for the rest of the journey, all needing to process what had happened to them on their own.

They stopped at the edge of the forest, knowing the wagon would only draw unwanted attention, and changed out of the guards' uniforms into more regular clothes. Before further heading out on foot, Kalani beckoned them all close.

"Have you heard of someone like Silac before?" she asked Rodrick. "About his... control?"

He stayed silent for a while, gaze downcast, thinking her question over.

"In legends and fables. There are abilities associated with the gods, but I never took them to be literal. Old stories always embellish reality. They are not meant as an accurate representation of life. I-I don't know why he was able to control us like this. That doesn't... comply with any known laws of the world."

"His face got all weird," Logan added, concern written plainly on his face.

"Is that also something mentioned in the legends?" Kalani asked.

"Not that I'm aware of." Rodrick shook his head. "But I'm really not an expert. I don't know enough about the gods to know if what just happened to us has ever been part of any of these stories. They talk about similar things, events that shouldn't happen, that aren't possible in our world, but controlling others' minds and bodies? I really don't know if that is part of the legends. But I don't feel comfortable drawing connections. I think we can all agree that these gods who people prayed to hundreds of years ago were never real, so there is no point in finding an explanation for what just happened to us in that part of history. These stories are allegories of human struggles to explain phenomena they did not understand yet. Natural catastrophes, inequalities, human behaviour that is out of the norm. Anything similar. It makes life easier to bear when you imagine there is a higher power responsible for such events."

"And then we end up with a million different *gods*," Asha mumbled, arms crossed over her chest, "'cause people can never take responsibility for their own actions. Gods of house pets, and broken toenails, and green olives."

"I don't know if I would fully agree," Kalani replied carefully. "Not every region has completely disavowed their belief systems. They might not be gods as you picture them, but people still believe in forces beyond our understanding that guide us on our way. And there certainly are malignant forces that could manifest as something like Silac, even though I pray we haven't actually drawn the ire of any of them."

Rodrick looked at her for a moment, then smiled amicably.

"Fair enough. I apologise, I did not mean to disregard any faiths or cultures. My statement might have been a bit harsh. What I meant is that these gods or higher forces, as you call them, aren't regular human beings and, if they do exist or ever existed in the past, probably do not hold a human form. Especially not one with a job and family."

"So, what do we think he is?" Logan linked his hands behind his head but then grimaced and dropped them again, one arm coming to rest around his stomach. "Just some freak of nature? The Crow's little experiment? Trying to turn him into a god to get back to how the kingdom was like five hundred years ago?"

A cold shudder ran down Rena's back. What had she gotten herself into? If that was really what Silac was doing, what chances did they have to fight him and the Crow? A knot formed tightly at the back of her throat, wrapping around her lungs, making it difficult to breathe. Just the same as when Silac had taken possession of her. She still felt the lingering energy that had tried to move her body, to make her cause violence. Was this what the Crow was working on? Turning people into gods? It sounded so implausible, and yet, they had just experienced something that they would have never imagined possible.

They looked at each other in silence, letting the question hang heavy between them.

Rena didn't know what to believe anymore. Even just an hour ago she would have scoffed at the idea that the Crow were burning down villages in the hopes of reviving their gods, but how could she deny the possibility now that she had experienced what Silac could do?

"They placed those bird figurines around the old church in Oceansthrow," Rena mumbled in a daze. "And they carved that symbol onto its walls, the one for that god you told us about, that we also found on the graves in Miller's Knee. Ta something."

"Tavuu'Moda," Rodrick said quietly. "Associated with chance, perseverance and survival."

"Was Tavuu'Moda ever able to... control people's bodies? Or had those strange green veins?"

"Not that I'm aware of, but again, I really don't know much about the old faith. There is a lot of scripture I haven't read. My interests as a scribe of the lands have always lain somewhere else, much more focused on the lived experience of common folks. But what I know is that each region had a different interpretation of the gods. It might very well be possible that some people somewhere believed him to have such abilities."

"The symbol they use is a regional one too, right?" Rena continued, remembering the intertwined triangles crossed with a line and dot. "Maybe their version of Tavuu'Moda has green veins around the eyes and can control people? Maybe they really are trying to make Silac into a god? To make *him* into Tavuu'Moda. And they're burning down the villages because the ritual needs sacrifices somehow? He talked about sacrifice. That it's needed for the greater good. And they kidnapped Maya for the same reason. Maybe they'll try to turn her into a god next and she'll have those ugly veins all over her face too. What if the ritual goes wrong? What if it kills Maya?"

Kalani stepped up to her and held her face in her hands, stopping her spiralling.

"Rena, look at me," she said calmly. "Deep breaths. We'll get your sister back before they can hurt her, I promise. Think about it. Why would they choose your sister to turn into a god when that honour should go to one of their acolytes? They won't turn Maya into such a monstrosity!"

"But how do we fight someone like Silac?" Rena answered in a weak voice, unsure if she believed Kalani's words.

"The second time around was much weaker," Asha replied behind Kalani. "I think the more people he controls, the weaker he gets."

"Yes, I would have to agree," Rodrick said, a deep frown settling on his brows. "The first instance was overwhelming. I had no control over my body whatsoever; it simply moved on its own. It was the worst feeling I had ever experienced but once he had also taken control of Asha's body, I could feel his control lessen. Not completely, but it became easier to fight against the movements."

Kalani's thumbs ran over Rena's cheeks. She looked deep into her eyes, then planted a soft kiss on Rena's forehead and stepped back to address the rest of the group.

"I'm not going to lie, he scares me, a lot, but that doesn't mean he's invincible. I don't think this is the last we've seen of him, so we'll need to be careful." She crossed her arms and looked down for a while, deep in thought. "We should make sure to never engage him one-on-one, not until we know more about him. Hopefully we'll be in and out of Hrevim before he can follow us."

They didn't linger near the caravan for much longer and commenced their long trek to the city, the ocean glistening in the sunlight to their right. Only the sound of the waves accompanied them, their exhaustion having rendered them silent.

"Rena." Rodrick leaned closer so only she could hear him. "There is something else I wanted to mention."

He looked at her with trepidation, his face twitching as if the words didn't want to come out.

"What is it?"

"You speak so confidently of finding your sister," he started, his voice soft but full of concern, "and although I agree that it is strange that you found her dress among the Crow's belongings, I don't know if that is enough proof to say with certainty that she is still alive."

"She has to be," Rena blurted out before she had time to process what he had said.

"I understand that you think so," he continued, his face growing grimmer, "and I do truly hope that you are right, but we have to acknowledge that the Crow might not have her."

A cold shudder ran down Rena's back, constricting her airways. She pressed her nails into the palms of her hands, needing the feeling so she wouldn't run ahead and leave him far, far behind.

"Of course we will do everything in our power to rescue her if she is still alive," he continued in a tone that was irritatingly compassionate, "but I don't want your heart to be broken if that isn't possible."

She pressed her teeth together and stared straight ahead, fixed on the curls at the nape of Logan's neck, hoping that if she simply didn't reply he'd leave her alone.

After a few seconds, he nodded and looked away, walking the rest of the way next to her without saying another word.

Chapter Twelve

Finn

Finn could already feel his mind building walls around what had just happened, punishing him every time he tried to decipher it. Best to forget about it, it seemed to say. He would have to comply, at least until he'd had some rest and could tackle the problem with a fully functioning brain. As they walked the rest of the way to Hrevim, Finn had had to fight with his body not to throw up. His vision had gone bright white a couple of times thanks to the headache blossoming behind his bruised eye, but his steps never faltered and so none of his companions noticed his condition.

Hrevim was a large city surrounded by walls of beige stone, larger than anything that existed in Vellashta. Every few metres, a rectangular tower jutted out from the top of the wall, dotted with tiny windows. The walls had been standing for centuries, although they weren't all of the same age. To their left, where the city grew inland, the stone looked newer, showing the city's age like the rings on a tree.

Baedan's coast wasn't like Vellashta's. Instead of cliffs separating the land from the ocean — except for the occasional coastal town like Hollowtooth — Baedan had flat, narrow beaches made of coarse sand that led to a verdant, hilly landscape in the centre of the province. It was more densely populated than Vellashta, with bigger cities and a long history of maritime trading.

Before the entire peninsula had been unified into the Kingdom of Kal-Hemma, the three southern provinces had been their own kingdom, with most of its activities concentrated along Baedan's coastline. The rest of the province was said to be uninhabited as the hills made it difficult to settle beyond the few valleys wide enough to accommodate villages. Exactly that had made western Baedan perfect for monasteries during the height of the old faith, as it led to a life free of distractions. It was unclear to most why so many monasteries had been built, sprinkled throughout the landscape as if believers who had flocked to the province couldn't agree about the minutiae of their beliefs with their neighbours, but most of the structures had long been abandoned and left to decay in the centuries since.

The road they'd travelled on led them to a gate flanked by two large, rectangular towers and even though the massive doors were wide open to let anyone pass through, a pair of guards stood in front of each tower, looking straight ahead, unmoving. Their uniform was reminiscent of the one from Vellashta with only a difference in insignia and some of the stripes running over the shoulders and chest. Each city and institution had their own insignia to quickly identify each guard corps, but the South had always tried to show unity through the overall design of the uniforms. A steady crowd streamed in and out of the gate, only worsening Finn's headache as his mind tried to be aware of every person around them.

Kalani marched them to the eastern edge of Hrevim, the one that was closest to the ocean, as if she knew the city's layout by heart. She led them past bustling markets and artisans' districts, through gates belonging to even older city walls, past streets with extravagant houses that had been built high instead of wide to fit into the limited space the city granted them, and all the while, on a hill in the distance, stood the shimmering white palace that belonged to Viscount Zarkid.

Their journey brought them to the docks where sailors and fishers gathered. The district had the same giant hangars as the one in Hollowtooth, only more of them. As a port city, Hrevim had also developed a vibrant ship-building tradition with its ships being used all throughout the kingdom and beyond. Their newest fad was following the developments in steam-powered vehicles. Bronze pipes ran over the hulls, two wide chimneys sticking out towards the sky exuding a stream of thick, dark smoke.

They walked past hangars and their workers, ships unloading their cargo, and the fisher boats bringing in the last catch of the day. They reached a square with taverns and inns frequented by those working in the district and ended their march at the Broken Mast inn. It was a strangely shaped building with one side taller than the other as if the initial plan had been to build two towers but they had run out of money halfway through.

While only one doorway opened onto a wide entrance hall, two passages led further into the building: the left one, where the tower stretched towards the sky, was dedicated to merchants in colourful coats and tights and shiny black shoes, while the right welcomed labourers who didn't have the luxury of worrying about the state of their clothing. The division remained evident in the entrance hall, the groups keeping to themselves.

As much as Finn was aware of their surroundings, he didn't much reflect on where they were going. While his body followed Kalani into the inn's core, his mind was blank of any thoughts beyond physical observations. They walked through multiple corridors, up and down stairs, through a long, narrow corridor with no doors or windows, until they emerged through a hatch in a square room. There were two doors on each wall to their left and right and one door on the walls in front and behind them. The room was sparsely furnished, with only a few old seats and a massive wooden chest placed next to a staircase that led to an upper floor. The room was illuminated with a similar system to the one in the archives — a cluster of milky-white bulbs emitting a dull yellow light. Faint noise could be heard behind the doors of some of the rooms, indicating that they were not alone.

Kalani walked up to one of the doors to their left and opened it with a key, then tossed the other key to Logan and pointed to the door to her right.

Rena suddenly hooked her arm through his and lightly pulled him towards the door on the right that Logan was opening. He flinched, not having expected the touch. He wasn't quite sure why she was pulling him towards that room, then his eyes fell on Rodrick and the dog heading towards the other one. He nodded once at her in gratitude, happy he wouldn't have to spend the night in the same room as the dog.

The room they stepped into was small and sparsely decorated, with one bed against the wall next to the door and the other two on the opposite wall with barely enough space between them to walk. The only other furniture in the room was an old wash basin in the corner opposite the door with a simple ceramic chamber pot placed underneath. There were no windows in this room either, and only the light from the entrance revealed the outlines of the furniture.

Finn slipped his arm out of Rena's grasp and sat down on the bed next to the door, burying his face in his hands and breathing deeply. He stayed like that for a moment, simply breathing, then a jolt ran through him that it wasn't polite to ignore other people in the room. He looked up but neither of the other two were paying attention to him. While Rena was looking around the room in concern and confusion, Logan had lain down in one of the other beds, feet dangling off the side so he wouldn't dirty it with his shoes. He had his arms crossed behind his head in a pretend show of nonchalance, but he didn't really fool anyone with it. His smile barely managed to hide the pain and discomfort their journey to Hrevim had caused him. His body was stiff, turned a specific way that was certainly meant to alleviate some of the wound's soreness.

Finn kept his eyes on them even though he couldn't keep his focus on them. His mind kept approaching the subject of Captain Silac and instantly retreating. What they had experienced simply couldn't be true. He had to have been dreaming or hallucinating, and if that was the case, there was no point in trying to understand it. He needed something else to latch on to, something that was familiar, something Silac had mentioned.

The captain had mentioned Finn's family and ever since, they'd been at the forefront of his mind again. He was aware just how dissatisfied they'd be with him once they learned of everything he had done, which words they would use to make him feel guilty, which looks they'd give him. And his actions wouldn't just reflect badly on him; they'd also shine a bad light on the administrator. She'd been tasked with putting his sister and him onto the right path in life, after all, and even though she'd clearly done a good job with Finn's sister, the last week had made clear just how much she'd screwed up when it came to Finn. At least, that was the angle the administrator's competitors would go with in the hopes that it would be enough to depose her. His family would know to put all the blame on him.

How likely was it that Silac would contact his family? He had mentioned getting a hold of Finn's sister, but could he find a way if he didn't go through Finn? And would his pride prevent him from telling anyone that Finn had stolen Kalani and Rodrick from under his nose, or would he use his sister's influence to go after him? Nara certainly wouldn't ignore an opportunity to show her superiority over her brother, but that didn't mean she would willingly work with Silac.

Finn usually kept track of where his family was, but he hadn't really had the opportunity over the last week to stay up to date with their locations. His parents and extended family didn't leave the capital much anymore except for special occasions, and he knew there hadn't been any over the last week, so it was safe to assume they were still in Mak-Hemma. Keeping track of his sister was a bit more complicated. She travelled a lot and had been in Jodash a little over two weeks ago, but he hadn't gotten any updates on her whereabouts since. Had she had time to travel across the kingdom in such a short period of time? It was always possible, but she had an aversion to the South and it seemed unlikely for her to be anywhere Silac could get to easily. Even if Silac had sent a messenger to fetch her the day he'd caught Finn, it would take that messenger a few days to get to wherever she was, then double that time for her to get to Baedan. In all likelihood, they had at least a week or two before Nara reached Hrevim. As long as Silac hadn't followed them into the city without them noticing, they would have enough time to gather information about the Crow and leave Hrevim before anyone could intercept them.

Chapter Thirteen

Rena

Rena stood inside Oceansthrow's old church surrounded by children cowering underneath their school desks, the faint sound of fire crackling somewhere far away. She was holding Maya's hand, gripping her tightly so she wouldn't lose her again. Heat kept her from breathing as the walls pulsed bright white, yellow and red, the crackle of the fire getting louder with every pulse. She turned, noticing that her brother Valerio was now holding her hand, staring at her in that way children do when they expect you to make sense of their world for them. Rena looked around in confusion, trying to figure out where Maya had gone, but she was nowhere to be found. Instead, she saw that triangles were slowly etching themselves into the walls, intertwining, a line running between them and connecting them all.

"It's going to be fine," she repeated in a daze to her brother. "We just need to find a way out."

Someone pounded on the door, the noise throbbing through her entire being.

"By order of Captain Silac and the Royal Council, I command you to vacate these premises at once!" the person shouted as horses neighed violently in the background.

Rena turned round and round, her grip tight on her second brother Savio's hand as she searched for a way out, but the light hurt her eyes too much. Fire had engulfed the furniture around her and the only ones that remained were the desks the children were hiding under. Lino, her youngest brother, was now holding her hand, silently crying as he stared at the door.

"We'll find a way out," she repeated as the room spun around her, the fire's roar drowning out her words. "They won't get to us, don't worry. I'll keep you safe."

With a sound that shook the earth, the church's tower collapsed in on them and Rena jolted awake.

The blanket on her chest felt like lead, holding her body in place, impossible for her muscles to move. She stared up at the ceiling with wide eyes but the room was too dark for her to recognise where she was.

A click, a hiss, and then a bright light pulled her back to reality.

"Rena?" a voice pierced through the silence.

She blinked rapidly until her eyes got used to the light.

She was looking up at a simple, off-white ceiling, a singular bulb emitting weak orange light in the middle. She didn't dare move, not just yet, as if the room around her could dissipate at any moment. Her mouth was dry, her tongue heavy against her palate. Her eyes shifted slowly, slowly, from one side to the other, from the wall to the empty bed next to hers, as if she wasn't entirely sure that what surrounded her was real.

"Finn?" Her voice was no more than a quiet croak.

"Is everything all right?" he asked hesitantly.

She closed her eyes and inhaled deeply, before answering, "Yeah."

"You were breathing so heavily, I thought you might be in pain."

Rena pushed herself upright, her muscles aching with every move. She pulled the blanket closer and buried her face in it before lifting her head to look at Finn. He was sitting on the bed next to the door, his back leaning against the wall, one leg angled up, staring at her with more curiosity than worry.

She tried to smile at him, to reassure him, but her face didn't want to cooperate. A deep exhaustion spread through her bones as if the night had left her wearier than she'd been the day before.

"I'm sorry," she said weakly. "Just a nightmare."

He didn't respond at first, simply observing her, no malice, no aversion in his eyes. She wanted to hold his gaze, but as so often happened when he truly looked at her, she couldn't stand it for long.

"Is there anything I can do?" he finally inquired.

"No, no. I just need time."

She forced her cheeks to move until they produced something resembling a smile, fighting against the dull ache in her muscles.

"How are you?" she asked him instead, directing the focus away from her. "Did you sleep well?"

"Well enough."

Rena shifted in her bed and stretched her shoulders, then her neck, before looking over at the third, empty bed.

"Where's Logan?"

"I don't know. He must have left before I awoke."

She frowned, annoyance mixing with her exhaustion. She couldn't understand why he refused to rest. He kept pretending like nothing was wrong when it was so clear for everyone to see that his wound wasn't just a little scratch.

"Maybe he's in Kalani's room," she said, hoping deeply that it was nothing more than that.

Rena stood up and walked over to the wash basin, her legs still shaky from the nightmare. The wooden floor felt cold and rough underneath her bare feet, but she didn't mind. It gave her body something real to latch on to.

Soon after, they both headed to the second room where Kalani, Asha and Rodrick were already awake and ready for the day. To Rena's great annoyance, though, Logan was nowhere to be found, but her feelings were somewhat remedied by the presence of fresh bread rolls filled with orange jam. She grabbed one — greeting everyone as cheerfully as she could muster — and walked over to where Vincent was lying next to Rodrick's bed. She sat down next to the dog, her back against the wall, and leaned down to kiss his forehead before running her fingers through his fur.

"Has anyone seen Logan?" she asked before biting into the still-warm bread roll.

"He's not in your room?" Asha replied, her brows furrowing.

Rena shook her head, her mouth too full to answer.

"When did he leave?"

Rena swallowed before replying. "We don't know. He was already gone when we woke up."

Asha looked over at Kalani, a conversation unfolding while their eyes met. Kalani carded a hand through her thin braids until they fell in neat rows down her shoulder, then she sighed.

"He probably just went to say hello to someone he knows in the city," she said but didn't seem too convinced about it.

"As long as it's a friend and not one of his *business acquaintances*," Asha grumbled.

Rena buried her hand deep in Vincent's fur, the sweet taste of the orange jam lingering on her tongue. In moments like these, Rena almost felt like Asha and Logan didn't get along at all, but then again, she'd had the same concerns about her younger siblings. At home she would have intervened, would have tried to force them to get along, but she pushed that urge down. She couldn't treat adults she'd met only a week ago the same as her siblings, no matter how much she wanted to, no matter how much it felt like the only thing she knew how to do, no matter how much she craved the familiarity of it.

Kalani stood up and shot Asha a glance, raising an eyebrow at her, before coming to stand in the middle of the room.

"I've been trying to figure out what we should do next." She paused, her eyes fixed on a spot on the ground. "There's so much we don't know, so much we aren't even sure how to approach, especially with Silac on our heels." Frustration rushed over her face and she huffed once before she looked up. "I don't like the idea of all of us running around in the city where anyone could see us. It might be best if most of us stay here and Asha and I go talk to the people we know. It will minimise our risk of getting caught."

"I'll go to the docks and talk to some old fisherfolk," Asha said. "If anyone knows what's going on in the region, it's them. All they do all day is gossip, even when they're out at sea. They probably even know how many mice enter and leave the city every day. And even if they don't, their spouses will know something."

Rena caught her objection in her throat before it could leave her lips. She couldn't simply let the words burst out, not if they were tinged so deeply by the chaos of emotion residing within her. She bit down on her cheek until she knew she had gained control over her words.

"I know you're right about us being safest here," she started, choosing each word carefully, uncertain about how Kalani might react, "but maybe if more of us went outside, we could find out where the Crow is staying quicker and then we don't have to stay in the city for long. I don't really see how we can contribute if we're stuck here."

"And how are you gonna contribute out there?" Asha asked, raising an eyebrow at her.

Rena opened her mouth, then closed it again. Asha was right. Rena didn't have any idea at all how she might be helpful, but she wanted to at least try. Staying safe indoors while others toyed with danger to solve *her* problem didn't feel right and she knew that she wouldn't be able to stay put for an entire day without clawing off her skin.

"I..." No words felt convincing enough. "I'm not sure. Maybe I could help you or Kalani, or talk to some other people in the city. Without giving much information away, of course, just to see who might know something. Maybe there've also been fires in Baedan. It could help if we gathered more information about what the Crow's been up to, right? To better prepare once we face them?"

"Rena," Kalani said, then sighed. "Yes, sure, it could help to find out what the Crow's plan is and we could work faster if more of us asked around for information, I can agree with that, but I don't know if the danger you might be putting yourself in would be worth it. If everyone's running through the city on their own, we won't even know until tonight if something happened."

"How about we go to the library?" Rodrick smiled at Rena, then turned to Kalani and Asha. "It would be quite safe if we stayed there and didn't wander the city, and I'm sure we could learn plenty about the Crow's objectives."

"You think so?" Rena wasn't sure about leaving one stuffy room for another but she was still grateful he was trying to help.

"Yes, of course! We could take a look at the documents you found in Halvint before we leave, then we might know what to look for in the library. As I mentioned, they have quite an excellent catalogue here!"

Kalani ran a hand over her face in exasperation but then conceded, "I suppose the library would be safe."

"If they don't get caught before arriving," Asha muttered under her breath.

"We'll be careful, I promise!" Rena said. "Captain Silac doesn't know where we went, right? So how likely is it that he's already followed us here?"

Rena wasn't quite convinced of her own words but hopefully they would be enough to sway Kalani and Asha. Even if Silac knew that their group was planning on crossing the border into Baedan, there were plenty of places they could have gone to. Sure, Hrevim might be the biggest city in the region and the likeliest place where anyone could gather information but there was always a chance Silac thought they would go directly to the Crow's hideout. And who was to say that Silac could even leave his post long enough to chase them? It could very well be that he would first need to arrange a reason for him to enter Baedan or find an excuse why his own troops wouldn't go look for him if he went after them on his own. And in the unlikely case that he had already found his way to Hrevim, the city was big enough that they might never run into each other.

Kalani looked at her for a moment and Rena couldn't quite decipher her expression.

"Fine," she finally said. "You know the risks; I trust you to take them seriously." She turned to leave but added with a look over her shoulder, "In case you run into Logan, tell him to come back here and rest before he jumps headfirst into his own death."

As Kalani and Asha headed out, Rodrick got up to fetch one of the knapsacks. He pulled a bundle of fabric out and unwrapped it, revealing the parchment rolls and the wooden bird figurine Rena had found in Oceansthrow. He sat back down on one of the beds and motioned for Rena to sit next to him. She picked up the carved bird and idly ran a thumb over the inscription carved from wing to wing as Rodrick unfolded the parchments.

The deep grooves on the figurine had to mean something, but was it just a word or an entire phrase? It seemed a bit short for a sentence — a few straight lines that intersected to form letters she didn't know — but what kind of word could it be? And how much would knowing the word help them understand why the Crow had left these figurines around the old church in Oceansthrow?

"Do you think we can find someone who can translate this for us?"

"Hmm, I'm not sure," Rodrick glanced at the effigy in contemplation. "But we might be able to translate it ourselves at the library. I'm sure they'll have at least some information on the old languages spoken in these parts of the kingdom. Well, *if* the Crow is using a language from around here and not something from the North. Of course, finding out which script this is would be easier if we could simply talk to an expert on ancient languages but I doubt we'll have much time before Asha and Kalani come back from their little outing."

Rena frowned at the thought. She couldn't see herself hunched over old, dusty tomes for days on end to find a translation for a single word that wouldn't even tell them much about the Crow's plan, not even if she had all the time in the world. There was always the possibility that all the inscription said was *bird* or *crow* or *fire*, that the figurines were simply meant as a signature of the tragedy.

Finn came to sit on Rodrick's other side, frowning at the document Rodrick was unfolding.

"Where did you find those?"

"In Halvint," Rena replied, "in the house where the Crow was staying. They had a sort of altar made of red and orange fabric that kind of looked like fire. Do you know anything about them? Can you read them?"

He looked at the unfurled scrolls in Rodrick's lap for a moment, then delicately picked them up and held them towards the light.

"No," he said pensively, squinting at the parchment, "but the prints resemble a lot of the tapestries hung in the palace in Mak-Hemma. There's a tapestry in one of the dining halls that looks similar."

"Oh yes!" Rodrick exclaimed. "Now that you mention it, I think I remember it! But it has been quite a while since I've been to that dining hall."

"This picture is older," Finn continued, absent-mindedly shaking his head. "I would say it's, maybe, three or four hundred years old, if it was created when that art style was popular. It could always be a newer replica, but the paper quality would indicate that it has a certain age. The tapestry in Mak-Hemma must be a depiction of the same myth from a different time period. Probably from when the dining hall was first built. The palace has only existed since the unification of the Royal Council, so it can't be older than, say, two hundred years. The lines are blockier in the tapestry and the human anatomy truer to life. Very clearly a different style."

Rena stared at Finn, then at the print with its swirling lines and lanky bodies, then back at Finn. The first time he'd been inside Rodrick's caravan, he'd also been able to tell exactly where the caravan had been built just based on its design. Rena knew nothing of these things, had never even considered that you could determine how old a picture was based on its colour or shape. She knew that different regions had different symbols associated with them — they'd learned that much in school — but she thought those had stayed the same since the kingdom's unification.

"Do you know what it depicts?" she asked.

"It must be the myth of Hama'Voshi creating the world. It's said that she gathered the loose energy that was floating in the vast nothingness and gave it its physical form. But seeing as Hama'Voshi was a real person who existed no more than six hundred years ago and that we have evidence that our world is much older than that, it can't be a true story."

"As I already mentioned yesterday," Rodrick interjected, scooting forward on the bed, "these legends and myths are often metaphors for human struggles or explanations for something we don't yet understand. Of course, Hama'Voshi didn't actually create our world." He chuckled as if even the thought of someone believing it true was preposterous to him. "That would be quite the feat."

Rena frowned at the print, at how the lines swirled from the edges of the parchment towards the centre and formed a sphere. A figure resembling a woman wrapped around it, the sphere forming in her arms. She was contorted, her limbs pressed against the borders of the image as if she could barely fit into the box it provided.

Could this image actually be of any help to them or had they stolen these documents for nothing? They could spend hours and hours and hours trying to decipher what they meant or why the Crow felt the need to bring them to Halvint, but would they tell them anything of use? She couldn't imagine how a myth about the creation of the world would lead them closer to where the Crow was hiding or why they were doing what they were doing.

She felt a headache approach, her exhaustion mixing with her confusion. Her eyes wandered over the edge of the image where a row of small symbols resembling those on her figurine created a border.

"I don't know how much these images can really help us," she murmured with a heavy sigh. "Maybe if we had all the time in the world, it would be nice to translate them, but I think it's best if we focus on something else."

"We can't know until we've investigated them," Rodrick replied, not taking his eyes off the documents. "There's no need to despair so quickly, my child. We'll get to the library soon enough, don't worry. These might help us understand the Crow's motives and once we know those, it will be much easier to understand their actions."

"Sure," she exhaled, unable to keep the defeat out of her voice, "but it will take us forever to find out *how* it could be relevant and by then Silac will have reached the city and Inkra will have gone back to wherever the rest of the Crow is hiding and they'll leave the province and then we'll never find them."

"Now, now, there's no need for so much gloom. The world isn't going to end just because we're taking our time to decipher these parchments."

Chapter Fourteen

Rena

It didn't take long for Rodrick and Finn to devolve into talking about hypotheticals to the point that it became white noise to Rena. *Maybe* the Crow was working with the Royal Council; *maybe* they had been burning down villages for centuries; *maybe* this or that other tragedy could also be attributed to them; *maybe* they had given strange abilities to more people than captain Silac; *maybe* they were kidnapping children to convince them of their cause and recruit them to their ranks; *maybe* they were responsible for all the misery in the kingdom; *maybe* they were trying to usher in a new age of the gods. They talked and talked and talked so much that Rena almost decided to go to the library on her own, but she had no idea where the building was and she didn't like the prospect of wandering the city until she stumbled upon it.

Logan came back just in time to save her from another myth Rodrick was trying to recite from memory that he had mostly forgotten. He looked tired but otherwise fine and didn't argue at all when Rena told him to get back to bed. She thought later as she was heading out with Rodrick that it might have been so Logan wouldn't have to explain where he had been and what was in the knapsack he'd brought back. She wasn't sure she really wanted to know, not if it would just make her angry with him.

Finn stayed behind at the inn, assuring Rena that he'd make sure Logan would actually rest. It took Rodrick and her quite a while to find the library even though Rodrick was adamant that he'd been to Hrevim before. The city had been built over several centuries, constantly expanding and rebuilding itself to fit all the people flocking to it, which meant that the streets had to adapt to its ever-changing form. Most buildings were tall and had been constructed close together, keeping the small roads winding between them in the shadows. The streets were well paved and clean, the houses painted in a multitude of bright colours and the passage of time could barely be seen even on the older buildings. They passed through a few old gates that were kept permanently open, indicating where the city walls had previously stood.

Emotions warred inside Rena. She was happy to be out and active, trying to help solve their problem as well as she could, but on the other hand she jumped at every shadow. She couldn't shake the feeling that Silac had already found them and was waiting behind every corner to pounce on them. She stayed close to Rodrick, her eyes darting from side to side in fear of recognising any of the faces around them. Even Rodrick's shoulders were tense and his face sombre, and he was so preoccupied with trying to find the right path that he didn't even try to reassure Rena.

A small voice in the back of Rena's mind told her that Kalani had been right all along and that they should have never left the safety of the inn, that it was much too easy to spot them in the broad streets of the city, but there was no going back now — the risk had already been taken. Rena simply had to hope that their expedition would be worth it.

The streets parted and revealed an open square with low, wide buildings in an older district in the North, close enough to the ocean that they could hear the waves and seagulls as they stepped closer. In front of them stood a rectangular building, its façade painted with a myriad of intricate, symmetrical patterns similar to the ones in the archives in Vellashta. Browns, blacks and yellows formed stars and flowers around the wide entrance and four white, round towers jutted out of each corner of the building's roof, a column of grey smoke rising out of one of them. By the quickening of Rodrick's steps, Rena guessed that they had finally found the library.

As they entered, she noticed that the patterns hadn't just been painted on but meticulously carved into the sandstone. She was in awe of the building, instantly forgetting the restlessness she had felt all morning. The library's entrance hall looked similar to the one in the archives, with patterned tiles covering the floor and the bottom half of the walls, although they had reddish tones instead of the archives' blue and green. Seats had been placed in the corners to each side of the entrance for visitors to sit on and a desk — much smaller than the one in the archives — stood to their left, with two clerks behind it who were busy talking to patrons.

Only one path led into the library, at the far end of the room, but there Rena saw something that she'd never even considered possible. A box, large enough for four people to stand in, rose out of the ground and disappeared into the ceiling. Next to it, another box emerged from the ceiling, two people stepping out of it when it was level with the floor. The boxes never slowed down, simply continuing on their path as patrons hurried to step in and out. The contraption made a sound that rumbled through the entire building, but not loudly. It was like a constant mechanical hum, as if the building itself was breathing very calmly. To its left and right were stairs, although not a lot of patrons were using them.

Rena barely even registered that Rodrick had gone to the desk and was talking to one of the clerks, too fascinated by these rising boxes. She wondered if they travelled through the entire building, but then, where did they go once they'd reached the roof or the basement? The only logical explanation was that they went in circles, but how was any of this possible? Did the same machine that had moved Rodrick's caravan also make these boxes rise and fall? It certainly had to be a machine; she couldn't imagine that human hands were strong enough to consistently make such heavy boxes move.

Rodrick turned back to her and gently put a hand on her back, urging her to move forward.

"What is that?" Rena asked, awestruck.

Rodrick frowned, then followed her gaze to the moving boxes and his face lit up.

"Oh yes, I heard there's a new addition to the building! They had to completely shut down the library for a few months to build it. Isn't it fascinating? Such a marvel of ingenuity. Do you want to try it out?"

"What?" Rena turned to him in dread and wonder.

"We only have to go up one floor but if we're already in the presence of such a marvel, why not use it, right?"

Rena stared at the contraption, fear rising in her at the thought of stepping into one of these moving boxes, although it quickly mixed with excitement. She nodded, not taking her eyes off the strange device.

As they approached, she took hold of Rodrick's arm, following his lead as he stepped into the box when it was level with the floor. She stumbled in, not used to the ground underneath her feet moving so abruptly, and lost her grip on Rodrick's arm. She fell against the back wall, quickly turning around and pressing her back against it. With wide-open eyes, she saw how the entrance hall disappeared and the box was plunged into darkness, although she could still see the texture of the wall in front of her. Before she had time to panic, light reappeared at the top of the opening.

Rodrick took her arm once more, leading her to the front of the box as a spacious reading hall appeared before them. Climbing out of the box was more daunting than climbing into it, and Rena ducked as she hopped out to make absolutely sure she wouldn't be crushed.

"Well, wasn't that fun?" Rodrick beamed at her. "Didn't I promise you that we would have plenty of fun at the library?"

Rena turned around and observed the boxes rising and falling at their leisurely pace as if nothing could ever go wrong. A wide smile slowly appeared on her face, dissipating the fear she had felt only moments before.

"I didn't know something like this existed," she said in awe, not taking her eyes off the machine.

"Oh yes, and a myriad other just as interesting things! I think that's what I miss most about Mak-Hemma. Working on these new marvels."

"You made these?" Rena asked, shocked, and turned to look at Rodrick.

"No, no, no, not this one. That was a friend of my son's who figured this beauty out."

"You worked on something similar?"

"Well, not exactly similar to this, but all of our new discoveries are built on everything that came before it, like bricks on a house. My research mostly focused on the engines that led me to my wonderful caravan." He drifted off in thought, then mumbled into his beard, "I will miss that thing."

"And your son?"

Rena was desperate to know more about her companions' lives, to know about their past and their families and what their lives had been like before they met. She vaguely remembered Rodrick mentioning his son before and how he'd lost him a few years ago. She wanted to know all about him but wasn't sure if the subject still caused Rodrick much heartache.

"Oh, yes, yes, he also worked on these machines. Helped me a lot with my research. He was a very diligent young man." A strange smile flitted over Rodrick's face. "You know, I also have a daughter."

"Oh, really? Does she still live in Mak-Hemma?" Rena pressed her lips together to not show the smile that wanted to surface.

"Yes, indeed."

"You must miss her terribly."

Rodrick's eyes drifted to the ground, a terrible sadness shadowing his smile.

Rena didn't care about the library anymore; all she wanted was to find a quiet place where she could talk to Rodrick for hours on end about his life. She wanted to know the names of his children, what his house had looked like, all the details of his work in the kingdom's capital. She wanted to listen to stories from his past, what his own childhood had been like, if he'd had any siblings or even where he'd grown up. Most of all, she desperately wanted to know why he'd chosen to leave his old life behind and wander the kingdom as a scribe of the land. If he still had family in the capital, why hadn't he stayed with them? If she understood it correctly, he'd worked as a tinkerer in Mak-Hemma's citadel before leaving. She couldn't imagine abandoning such a job. It sounded so fascinating to her.

A clerk suddenly approached to greet them and Rodrick seemed all too eager to follow him to an empty table. Rena sighed and followed them, knowing she shouldn't push the subject too far.

As they sat down, Rena looked around in confusion, wondering where all the books were. The room was deep and had multiple rows of tables, all facing towards the moving boxes, and a handful of bookshelves lining the walls, but there couldn't have been more than a few hundred books. She wondered if she had misunderstood the purpose of the building and that it instead worked like the archives, where patrons needed a special authorisation to study the majority of the documents. Rodrick explained that the interesting books were being held in rooms in the back that patrons weren't allowed to enter. They were instead supposed to tell a clerk what they were looking for and the clerk would then bring them the books, which would be chained to the table to make sure no document would go missing.

Without hesitation, Rodrick turned back to the clerk and explained what they were looking for. The oppressive silence in the room as they waited for the books made Rena realise just what she had signed up for. The excitement of the moving boxes had overshadowed her reluctance to follow Rodrick into the library but suddenly the reality of their task flooded back to her. She tried not to think of it, to tell herself that at least they were safe at the library and they had a great view on anyone entering the room, that they were contributing to their investigation and not simply wasting their time. If she told herself that often enough, she'd start believing it.

The books arrived a few minutes later and the clerk chained the six volumes to their table before stepping away. Rena observed the heavy, leather-bound volumes for a moment, too afraid to touch them in case she ripped one of the pages, but then Rodrick placed a heavy volume with a deep red cover in front of her and informed her that she should be able to find information on the figurine's inscription in it.

Rena wasn't quite sure how much time had passed. The silence around them heightened her nervousness, but Rodrick's deep focus on his research had kept her from begging him to leave again. She tried to keep her mind busy with the books in front of her but all it brought her was a headache.

The symbols of the old language — the one she'd found out was called *Mohrishim* — had started to flow together, becoming one big mass on the page. She'd managed to piece together how the letters on the bird figurine should be pronounced: *Vöshek*, if she wasn't mistaken, although by the time she was done deciphering the word, she was certain that Mohrishim used sounds that her own language didn't have.

But finding an approximately correct pronunciation seemed to be the easy part. Figuring out what the word actually meant was a thousand times more difficult. Of course, Mohrishim hadn't simply been one language. No, that would have been much too simple. There had been regional differences that all evolved over time so that the same pronunciation meant slightly different things in ancient eastern Mohrishim than it did in the more modern form of southern Mohrishim. According to her research, Vöshek could either mean *endurance*, *he survives*, or a very specific form of chance that was tied to the concept of living and birth that Rena didn't quite understand. Which meaning the inscription on the figurine held was impossible to know.

It wasn't clear whether the word had ever been used as a prayer or charm, although other words seemed to have been used this way. Rodrick had told her once that there used to be a custom where people would etch symbols or words into objects over and over while praying to strengthen their worship. It seemed quite likely that the Crow had done the same with these bird figurines — the same way they'd carved the interlinked triangles into the grave in Miller's Knee and the church ruins in Oceansthrow — but realising that didn't tell them much about *why* they'd done so.

She could see the connection between the figurine's inscription and the intertwined triangles, — which were linked to Tavuu'Moda, the god of chance and survival, — but knowing that all of this had *something* to do with chance or survival or endurance or perseverance didn't help her in the slightest, not when she didn't know why they were carving those words into the bird figurines and why they had placed them around Oceansthrow. It had to be a ritual, but which one? And what for? To have Tavuu'Moda bring them luck? To give people like Silac strange abilities that no other human had ever had before? How did survival or chance connect to being able to control other people's movements? And if their god truly existed — which Rena doubted, but at this point, she had to admit that anything could be possible — why did he agree to help such heartless murderers? And why did they need her sister for any of this?

"I can't do this anymore," Rena muttered and leaned back in her chair, burying her face in her hands.

"Hmm? What did you say?" Rodrick replied distractedly, not lifting his eyes from his book.

"The books are giving me a headache," Rena whined through her hands. "Knowing what the inscription means doesn't help us figure anything out. Maybe in the long run it could, but it feels like we're just wasting the little time we have. It would probably take us months if not years to understand what the Crow is doing and why they're doing it and we don't have that time. I don't want to leave my sister with them for that long!"

"One little piece at a time, my dear child," Rodrick muttered, clearly not feeling the same desperation. "Finding the link between the inscription and Tavuu'Moda's symbol is already a wonderful discovery. We just need to keep finding such connections until we can see the full picture."

"But it takes so long!" she whispered, trying not to have her emotions get the better of her and draw everyone's attention to them. "Silac will have found us before we've figured anything out. What do any of these symbols have to do with burning down entire villages and killing hundreds of people? Sure, we can try to understand their motives, but is that really helpful if it doesn't tell us where they are?"

"Patience, my child. Patience. Knowledge wants to be chased. It wouldn't be very rewarding if there were no sacrifices in our pursuit of it, now, would it? And our current sacrifice just happens to be our time. I'm sure these books will help us resolve the mystery — we just need to find the right ones. And as luck would have it, this building is filled with all sorts of books. You just have to think of it as similar to the archives. Jumping from one document to the next. Only this time, we don't have the margins telling us how to continue but I think that makes it more fun."

"I can maybe see how it could be fun if we had more time on our hands, but—"

"Listen, Rena," Rodrick interrupted her, no malice in his voice. "I know that what we're doing might seem pointless but the better we understand them, the better we can predict what they'll do next. Especially with people like the Crow, we need to try to understand what the logic behind their actions is, even if we cannot empathise with it and none of it seems rational to us, otherwise we will never be able to anticipate their next move."

Rena conceded and huffed in frustration, looking around at the other people in the room, some meeting her gaze to glare at her. She wondered what they were researching and if they were also disheartened by it. She could imagine that this chase might be thrilling to some but even if her situation wasn't so dire, she wasn't sure it could ever be fun to her. She would much rather have followed Asha or Kalani to talk to people than sit in a badly lit room where she was forced to stay quiet. All her energy had balled up in her core into a restless mass that made her want to jump out of her own skin.

"I need a break," she said, then sighed, her hand coming up to play with her necklace. "I'm sorry, Rodrick, I really tried my best, but I need to make sure Logan is doing better and someone needs to look after Vincent because Finn doesn't seem to like dogs all that much and I need to buy us some supplies for the journey and staying here feels like I'm going to suffocate."

She carefully closed her book and placed it back on the pile, making sure the chains didn't get tangled, then got up.

"I think that's a brilliant idea, my dear," Rodrick mumbled, still engrossed by his research. "And once you've walked off your frustration you can come back and help me figure out the rest of this mystery."

She glanced over at him, debating with herself whether she should simply agree with him or tell him the truth about her passion for research. In the end, she thought it best to get out of the library as quickly as possible.

"Sure, but we really shouldn't stay too long. Kalani and Asha will be cross with us if we're not back when they return."

"They'll understand," he replied absent-mindedly and waved her off.

Rena was happy that she at least got to use the moving box again as she left the building. Stepping into it on her own was a million times more daunting than having Rodrick by her side, and she let two boxes pass by before she found the courage to move forward. She couldn't keep her face from smiling, however, even though a nervous knot had formed in the pit of her stomach. On the ground floor, she quickly stepped out, afraid that if she didn't exit where she was supposed to, she'd disappear somewhere she could never get back from.

She turned back around and stared at the boxes as people streamed past her, some more confident than others. Out of all of the new inventions she'd gotten to experience since starting their journey, she thought she might like this one the most. Rodrick's caravan had been a fascinating object, but it had been loud and slow and she'd always thought in the back of her mind that a regular horse-drawn carriage could have done the exact same job. But these boxes made her giddy with their simplicity. They rose and fell, going round and round in a circle, never wavering.

She turned back around, a soft smile on her face, and stopped right away. Her eyes had landed on another visitor at the other end of the hall, someone wearing a dark-blue robe with golden inscriptions — the uniform of the Historical Academy. The knot in her stomach tightened momentarily, afraid that it might be the woman they'd stolen the decree from in the archives, but she soon realised that it was a completely different person. Then her eyes moved slightly to the left and she froze, her smile falling instantly.

"Jesper?" she whispered, stunned.

At first she thought she was dreaming, but the vision never disappeared no matter how often she blinked. In the same room as her stood a person she thought she'd never see again. Her father's friend who had owned a goat farm in Oceansthrow. His face looked different, with short-cropped hair and a bandage wrapped around half his face.

Before her mind had fully comprehended the situation, her body had already rushed forward, disregarding any caution she should have had.

"Jesper!" she shouted in excitement.

The man turned around to look at her, first in fear then in confusion.

"Rena?"

His green eyes were bloodshot and a fresh burn wound peaked out from underneath the bandage.

"You're alive!" If he hadn't been holding himself upright with crutches, she would have jumped into his embrace.

She wanted to hug him and never let go. She couldn't believe what she was seeing, couldn't believe that she truly wasn't the only one who had survived the fire! And if Jesper was alive, maybe so were others.

"What are you doing here?" he asked her, as if he couldn't fully believe what he was seeing either.

Before Rena could answer, a third person — who had been standing next to Jesper this entire time but whom Rena hadn't registered at all — pushed himself forward and held out a hand.

"So, you're the infamous Rena," the man said, his speech nervous and quick. "Hello, hello, so nice to finally meet you."

Rena looked at him in confusion, her eyes darting between this stranger in front of her and Jesper, letting the man shake her hand out of habit. He had pale skin with a reddish tint, a patchy, reddish-brown beard and clothes that looked like they'd been stolen from a nobleman's estate fifty years prior and had since been kept in a humid cave.

"My name is Deacon. I believe you're travelling with an acquaintance of mine, is that correct?"

Chapter Fifteen

Finn

For the first hour of Logan's nap, Finn had kept a vigilant eye on the dog until he could be sure the animal wouldn't do anything erratic. The dog had looked back at him with the same mistrust but then settled down with his head atop his paws and dozed away. It had taken Finn a while to do the same but couldn't keep denying himself the rest he desperately needed over a potentially unfounded apprehension.

His eyes shot back open when he heard rustling in the room, his muscles instantly tensing, but he soon realised that it was only Logan waking up. The other man pushed himself upright, his face contorting into a grimace from pain. It took him several moves to find a comfortable sitting position on the bed, and he sighed heavily when he finally settled, his hair a wild cascade around his face.

He only then lifted his eyes and noticed that Finn was observing him.

"Good morning, handsome." The corner of his mouth lifted into a wicked grin. "Have you been staring at me this whole time?"

"How are you feeling?" Finn asked, not deigning to stoop to his level.

"Well, you know." He shrugged, his smile softening. "The way someone might feel after getting their guts carved open."

Finn squinted at him, his gaze falling to Logan's midriff, wondering just how bad the cut actually was.

"All right, maybe that's a bit dramatic," Logan clarified with a chuckle. "It's just the skin, really not that deep. It just needs time to heal."

"No fever?" Finn inquired because he knew that asking about pain would be redundant.

"Don't think so."

Logan slid out from under his covers and stood up. He stretched his arms and shoulders back and forth, making sure not to move the rest of his body too much.

"How long was I asleep?" he asked.

"A few hours but I'm not sure. I drifted off for a bit too."

"No one's come back yet?"

"Not that I know of."

Logan hummed in acknowledgment and braced his hands on his hips, looking around the room as if in search of something.

"What do we do now?"

"We wait?" Finn replied, unsure of what else there could possibly be.

Logan sighed and rolled his eyes in a big dramatic arch.

"That's boring."

"And safe."

Logan looked over at him, something in his eyes that he couldn't quite decipher. Was it annoyance? Or resentment? At the situation itself or that Finn was reminding him of it?

"When do you think they'll be back?" Logan asked in the end, turning away from Finn to pick up the knapsack he'd come back with.

"Impossible to know if we can't even be sure of the time it is now." Finn watched him put the sack on one of the beds and rummage through it. "Where did you go this morning? I didn't hear you leave."

"I can be sneaky."

"That doesn't answer my first question."

Logan huffed and turned towards him, one hand on his hip, the other on the knapsack.

"So... I have an idea," he started, and a bad feeling instantly ran through Finn. "Silac's family has a high standing, right? Or had, whatever. So if we want to learn more about him, shouldn't we ask other people of high standing?"

"I don't really see—"

"I'm sure you've noticed that it's almost Tide-bringings and with Tide-bringings come celebrations."

"What does that have to do with anything?"

"Well, there'll also be one at the palace. In fact, it's a week-long celebration and it's already started and where there's a party, there's nobles without a job loving nothing more than gossiping."

Logan looked at him expectantly with a wide smile as if he'd just proposed something that would solve all of their problems. As much as Logan's idea had some merit to it, it would also increase their chances of getting spotted tenfold.

"Kalani instructed us not to go out if it wasn't strictly necessary," Finn replied weakly, knowing he had no chance to change Logan's mind.

"Sure, but how likely is it that Silac has already followed us here? I think today might be the safest day to go to that party. Each passing day just makes it more likely for Silac to show up, so if we don't go today we'll probably have missed our chance."

Logan's argument wasn't without logic, but it started from a premise that they'd find out anything important at the palace and Finn doubted that that would be the case.

"I've got us new clothes." Logan turned his attention back to the knapsack. "We definitely can't go to the palace the way we're dressed now, except maybe you, so I thought I'd get us something fancy. Also, it's always nice to have a change of clothes on the road, for the smell and all."

"I don't think going to the palace is a great idea," Finn got off the bed to join Logan, who was busy fishing the clothes out of the knapsack. "I'm not saying your idea is without merit, but I don't think the information we can get out of these people is good enough to risk our necks for it."

"You never know."

Logan held up a long, red dress embroidered with black beads to the light, inspected it for a while, then dropped it back on top of the rest of the clothing.

"Look," he said, his tone almost defeated. "I know that you're right and that Kalani's right and that it's unlikely we'll get anything of real importance out of these guys, but I've never been good at sitting calmly in one spot with nothing to do, especially not if it's a tiny room with barely any furniture in it. Maybe if we'd stayed in a house somewhere I could have dealt with it, but not like this. So either you want to deal with me losing my mind over the next few hours or you don't fight me when I try to leave. I won't force you to come with me — it would just be more fun."

Finn thought about it for a while. The people who would be attending festivities at the palace on a random day before Tide-bringings had even started wouldn't be the type who had intricate knowledge of Vellashta's internal politics. At most, they'd get to hear all the rumours floating around about Silac and as much as he knew that there was usually a kernel of truth hidden somewhere in rumours, he doubted that kernel would be interesting enough for their cause. They didn't need to know anything about Silac's family history or his romantic life and the likelihood of any rumours involving his connection to the Crow was extremely slim.

On the other hand, Viscount Zarkid was a significant player in the politics of the southern provinces — there was always the chance that he'd invited someone of real importance for an audience. What he wasn't sure about though, was whether that chance was significant enough to outweigh the risk of running into Silac. Especially considering that *if* Silac had already reached Hrevim, the palace might be one of the first places he went to.

Finn's gaze fell on the dog, who still had his head down but was looking at them with one eye half-opened. If Rodrick had left the animal on his own, it logically followed that he was used to it and wouldn't start randomly freaking out, but Finn couldn't be sure of it.

"I'll come with you."

"Fantastic! Let me show you what I got for you."

He pulled out the rest of the clothing and spread them out haphazardly over the bed.

"You were gone all morning to get us these?" Finn asked, frowning down at the chaos before him.

"It takes time to find true quality in this city."

Finn stared at Logan for a moment, waiting for more details to explain the hours Logan had been gone. Logan just stared back, a pleasant smile on his lips. They both knew he wasn't telling the whole truth, but he would clearly not be saying anything more without further prompting. Finn decided that he didn't really care enough to start an argument over it.

He turned his attention back to the clothes and ran his fingers over the red dress. It was clear that it had lived a rich life before ending up in Logan's knapsack — the colour had faded from a deep vermillion and some of the black beads were missing.

"That one's for Rena," Logan explained. "Tried to find something that wasn't too long so she wouldn't trip over it, but I'm sure we can make it fit somehow. I could try to rehem it if it's really necessary."

"These aren't new," Finn said as he eyed a shawl that matched the dress, "or... *true quality.*"

He couldn't school his face from showing his aversion to some of these garments. He picked up a pair of blue trousers and held them up to the light to inspect the holes near the waistband that the store hadn't bothered fixing. "Where did you find these?"

"In a store," Logan replied with a shrug. "Rich people throw their old clothes away when they don't like them anymore, others rescue them from their tragic fate before the smell becomes unbearable, and we are the lucky ones who get to spend money to own someone else's rubbish."

Finn couldn't believe that a store like that existed and even less that it had enough customers to survive. Surely fabric couldn't be that expensive that people had to resort to *this* to clothe themselves?

"Someone else's rubbish," he repeated under his breath, unsure if he should keep touching any of it.

"Don't worry," Logan chuckled, clearly amused by Finn's revulsion. "They get washed before they get sold. We need something a bit fancier to blend into the crowd at the palace. This was the easiest and cheapest way to achieve that. And I made sure to pick pieces that wouldn't look bad at a glance. I got that coat for you."

"We're not going to blend in wearing *rubbish*," Finn muttered as he pulled said coat out of the pile.

"It looks like yours," Logan said softly as he sat down on the bed next to the clothes, one arm wrapped around his stomach. "The colours are just reversed. I thought it would look good on you."

The coat, indeed, had a very similar style to his own, but where his was mostly royal blue, this one was a golden yellow with deep blue stitches and lining. He unfolded the coat and inspected it. Out of all the pieces Logan had brought back, it seemed the least used. There were no visible holes and the colour seemed to have held up quite well over the years. The only thing that indicated that the coat had previously been worn was the looseness of the fabric and even that wasn't too noticeable.

"Thank you," Finn murmured and folded the coat neatly before placing it back on the bed.

"Couldn't have you running around looking like a common peasant, your highness."

Finn stiffened for a second, then shot daggers at Logan. It was met with a smile that effortlessly won the war as Finn looked back down a moment later, his lips quirking up in a small smile of his own.

"I'm serious, though." Logan leaned back on his elbows and let his head fall back. "It'll be easy for you to fit in at the palace as long as your clothes look the part. You've already got the attitude; no one's going to question your presence. And I'm sure some of them will recognise you, your lordship."

"So it seems," Finn mumbled, distracted as he rubbed the coat between his fingers. "The fabric is different from mine."

Logan's eyes narrowed and he glanced down at the coat. He sucked air through his teeth, then asked, "Is it... a bad fabric?"

Finn regretted having said anything. He had been too in the moment, had forgotten that he barely knew Logan. His sister had explained to him in great detail what strangers thought of him, especially when he let words just tumble out of his mouth before thoroughly vetting them.

"No," he replied, hoping Logan wouldn't linger on the moment. "Just a different one. I'll get used to it."

"All right, if you say so," Logan answered reluctantly, then added for good measure, "but I could get you a new one if you don't like it."

Finn stopped, still for a moment, then turned his attention back to the rest of the clothes.

"It's just a coat," he muttered and looked through the pile until he saw brown trousers that might match the coat.

The second his fingers touched the fabric, he recoiled, a shudder running through him. He froze, his hand hovering over the trousers. He stared at them with wide eyes, his mind screaming at him to never touch them again.

"There's also some beige ones," Logan said carefully, and leaned over to pull the offending trousers away from him.

Finn's eyes darted quickly to Logan, then to Vincent, horrified that anyone had observed his reaction. He forced himself to reach for the trousers a second time, adrenaline coursing through his veins.

"I just got a shock," he dismissed. "There must be some tension in the air."

He gripped the trousers and pulled them towards him, before his stomach clenched tight, threatening to make him vomit, and he had to let go to stop his mind from yelling that he was in danger.

"Are you sure?" Logan asked, genuine concern taking over his face.

"Don't be ridiculous, it's just fabric," Finn replied, getting angry at himself. "I will get used to it while wearing them."

He eyed the trousers with concern, then upset, then disgust, before he circled back to concern and all the while his hand didn't move closer to the trousers. He hated that he couldn't force himself through these feelings, that something as stupid as fabric could be his downfall. His sister had been right — he was ridiculous. No one else had a problem with these things; it was just him, trying to be special. He had overcome so many of his childhood quirks over the past years. Why couldn't this have been one of them?

"You really don't have to," Logan tried to reassure him. "The beige ones would work just as well with the coat."

He pulled the brown trousers away from Finn and threw them to the other side of the bed before leaning over to rummage through the knapsacks. Finn clenched his jaw tight, his whole body feeling rigid, on edge. He didn't dare look at Logan when he presented the other trousers to him. Finn pulled them closer to run a hand over the fabric and slowly his muscles relaxed.

"It's unfortunate those got some stains," Logan explained, pointing towards the backside, "but the coat should hide them."

Finn turned the trousers around and indeed there were some light green stains from someone having sat in grass. The stains were barely visible in the weak light of the gas lamp, but who knew what daylight would reveal.

"These will do fine," Finn replied, his voice hoarse, and folded the trousers neatly before placing them on top of the yellow coat.

"Good," Logan whispered and Finn could hear the relieved smile in his voice.

"What's your plan for once we're at the palace?" he asked instead, needing a distraction.

"Not sure." Logan carefully lay down on the bed and carded a hand through his hair. "Anyone can just go to the festivities. I don't think they'll stop us from getting into the inner court. As long as we look like we belong there, no one will give us any trouble. Then we kind of just have to find the right people to talk to."

"And how do we find those?"

"I don't know. We'll figure it out when we're there."

Finn glanced over at him out of habit, then quickly looked back at the clothes. Logan had closed his eyes, a small look of discomfort tightening his eyebrows but otherwise he seemed completely at peace.

"So you don't have a plan?"

"Not really, no. I don't think you can plan something like this in advance without knowing who's there."

Finn pressed his lips tightly together. He very much disagreed. Everything could be planned, even when you knew the plan might have to be adjusted later.

"You want to talk to people, right? So what do we tell them if they ask why we're in the city? Who do we tell them that we are? We need at least the foundation of a plan if we want to start conversations with strangers."

"You're overcomplicating things, Finn."

"You're undercomplicating them, Logan! If someone asks you why you're in Hrevim, what do you tell them?"

"I don't know, I'll come up with something on the spot."

"Not good enough. What if you can't come up with anything on the spot? We need to establish an identity for you. I won't be able to adopt a new identity since some people might have seen me before, but we can still reinvent who you are. Someone with a high enough rank to justify your presence at the palace but that most people there might not know. A minor son of nobility, from the North perhaps."

"How about Jodash?" Logan proposed. "That's small and unimportant enough as a province."

"I wouldn't exactly call it *unimportant*, definitely not these last few years, but it might not be a bad idea. It hasn't been the strongest province historically. Are you familiar with its nobility?"

"Familiar enough. I can just make up the rest."

Chapter Sixteen

Rena

Rena stared at the man in front of her in confusion, a wide grin splitting his patchy, brown beard in two. He kept a hold of her hand so that the spot where their skin met grew hot and sweaty, making Rena wish he would finally let go.

How did he know her name? And why was he excited to see her? He'd introduced himself as Deacon, a name Rena recognised but couldn't place. Only after an uncomfortably long pause did it hit her that Logan had had an argument with a person of that name back in the city of Rancor. Rena schooled her expression and politely smiled at him while her eyes darted between Jesper and the woman from the Historical Academy who was accompanying them.

She couldn't believe that he was so close to her, in a city so far away from their hometown. What luck it was that they'd both found their way to the same place at the same time! She'd seen his house in ruins, had seen how the fire had eaten away at it, but somehow, he had survived. Clearly, not without injury, but still, he was alive! Breathing and conscious! Someone who had survived the same tragedy as her was standing right in front of her!

Her heart swelled with hope and happiness and confusion and dread. There was so much she wanted to ask him. So much they needed to talk about. A million words almost spilled out of her, but then her eyes darted back to Deacon and his eager stare.

"Ehm," she stammered, unsure how much she should admit to him. "I don't know who you're referring to."

"Right, right, how could you know who my acquaintances are?" His words tumbled out of his mouth, one faster than the other, as if they were scared to be locked inside his body. "I'm talking about a fella named Logan. Might have introduced himself to you by another name, though — you never know with his sort. Tall fella, with wavy hair, pretends to get along with everyone. I'm sure you know who I mean."

"Eh... I..."

"Listen, missy. There's no point pretending you don't know who I'm talking about. I *know* that you're travelling with him. There are enough little mice in Vellashta who saw you together. And *all* the little mice like reporting back to me. I've been looking for him for long enough, it's starting to get annoying. He probably hasn't mentioned me before, doesn't want people to think ill of him, does he? He owes me. A lot. You really don't have to protect him; he isn't as innocent as he makes himself out to be. And I just want to talk to him, I promise. I won't hurt him. But he keeps running away so I have to keep chasing him and if you just helped me, it would all be over so much faster."

"Don't pressure her like this," Jesper interjected, a deep weariness in his voice. "She's just overwhelmed. Give her some time to adjust."

"All right, all right, all right."

Deacon finally let go of her, raising his hands in surrender, a strange smirk distorting his face as if he was forcing himself to appear amiable.

Rena clasped her hands in front of her, discreetly wiping the hand Deacon had been holding on her dress. She shifted, her gaze wandering to the ground and back up, trying to play the part so he'd give her more time to think.

Deacon was probably right. There was no point in denying she knew Logan, but that didn't mean she had to tell him where he was. She wasn't sure what the right decision was, whether he was telling the truth or lying about not hurting Logan, but she didn't really want to find out.

"I don't currently know where Logan is," she started, forcing the words past the lump in her throat, "but if I see him again, I'll make sure to tell him you're looking for him. I'm not quite sure when that will be, though. We're not travelling together anymore, so I can't make you any promises. But I'm sure he's already aware that you want to talk to him. He'll probably come to you once he's less busy."

"No, no, no, no." Deacon took a step towards her, then stepped back just as quickly, his movements jerky and nervous. "I need to talk to him now. You see, it's about an important matter, so it would be best for all if you thought *really* hard in that pretty little head of yours about where you saw him last."

She suddenly felt like crying and she wasn't sure why. She had faced worse than Deacon — it had barely even been twenty-four hours since their encounter with Silac — but it suddenly all felt too much, like her body couldn't take it anymore. She cursed Logan and all the decisions he'd taken in his life. As much as she was grateful that he'd paused his own life to help look for her sister, she wished he hadn't come with so much baggage.

She pressed her nails into her palms and breathed deeply, even though her breaths were shaky. She couldn't allow herself to cry, especially not in front of strangers.

"Now, now, Deacon, that's no way of talking to a young lady." The woman from the Historical Academy smiled warmly at Rena, stepping forward to put herself in front of Deacon. "But maybe we could find a nice, quiet tavern where we could all get acquainted properly. Loitering in the entrance hall of a busy library isn't very conducive to a thoughtful conversation, wouldn't you agree?"

She was a short, middle-aged woman, the dark blue uniform of the Historical Academy tight against her arms and chest. Her skin was a dark olive shade and dark brown hair reached her shoulders in thick coils, held back on her head with a headband that matched her uniform. Her smile was warm, but Rena didn't fully trust it. Was it something about the woman herself, or did the whole situation make Rena too uneasy? She couldn't tell anymore.

"Maybe we can find a solution to Deacon's problem over a calming cup of Elderflower tea," she continued, looking at all parties with her warm smile. "And I'm sure you have plenty to discuss with Jesper. It must be such a relief to see him again."

Rena glanced over at Jesper, horrified at the proposition laid out before her. She didn't want to leave with this woman — not on her own, not knowing the danger that could be lingering on the streets of Hrevim — but she just as much didn't want to lose track of Jesper. Who knew if she would ever find him again if their paths split?

"Okay," she said weakly.

She would try to keep her head down and keep their conversation as short as possible, but she needed to know how Jesper had survived. What had happened that he was now travelling with Deacon and the Historical Academy and why had they ended up in Hrevim? Did he know about the Crow? Had he maybe seen other people from their village who'd survived? There was so much she wanted to ask him; she couldn't let this opportunity slip through her fingers.

Rena looked back towards the moving boxes, staring at them for a moment. Would she need to notify Rodrick of where she was going? It would certainly be the safer decision, but if Rena was truly in trouble, she didn't want to drag him into the situation. Not right after he'd just been freed. No, she would need to overcome this on her own. Find out more about Jesper's situation then escape and find Kalani or Logan or anyone else who might know what to do next.

"Are you waiting for someone?" the scholar asked amicably.

"No, no," Rena answered, turning her attention away from the boxes and forcing a smile onto her face. "We can go."

"Wonderful, and I think I know just the place where we could have a delightful chat." The woman passed Rena to head towards the library's entrance and gestured for the rest to follow. "We will just have to walk for a little bit, but it's such a lovely day outside, I'm sure it will do us all some good to enjoy this splendid weather."

They exited the library and the woman waited for Rena to catch up to continue their conversation as she guided them through the city.

"It truly is an amazing coincidence that we ran into you, Rena. It's such a shame that the Historical Academy hasn't had an opportunity to talk to you yet. What happened to Oceansthrow is such a tragedy. My deepest condolences. I won't ever be able to grasp what you and Jesper must be going through, and all of it because of some mindless accident. But that's just the fortune life hands us sometimes. It doesn't always play out the way we imagined it would."

"Thank you," Rena forced out.

The knot in her stomach tightened, threatening to overturn her stomach. Hearing this woman talk so confidently about the fire being an accident felt like she'd been stabbed. Of course she'd think that. Rena had been warned often enough that that was the story the Historical Academy was going with, but it was something completely different to come face to face with it.

"You know," the scholar rambled on, "we're trying to get Jesper back on his feet. That's the least the kingdom can do after such a horrible event. We could do the same for you. It would ease my mind if you'd accept our help."

"Thank you." All Rena wanted to do was yell at this woman, tell her that the fire couldn't have been an accident and that the kingdom was letting a fanatical group destroy towns without doing anything about it, but she knew that wasn't the right thing to say if she wanted to stay close to Jesper. She would have to play along with whatever this woman said, no matter how much it'd hurt her. "I-I'll think about it. I do have an aunt in Lomen who I could stay with."

"Your mother's sister, right?" Jesper asked, appearing on her other side, struggling to keep up with the group due to his crutch. "Wasn't she much older than your mother? And sick?"

"Yes, but I wouldn't be a burden!" Rena assured him. "I'm old enough to find work. I'm sure my aunt wouldn't mind me staying with her for a bit."

"But shouldn't a bright, young girl have the opportunity to finish her education?" the scholar asked earnestly. "There's no need for you to inconvenience your poor aunt. The kingdom takes care of its citizens. You don't have to deal with this tragedy on your own."

"That is very kind of you," Rena answered, knowing she would have to pretend to be grateful for the offer if she didn't want to upset the woman. "I've always dreamed of going to the citadel in Mak-Hemma but with my family's meagre earnings, we've never had the opportunity to travel far."

"I'm sure that can be arranged, my dear. There are a few highly regarded academies in Mak-Hemma. Maybe you'd be interested in becoming a tinkerer? They're a highly valued profession at the moment. Or maybe you like numbers better and would like being a bookkeeper. You can never go wrong with becoming a bookkeeper."

Without waiting for Rena to weigh in, the scholar turned to Deacon at the back of their flock and waved him forward.

"Deacon, as soon as we're back in our rooms, remind me to write a letter to Aminah Burhan to inform her of this new development."

"I'm neither your servant nor your notebook, Aldara," Deacon growled but complied and walked up to the scholar's other side.

"And then we'll have to contact one of the schools in Dam-Vala. I'm sure at least one of them will be more than delighted to help out our new friend."

As Aldara rattled off potential schools and their respective deans, Rena glanced from side to side to memorise the route they were taking. Her heart was hammering wildly, her stomach in knots to the point she feared she might be sick. Hrevim was so much bigger than any other city she'd ever been to, that she couldn't really keep up with all the places they passed. She grew scared that she might lose her way and neither find the way back to the library nor the Broken Mast inn.

With every step, she regretted having agreed to follow Aldara. A million things might happen to her and none of her companions would know about it, exactly what Kalani had been scared of happening. She kept an eye on the people they passed, ready to hide herself if she recognised Captain Silac or anyone else, but what if Aldara and Deacon were working with the Crow and leading her towards a trap? Had they known she and Rodrick were in the library and had brought Jesper along as bait? It sounded cruel and irrational, but not impossible. If Jesper hadn't been on crutches, she could have grabbed his hand and run away with him to safety but with the way things were, no matter how much she racked her brain, she couldn't come up with any solution that wouldn't separate them again.

With alarm, she noticed that the city was preparing for Tide-brings, the festival celebrating the return of the fire mackerel to their waters. Blue, white and red ribbons were being hung high up between buildings, shading the streets and flowing in the wind, imitating the scarlet fishes' journey through the ocean waves. Some shops had already started setting up stalls in front of their establishments. Rena counted the days she'd been on the road with her companions and realised that the festival had to be less than a week away.

A knot formed in the pit of her stomach. She'd loved the festival back home. It had been a big celebration for the entire family as they travelled to Halvint or Hollowtooth, meeting extended family that would visit them from far away. They'd often talked about going to a bigger city to witness the splendour of their festivities — some places were said to have parades with giant fish swimming through the streets — but had wanted to wait until her younger brothers were older.

Rena averted her eyes, not wanting to continue that train of thought, and focused her attention back on Jesper. He had fallen behind, beads of sweat running down the side of his face as he struggled to walk. Rena adapted her pace so she could hold his arm but then Jesper leaned closer to whisper to her.

"How have you been, Rena? Are you hurt?"

"No, I'm fine," she answered in a hushed voice, keeping her eyes fixed on Aldara and Deacon, who were distracted by their own conversation. "But what about you? What happened to your face? Is it bad?"

"It's... not good," he answered after a pause, his gaze to the ground. "But it will heal. Eventually. At least the skin, it's... ehm... difficult to tell if my eye will heal. But that's why we came here. Apparently, Aldara knows a very competent healer in this city. With the correct ointment, I might be able to regain some of my sight."

"I'm so sorry I didn't come to your rescue!" The words burst out of her and it took all her strength to keep whispering. "The town was already in ruins when I arrived, and I tried to enter your house but it seemed so dangerous to step in and I didn't know if I could help. I couldn't even move when I first saw the fire. I know I should have! I feel so horrible that I couldn't help anyone. I should have tried harder.

Maybe your face wouldn't be hurt so bad if I'd managed to just get up, maybe your eye—"

"Rena. Rena! Calm down. You wouldn't have been able to help me. I was trapped in the basement with half a house on top of me. What do you think you might have been able to change? It would have been impossible for you to lift the beams on your own."

"I know, but I didn't even try." The words just kept spilling out of her, tumbling over each other. "I shouldn't just have given up. I might have heard you and gotten you help sooner. I could have told the people in Halvint to go look for you, even if you had been buried. I didn't even look for my father or Valerio or Savio or even Maya. I just saw my mother and Lino on the ground and ran. I didn't even look if they were still breathing. Maybe they were still alive. Maybe I'm the one who doomed them. Why did I think I was the only one who had survived? How many people could have been saved if I'd done more? If I had gone back to help search for them? If I had—"

"Rena, stop," Jesper hissed, then looked at Aldara and Deacon, waiting to see if they'd react before he continued in a hushed voice. "It doesn't help anyone if we start thinking like that. What has happened has happened. You blaming yourself isn't going to bring them back, either. I know it's harsh but it's the truth. It's not your fault that they're dead. We can't rectify the past, Rena. Luck abandoned us on that day and there is nothing we could have done to change it. Sometimes that's just how life is. Cruel and without logic. The smallest incident can lead to the worst outcome, and we have no influence over it. It'll just eat us alive to think about what could have been different. There's so little we could have actually changed. And what could the people from Halvint have done if you'd warned them? They couldn't have entered any of the buildings while they were still on fire. Even after a fire, it's extremely dangerous to enter such buildings."

She wanted to argue, to rebuke everything he had said, to cling onto hope that life could have been different, but deep down, she knew he was right. It made her feel sick, thinking that there was absolutely nothing she could have done to save anyone.

"I just can't help myself," she murmured, her breaths shaky, focusing hard on not crying. "I know that I wouldn't have been able to lift any of the beams on my own. I tried at the church and it barely moved at all."

"You tried your best, Rena," Jesper said, his voice drenched in sadness. "There's nothing any of us could have done differently that would have helped. But what happened to you? You seem unhurt."

Her gaze fell to the ground, her face distorting in anguish. She didn't want to tell him what had happened, didn't want to admit that she'd never been in any danger, but it wouldn't be fair to keep the truth from him.

"I'm sorry," she stammered out. "I wasn't in town when the fire happened. I was out gathering herbs for my mother and when I came back, the town was already in flames. I tried to help people, I swear, but my body didn't want to move, and once I'd finally found the strength, the flames had already eaten away most of town."

"Good," he interrupted, relieved. "That's good to hear. I'm glad you weren't in town when the fire started. Maybe you weren't the only one."

She'd barely considered that thought before. People had tended to stay in Oceansthrow most of the time but someone might have gotten out, might not even have heard of what happened to their hometown and come back from their long travels to discover it completely gone, only the ruins of the old church still standing.

"I don't know if the Crow would allow that," Rena said solemnly.

Jesper looked at her, his one unbandaged eyebrow drawing down.

"The... what?"

"The Crow. The people who started the fire."

He looked away, staying silent in confusion, before he turned back to her.

"What are you talking about?"

Rena suspected that Aldara hadn't told him the truth but hearing his utter confusion still broke her heart.

"The fire wasn't an accident," she hissed, keeping her eyes on Aldara to make sure she wouldn't turn around. "I know that's what the Historical Academy claims, but they're trying to cover up the truth. There's this organisation called the Crow that has something to do with the old gods and they set these fires for some reason — we're not exactly sure why yet — but Oceansthrow wasn't the first town they destroyed. There was this other town, Miller's Knee, near the Plains, that they destroyed a few years ago. And there have been others before that too. And I'm pretty sure they've got Maya. That's why I'm here."

She couldn't bear the way Jesper was looking at her. It wasn't simply that he didn't believe her; he was also clearly reconsidering everything he'd ever known about her.

"Rena," he hesitated. "I don't know about that. It all sounds... a bit outlandish. And who is *we*?"

"I know it's difficult to believe but you need to trust me! I've found some people who're willing to help me find Maya and uncover the truth. There's something else going on, something hidden that the Historical Academy doesn't want us to know about. Or maybe they don't know about it either, but I don't think they want to help us find out the truth."

Aldara and Deacon were several steps ahead and engrossed in their own conversation. Rena wondered what they could possibly be talking about. Her old fear that she was being led into a trap resurfaced, scared that they were rejoicing in how easy it had been to lead her away from her companions, but she couldn't let her mind run rampant with these hypothetical scenarios. She had more pressing matters at hand.

"I know this has to sound strange to you," she continued hastily after realizing the look of confusion on Jesper's face was turning into worry, "but how could the fire have spread through the entire town without being stopped? It was the middle of the day. People would have noticed."

"Sometimes fire spreads very rapidly," Jesper answered carefully, his eyes narrowing at her.

"But more people would have survived! They would have run out of their houses and tried to get to safety. Something or *someone* must have stopped them from exiting the buildings."

He looked away from her, then looked back and away again, as if he wasn't sure how to react.

"But why? Your theory makes no sense, Rena. Who would choose to burn down an entire village? Oceansthrow was nothing special."

"I don't know yet. We have theories — nothing concrete — but I found figurines near the church! These sort of hand-carved bird figurines that were deliberately placed in a circle around the church for some reason, with some inscription in an old language across their bodies. An accidental fire can't explain how those got there."

"You found... figurines?"

"Here we are!" Aldara exclaimed and put an abrupt stop to Rena and Jesper's conversation.

Chapter Seventeen

Rena

Rena looked around, breaking out of her daze, and realised that she didn't recognise the part of Hrevim they'd ended up in. The teashop was at the end of a busy road where stores sold delicate goods more expensive than anything Rena had ever owned — hand-crafted jewellery and ornaments made from lacquered wood with iridescent pearls and rare stones in all kinds of colours that imitated seashells and fish. Even the ribbons for Tide-bringings seemed to be crafted from finer fabrics, glinting in the light like fish scales and shading the street with soft colours.

As they stepped into the teashop, Rena felt entirely out of place. White, purple and light blue tiles decorated the floor and walls of the room and a subtly sweet smell enveloped them, the fragrance of honey and almond cakes mixing with the floral essence of the teas. To their left, the tiles formed a mural of the ocean and the city from centuries prior. A few tables were scattered around the room, most already occupied.

Rena couldn't keep herself from staring at the décor, the stark contrast to the inns and taverns she'd visited in her life almost knocking the air out of her lungs. She didn't know why Aldara had brought them here, didn't even want to imagine how much any of these sweet-smelling cakes and teas might cost. She knew she would never be able to afford them herself, but sure Aldara wouldn't demand that she do so.

The scholar led them to a table at the rear of the room and ordered elderflower tea and almond cakes for the whole group without asking anyone else's opinion.

Before the host had fully stepped away, Deacon turned to Rena and stared at her with intent.

"So, about Logan. I'm sure you've remembered by now where he might be."

Aldara tutted, lightly shaking her head at Deacon.

"We shouldn't start this conversation with your personal grievances, Deacon." She turned to Rena. "Tell us how you've been. It must have been such a difficult time for you. But why didn't you stay in Halvint after the fire? The Historical Academy could have taken care of you."

"I..." Rena hesitated, feeling so out of place that it kept her from thinking straight. "I needed to know what actually happened. How the fire started."

"That's why you should have stayed in Halvint." Aldara smiled at her reassuringly. "We could have told you what we found out after the guards finished their investigation. There's no need for you to figure this out on your own."

Rena didn't want to reveal much to this woman, but at the same time she wanted to find out what the Historical Academy's official statement about the situation in Oceansthrow was. How much did this organisation know and why were they so adamant on hiding the truth?

Was it just that they wanted to prevent panic spreading through the province or was it something more sinister? If Rena had already risked her safety by following strangers to a part of the city she'd never been to before, she could at least try to make her excursion useful for the rest of her group.

"And what did your investigation reveal about the fire?" Rena asked as innocently as possible.

"Well, it isn't completed yet, so I can't tell you much, but certainly not because I don't want to. I just really don't want you to get the wrong idea. But one thing we're certain about is that it was just a careless accident that sadly spread from house to house. We just don't know the specifics of it yet."

As the host came back with their teas and cakes, Rena dared a quick glance at Jesper. He was sitting next to her with his hands clasped in his lap, his gaze vacantly fixated on the table. His brow was lightly furrowed as if he was mulling something over in deep thought. Deacon sat across from him and never took his eyes off Rena, even when the host put his dishes in front of him. His face was neutral, with a hint of annoyance, and only changed into a quick, cocky smile when Rena looked over at him.

She smiled back and quickly looked away, focusing her attention instead on the small clay cup filled with elderflower tea in front of her on which a short branch with white flowers had been placed. The rectangular honey cake next to it glistened in a delicious orange and Rena didn't dare touch either of them.

The entire situation felt too strange. She was increasingly aware of all the grime and dirt on her skin and under her nails and how long it had been since she'd been able to properly clean herself. She was sure all the other patrons had already noticed how little she fit into this place, could smell her long journey on her. Any minute now, the host would ask her to leave because someone had complained about her stench.

Aldara had started eating the cake in small chunks and Rena forced herself to follow suit to not seem impolite. She slowly lifted her hand to grab her spoon, as if any rash movement could startle Deacon into pouncing on her. As if he were a lynx just waiting for the rabbit to hop out of its den. She carved off the corner of her cake and let its sweetness melt on her tongue. She instinctively closed her eyes to savour the taste. It spread throughout her mouth and further until it had touched every corner of her. It momentarily reminded her of her mother's dried fig cake, even though the desserts didn't have that much in common. She let herself remain in the memory for just a moment, then opened her eyes to this new reality she found herself in.

She turned her attention to her tea, stirring it to fake nonchalance, then asked, "How could a fire started by accident have spread through an entire village?"

"A strong wind could have spread it to some drying hay," Aldara replied with deep regret and Rena had to admit that the scholar was very good at playing her role.

"I don't remember there being much wind that day," Rena said innocently.

"It must have been quite localised. You might not have noticed it from inside the forest."

A deep anger clawed at Rena's belly, something she'd never felt before — the feeling almost scared her with how visceral it was. She wanted to scream, to thrash, to throw her delicate clay cup against the pristine mosaic. What Aldara was saying was complete nonsense, anyone had to see that. But how could she argue? The woman seemed so deeply convinced by her statements. Of course Jesper had believed her.

"I also don't remember there being any drying hay lying around," Rena said, controlling her voice as best as she could. "It would be a bit early in the season for it. Do *you* remember it, Jesper?"

He looked at her, startled, not having expected to be addressed. He glanced at Aldara for just a moment and Rena wanted to scream at him to forget about the scholar.

"I have to be honest, Rena," he said hesitantly, "it's all very much a blur for me. Not just the fire itself, but also the days prior. I couldn't tell you if there had been hay lying out to dry or not. Or how the wind felt."

How could he say that? No one in their town had started drying their hay yet, it was just too early in the season. It wasn't something that could just be overlooked or forgotten.

"Jesper suffered some heavy injuries to his head." Aldara smiled gently at him. "It's perfectly normal if he has trouble remembering certain things."

Rena breathed in deeply, hiding her shaking hands under the table. She shouldn't grow angry at Jesper, not after what had happened to him. She knew how exhausted she was herself and how much the memories of the fire weighed on her mind; she could only imagine how much worse it was for Jesper who had actually been in town during the attack.

"I'm sorry," she said, mirroring Aldara's smile. "Jesper, I know that it has to be difficult for you to remember details. I'm sure it'll come back to you once you've had plenty of rest." She turned her attention back to Aldara. "But, uhm, I still think it's a bit unlikely that anyone would have been laying out hay at this time of year. The grass is still growing — it doesn't make a lot of sense to already harvest it."

"Well." Aldara chuckled lightly, her annoyance peeking through her feigned warmth. "It is just one of our theories. It could also have been caused by an oven. As I said, I don't want to discuss the details of what we think might have happened too much, exactly because of this. People tend to focus on the wrong details. Once we have reached a conclusion, I'll personally make sure to discuss it with you."

Rena glanced at Jesper again, hoping their eyes could meet, but his gaze never strayed from the cup of tea in his hands. She just needed to make him wonder about the fire, make him realise on his own that the Historical Academy was lying to him and that an accident couldn't have caused that much damage.

"Can we talk about Logan, now?" Deacon asked, voice dripping with frustration.

Aldara turned to him. "This person you keep mentioning, he's travelling with Rena?"

"He sure is."

"Is he a trustworthy person?" It sounded like there was genuine concern in her voice, but Rena didn't trust it.

Deacon laughed but it felt wrong and grating.

"Oh, I don't know about *that.* How much can you really trust someone from Rancor, right? He sure has a mind of his own."

Aldara turned to Rena and gave her a look she had gotten plenty of times from her mother.

"Do you think it's a good idea to be travelling with someone like that, Rena?"

"But Deacon is also from Rancor and you're travelling with him," she replied, not able to keep the bite out of her voice.

"Certainly, but we are adults."

"I don't see how that has much to do with the situation. I'm not a child anymore."

"No, but you are still young and just experienced a very terrible event. Don't you think it's a bit concerning that you are travelling through the kingdom with strangers?"

As much as she hated it, if Rena didn't want to draw any ire, she would need to play along. She had to set her feelings aside, no matter how angry Aldara made her. The longer she argued with them, the longer it would take to get back to her companions. She needed to tell the others of Jesper's existence so they could find a way to rescue him before the Historical Academy had completely influenced his mind.

She held Aldara's gaze then sighed a bit too dramatically, looking down at her hands.

"Maybe you're right," she murmured. "They've all been very kind to me but it *is* quite dangerous out here for someone like me." She paused, then looked up at Aldara. "I like what you proposed earlier, about getting to finish my schooling and maybe trying my luck at an academy."

"That would be wonderful, Rena," Aldara replied with a soft smile. "I'm sure you would do fantastically at any of the academies, don't you agree, Jesper?"

"Oh, eh, yes," he replied, startled once more as if his mind kept wandering off. "She's very smart. Always helped out the other kids at school. Your, uhm, teacher... Uhm, what was her name again?"

Rena startled at his confusion, shocked that he couldn't remember their teacher's name.

"Miss Kaari," she replied carefully. "She lived in Oceansthrow all her life. Don't you remember?"

"Yes, right, her name had just slipped my mind." He looked concerned for a moment, then smiled up at her. "She always seemed very proud of you."

A strange heat rose from the pit of Rena's stomach, spreading through her body and into her cheeks. She couldn't keep herself from smiling, although her joy was soon tinged with the bitter aftertaste of grief.

"Thank you," she replied softly. "I always tried my best."

"Then I'm sure you could even become a teacher yourself!" Aldara said joyfully. "It will take us a few days to get back to Napahrit. I might send a messenger ahead so all the procedures to get you back to school can be arranged. You'll join us, right, Rena?"

"Oh, yes," Rena stammered, suddenly afraid that Aldara would not let her leave. "But I need to get my belongings first. We could meet tonight? At the place you're staying at, maybe?"

"Or we could accompany you," Deacon replied, his eyes fixed on her, unblinking.

"Oh no, that won't be necessary," she replied, waving off his proposal, her heart hammering so loud in her chest she was afraid the others could hear it. "I'm sure you have better things to do. You didn't come all this way to waste your time watching me pack my stuff, especially not considering Jesper's injuries. And Logan wouldn't be there anyway if that's what you're hoping for. Like I said, I really don't know where he currently is."

"How do we know you won't just run away?" he asked, narrowing his eyes at her. "I don't particularly feel like chasing you over another border."

"Why would I do that?" Rena replied, forcing humour into her voice, her palms uncomfortably sweaty. "I've known Jesper all my life, he's one of my father's dearest friends. Why would I abandon him after having found him so unexpectedly? I thought I was the only one who had survived but now I know better. It wouldn't make a lot of sense to run away now. Where would I even go?"

"I know, child." Aldara reached forward to hold Rena's hands. "I know. Deacon is just a very stubborn man. Why do you care so much about this Logan fellow anyway?"

"He owes me something," he grumbled, his lips pulling up in a snarl.

"Well, I'm sure it can't be so important to threaten a young lady over it."

"It will only take me a few hours to pack all my belongings," Rena said. "We could meet up again before the sun sets."

"Why don't we assemble again here?" Aldara asked.

"Wouldn't it be easier if I came to the inn you're staying at? Just so I could store my belongings in your room."

"It's near the palace," Jesper replied and Aldara's smile faltered for a split second. "I don't remember what it's called but it has a mechanical statue of a yellow flower in front of it that opens and closes. Strange object. Quite loud if I'm being honest."

"Right, yes," Aldara replied, staring at Jesper for a moment before turning back to Rena. "We will wait there for you. Just let the innkeeper know you're looking for me and he'll escort you to the correct room."

Chapter Eighteen

Rena

Rena hurried back to the library as fast as she could. She looked down every side street she passed, afraid that Silac or Inkra were waiting there for her. Her mind jumped from Jesper to Deacon to the Crow to Maya in a panic, trying desperately to find a way to keep the ones she loved safe but never coming to a real conclusion.

She had considered Jesper's reappearance from every angle but couldn't quite figure out how to save him from the Historical Academy without delaying Maya's rescue. She tried to determine which of them was in greater peril but there was so much she didn't know about either's circumstances. As much as she hated herself for it, she knew she had to focus on Maya first, even if it made her feel incredibly selfish. The Historical Academy seemed to be treating Jesper fine, even though they were lying to him, but no one knew what the Crow was planning to do to Maya.

Rena hurried inside the library, past the reception desks and stepped into the moving boxes at the end of the hall without hesitation. She was too preoccupied to still be afraid of them. She leaned against the back wall and kept her gaze fixed on the library's entrance, but to her relief no one seemed to be following her. Her body was tense, her mind racing from one outlandish idea to another, begging the universe to let her find a way to save both. There had to be a way, she was certain of it, she just couldn't see it. But maybe Rodrick could, or Kalani, or Logan, or even Asha or Finn. They had lived through so much more than she had — they had to know how to best proceed.

She re-emerged on the first floor and even though she wanted to run towards Rodrick, she walked slowly so her footsteps didn't break the silence of the room. Rodrick was still sitting at the same table, hunched over an ever-growing pile of books. He'd somehow acquired a piece of parchment, a quill and an ink pot and had filled the page with notes in a barely legible script.

"Rodrick!" Rena hissed as she sat down next to him.

He jerked up as if she'd screamed in his ear and looked at her in total shock, but his features quickly softened to a mild confusion.

"You're back already? I hadn't expected you for another couple of hours. Or did time fly by so quickly?"

"No, no." She shook her head violently. "I didn't go back to the inn. Something happened."

He tilted his head, then glanced back at the moving boxes before looking at her.

"Something happened?" he whispered, his voice full of concern.

"Yes, I ran into someone." She scooted closer to him, keeping an eye on the clerk overseeing the room who was already regarding them with apprehension. She described what had happened to her but realised halfway through how far-fetched it must sound.

Rodrick's mouth opened and closed, too bewildered to respond. Rena wrung her hands nervously in her lap, desperately trying to find words to make the events sound any less outlandish.

"What are you talking about, child?" Rodrick finally replied, voice low as he leaned closer to her. "Where did you meet those people? When did this happen?"

"Here in the library, in the entrance hall, but then we went to a tea shop."

"Rena!" Rodrick exclaimed but quickly pressed his lips together when the clerk cleared his throat at them.

"I know, I'm sorry," Rena pressed on, not waiting for Rodrick to scold her further. "It was stupid to follow them on my own but I didn't know what else to do. I couldn't lose track of Jesper after just having found him again. Rodrick, I'm not the only one who survived."

She looked at him with such desperation, thinking that he must inevitably realise that she'd had no other choice considering the circumstances. Surely he could not hold her actions against her?

He opened his mouth again but didn't say anything, then sighed and looked at her full of pity.

"Oh, Rena," he said quietly and it almost broke her.

"I needed to find out why he's travelling with the Historical Academy," she continued quietly, averting her eyes from his. "They got to him after the fire and are telling him all kinds of lies about what happened to Oceansthrow. I just need him to realise that it wasn't an accident like they say it was."

"You told him about the Crow?"

"I had to! But I made sure the lady from the Historical Academy didn't hear us."

Rodrick hesitated, then said, "I don't know if that was—"

"He deserves to know!"

Rena wasn't sure where her resolve was coming from but the thought of Jesper not knowing the truth of what had happened to his family and friends filled her with a rage she'd never felt before. All day she'd felt like a different person. She would have never been this way a week ago but how could she fault herself for having changed after such a horrible event? But what if they got to Maya so late that her sister wouldn't recognise her anymore? What if the changes stayed and she would be angry for the rest of her life? How could she keep on living with these feelings burning away at her?

"I know that I'm already asking a lot of all of you," Rena continued, the words spilling out of her, her thoughts not wanting to slow down, "and I'm so, so grateful for all the help that I'm getting but I'm not sure Jesper is safe with the Historical Academy. They told me where they're staying and I agreed to meet them there tonight but of course I won't, I just needed to know how to get back to Jesper. I was trying to figure out how we could save him. I don't want to lose track of him — who knows what'll happen to him if he stays with the Historical Academy — but it would probably put us into more danger than we already are and we need to get to Maya as quickly as possible and I just can't wrap my head around how we could save both of them but maybe someone else will know. Maybe we can find Kalani or Asha and talk to them about it. They'll know what to do, right?"

"I understand, Rena," Rodrick interjected, holding his hands up to slow her down. "I understand. You are not wrong; we just need to be careful. I am not saying that I do not trust you, however, we don't know whether we can trust Jesper. Situations like these often make people act in strange ways. It wouldn't astonish me if he were to side with the Historical Academy over you. Not because he doesn't cherish you, but in his eyes the Historical Academy is the one who saved him."

"But—"

"We cannot assume that he won't repeat what you've told him — and I do not blame you for having told him; he deserves the truth — but we need to be more careful about who we tell what we have found out. I know that is not what you wanted to hear, my child, but we need to play our cards right if we want to save your sister."

Rena sighed and slumped against the back of her chair, her body deflating. She looked up and her eyes met the clerk's. He had a grim expression of annoyance on his face, then placed a finger over his lips. He clasped his hands behind his back again, shooting one last meaningful glance at her before looking out over the reading room. Heat flushed into Rena's cheeks and she quickly averted her eyes.

Her anger was still simmering underneath the surface but she wasn't quite sure what to do with the energy. The world felt so unfair to her. She shouldn't have to choose between saving Maya and Jesper. They both deserved such a long and happy life and Rena wished so desperately she could provide it for them.

Rodrick patted her shoulder and turned his attention back to his books. He closed the one in front of him and carefully placed it on another, the chains holding the books to the table softly clanking together.

He pulled the piece of parchment closer and squinted at it, brushing his finger over the neatly written rows as he reread his notes. From close up, Rena could see that they were written in the same script she'd found in Rodrick's notebook a week ago, the one she couldn't read.

"What did the books tell you?" she asked, hoping the distraction could calm her inner turmoil.

Rodrick leaned over to show her his notes, disregarding the fact that Rena couldn't read them.

"It is quite fascinating," he whispered, the excitement breaking through his voice. "I couldn't find much at first because the manuscripts I read in the beginning kept their information quite broad, talking about the history of the old faith without going into much detail, but I found one that discussed its place in this region more specifically and that led me down a rabbit hole. I hadn't expected to find much about body-controlling abilities or other such strange talents, or even about any rituals, but there's actually quite a lot of information on both if you know where to look. How trustworthy that information is, however, I still haven't fully decided.

"One of the resources I found talked about the gods of the old faith and which miracles they could enact. As far as I know, this belief in miracles and influences that the gods had wasn't universal. Some regions believed in it, others didn't. But the southern provinces seemed to be quite fond of the belief. How ahistorical or metaphorical those beliefs were, however, is quite difficult to parse."

Rena wasn't sure she truly understood everything he'd said. She found herself squinting at Rodrick's notes as if that could clarify the situation, but they only confused her more. She noticed a few instances where the script changed to Mohrishim, but the notes never changed into anything she could read.

"So, there is a god who can... control people's bodies?"

"In a sense. It's described more as guiding but you could interpret it as taking over someone's body and mind. I'm sure I mentioned her before. Kaepi'Pari. Tavuu'Moda's twin sister. Which, I suppose, if the Crow is so focused on Tavuu'Moda, it makes sense that they'd also be interested in his sister."

Rena vaguely remembered having heard that name before but couldn't recall what Rodrick had said about her.

"So..." Rena hesitated, trying to connect their research to what they'd experienced. "The Crow has given Captain Silac Kaepi'Pari's abilities? Or similar ones? Does that mean... he's a god?"

She frowned at Rodrick, finding her own words too strange.

"No, no, no." Rodrick shook his head but then paused. "He's certainly not a god, but the Crow might think that's what they're doing, even if it sounds impossible. There seem to have existed some obscure rituals that either tried to imitate the gods' abilities, turn someone into a god or create a new one. The sources I found weren't very clear about it; they mostly talked about how these practices were heretical and should be shunned. But I would have to spend more time researching the subject to come up with any legitimate theories. It is all very unclear at the moment — too many sources contradicting each other, and I'm not sure we can trust any of them. If only we had more time. I would appreciate losing a few afternoons on this research, but alas."

"I don't suppose any of this is actually helpful to us?" Rena asked, defeated, feeling like they had just wasted hours on nothing.

Rodrick tried to protest but then thought better of it.

"Not anything that could help us directly, no," he replied apologetically. "It might help us understand how Captain Silac became the way he is, but I don't think that will help us if he attacks us again. At least not unless we pour many more hours into this subject and even then it's uncertain we'll get a clear answer."

"What if they want to do the same to Maya?" she said quietly.

Rodrick looked at her as if he had never even considered that possibility.

"Why would they do that?"

"I don't know," Rena replied, trying to keep her mind from panicking over something so ridiculous. "But why else would they have taken her?"

Rodrick turned his attention back to the parchment, dumbfounded by Rena's idea.

"Well... I'm not sure. It might have simply been an accident or this is how they gain new recruits. She might not be the only person they took from Oceansthrow. And Rena, I do not want to disrespect your sister, but they would probably keep the privilege of becoming the god they so admire for one of their own."

Rena hated this, hated how little she knew about what was going on, hated that every day they learned something new that made no sense to her. Reality had completely shattered and she was supposed to simply keep moving on. All she wanted was to get her sister back but she couldn't even do that. Her mind spiralled thinking about the Crow trying to turn Maya into a god, trying to make her something that isn't human anymore. Rena didn't want her sister to become like

Silac, certainly didn't want her to have those ugly green veins all over her face. Whatever the Crow was planning, Rena needed to stop them.

Her heartbeat started racing, her fingers turning ice cold as sweat ran down her back, and her mind went blank. Maya had to be alive, and they had to save her, or nothing they had done had any meaning at all. How unfair would life be if she'd survived but her sister hadn't? How unfair would life be if Jesper had survived but Maya hadn't?

Her lungs clenched tight at that thought, pushing out all the air in her body. How could she think such things? How could she value Jesper's life so little? She was a horrible person if such thoughts even dared cross her mind. She'd survived the tragedy without a bruise and yet she blamed a man who had lost an eye and had burns all over his body for surviving instead of her sister? What a selfish girl she was.

"I'm sorry, Rena," Rodrick whispered in a soft voice. "I didn't mean to make you feel uncomfortable. I do hope we can find her, but it isn't a guarantee. Of course, we'll do everything to figure out if she is still alive and to keep the Crow from continuing on their wretched path, but it might all lead to more heartache. Can you promise me to keep this in mind? I don't want you to obsess over something that might only devastate you."

Rena stared out into the nothingness in front of her, her eyes unable to focus. All energy had been drained from her and all she managed was a weak nod. He was right, she knew that, but what was the point of discussing it? Why did she have to consider that Maya might be dead when it was the only thing keeping her going?

After a few minutes of silence, Rodrick pulled a book closer and opened it partway through. She observed him for a while, every passing second feeling like it was ripping at her soul.

"We should try to find Kalani," Rena whispered, her body too exhausted to lean closer to make sure Rodrick would hear her. "She'll know what to do next."

"Yes, certainly..." Rodrick whispered back, distracted by his notes. "The others might have discovered something important as well."

He paused, then frowned at the parchment. He pulled a book from the middle of the pile, the chain entangling itself with those of the other books, and opened it. He turned the pages hectically until he stopped towards the end of the book and leaned in closer.

Rena wasn't sure what he'd found but she also didn't really care. All she wanted was to leave the building, even if Deacon was waiting for her outside, even if they would run into Silac.

"I can just find Kalani on my own," she muttered and pushed her chair back.

"No, there's no need for that," he told her but didn't move away from his book. "Just give me a second."

She paused, waiting for him to move but something new seemed to have captured his attention. She sighed and stood up and only then did Rodrick snap out of it. He looked at her in astonishment, blinking a few times, then shook his head.

"No, no, let's not be foolish. I can come back to the library at a later time. Maybe tonight once we've had a chance to catch up with the others."

Rodrick gave the books back to a very annoyed-looking clerk and led Rena out of the library.

She kept her gaze low but analysed every pair of shoes and trousers they passed, hoping she would be able to recognise Deacon's or Silac's before they could get a good look at her face.

Chapter Nineteen

Finn

Logan and Finn marched straight to the palace, walking with determination as if they had an important meeting. Finn scanned the crowds around them from the corner of his eye. He wasn't sure what they would do if they ran into Captain Silac, especially since he'd opted to leave his rapier at the inn — it would just look suspicious if he had it on him at a celebration. If they saw him before he saw them, they could always give up on Logan's plan and sneak back to the inn. If Silac saw them first, however, there wasn't much they could do besides run away, and Finn didn't dare calculate their chance of success considering Logan's injury.

The fortress stood higher than the rest of Hrevim, built centuries ago on a small hill with the city growing around it. With constant renovations, it barely showed its age. The white walls still shone brightly in the sun as if no fleck of dust or dirt had ever dared touch them. A cobbled path — red and white stones forming an intricate pattern — led to massive cast-iron doors that probably remained of the palace's first iteration. They stood wide open, two guards standing to either side of them as masses of visitors flooded in and out of the first vestibule.

Logan and Finn let the flow move them forward into the inner court while guarded doors to either side barred entrance into the actual palace. With a light touch on his lower back, Logan guided Finn through the crowd. The centre held a garden large enough to fit a small village. It had already been decorated for Tide-bringings; thin poles jutted out of the ground every few metres, adorned with red fish-shaped streamers that fluttered high in the air. Several metal sculptures of fire mackerels stood around the garden, their motion conveying a feeling that a swarm was circling around the court.

"You know, I never really got the point of Tide-bringings," Logan said, looking around at the decorations. "Fire mackerel tastes just like any other fish, why do we specifically celebrate that one? Why does the South care so much about where it's at in the ocean? The rest of the kingdom doesn't even care and here people get so heated about *how* to celebrate this stupid fish. I've gotten into actual arguments with people over it. It's so strange."

Finn hummed, half in agreement, half because he couldn't fathom why that was on Logan's mind. He didn't much care for the celebration either but there were more pressing matters they should be focusing on.

They were surrounded by groups of visitors who stood in deep conversation all throughout the inner court. Balconies ran along the inner side of the square building and held further flocks of people, looking down upon the ones unworthy of entering the palace proper. Blue, white, and red ribbons had been tied between the balconies, hanging down into the court.

"I knew Viscount Zarkid liked company, just not to this extent." Finn's eyes darted from person to person, his efforts to avoid bumping into people becoming increasingly fruitless with every step they took.

He recognised a handful of people, although he wasn't sure he could name them. It was no one he'd had any significant contact with, just patrons of the archives that had shown up often enough for him to memorise their faces.

"It's incredible that he really still uses *Viscount*," Logan said, grabbing Finn's arm to slow him into a leisurely pace.

"It's a historic title tied to the region," Finn replied automatically, his mind occupied with scanning the crowd for anyone more important. "There's no reason to abandon it."

"It just sounds a bit pompous, don't you think? Everyone else is just a lord or lady."

"Not everyone. Jodash has an exalted count. You should probably know that if you're gonna pretend to be from that province."

"And that guy must be a really arrogant prick," Logan retorted. "Imagine using *exalted* in your name. Like, what the fuck? No one's that important!"

"Can we focus on why we came here?" Finn hissed under his breath. "I don't want to waste all day strolling through this pointless celebration."

Logan glanced at him with a small smile Finn couldn't really decipher. He didn't notice any tension in Logan's body, as if not even his wound was bothering him. It almost seemed to him that the crowd was giving Logan more energy instead of sucking it out like it was doing to Finn.

"I don't know about you, but I'm already hard at work," Logan said with a wink. "We can't simply walk up to a random person a second after arriving. We need to be in the space, let the others see us, wonder who we are and why we're here until they get bored and move on to the next people who come in. It's all part of the game. Pretend we belong here until we blend in."

Finn balled his hands tightly into fists and let his eyes wander over all the faces, noticing how some gazes quickly looked away as if they'd just been observing him. He came to the realisation that this wouldn't be a quick and easy job that would have them on the way back to the inn within the hour. He hadn't actually been naïve enough to think that it would be *easy*, but not in his wildest dreams had he considered that they'd need to stroll through the celebration as if they were actually enjoying it. This event was the furthest from what he considered fun. There were too many people, the surrounding walls trapped the noise and amplified it tenfold, and there wasn't even anything interesting to do. He had seen stalls selling drinks and food along the walls but that was about all that the palace offered its guests. The whole point of the event seemed to be to just stand around and talk, and Finn despised that some people genuinely enjoyed that activity.

It all brought back memories of his childhood. He'd been to more than one of these functions when he had still lived in the North and all of them had come with the disappointment of his parents. They criticised him for things he hadn't even noticed he was doing — for the way he was standing or talking or eating or looking at people. He had tried to follow their instructions but none of it came naturally to him, not like his sister. She'd always been so good at pretending. She could smile and laugh at someone's jokes and then turn around and tell Finn all about how much she hated them. It had all been a game to her and she had never tried to teach Finn the rules.

"I don't get any of this," he muttered under his breath, his mouth running dry at the old memories.

"You don't need to — that's my job. You just need to look pretty and important and give me a justification to be here."

Finn hummed in acceptance, wishing desperately he could come up with a better plan that would distract Logan from his own. The thoughts of his childhood had accelerated his discomfort. His throat was constricting, making it hard to breathe, and all he could think of was trying to get away from the crowd.

His gaze drifted up to the balconies at the groups of people looking down upon them. He recognised a few — people of actual rank who didn't just hold a title with no power.

"We should head up," he murmured as he leaned closer to Logan. "We'll get much more out of the people up there than down here."

Logan looked up and scanned the faces, the sun making him squint.

"Maybe," he said pensively, "but it'll also be much more difficult to talk to them. Finding someone down here who's keen to gossip will be a million times easier."

"What use is gossip to us? We need something concrete, not the millionth speculation why Silac's family fell from grace."

Suddenly the inner court fell silent and everyone's attention gravitated towards the entrance. Finn's heart dropped, afraid Silac had found them, but a second later he realised that made no sense. Silac wasn't well known enough for the entire crowd to know him and his presence certainly wouldn't have elicited such a reaction. He was simply on edge; he desperately needed a way to calm himself down.

The murmuring resumed but it had a different undertone to it — more hushed, more covert. He turned to look back at the court's entrance and craned his neck. An older woman had entered and was striding through the crowd with purpose, two servants hurrying after her.

"That's his mother," Finn heard from someone behind them. "Stars, she really thinks she's someone. They're not even married yet."

"This wedding is such a farce anyway," a second voice responded. "Zarkid barely even cared about his second husband; he's certainly not going to care about the third."

Finn tilted his head to better hear the conversation, pretending to be following the woman's path across the court.

"I've actually heard that the wedding's all Kyrec Sitec's idea. He's probably given up trying to be Zarkid's favourite so now he's dragging his lover into this mess. It's so impertinent."

"It really shows how little Zarkid's aware of what's going on around him to let these crooks walk all over him and steal the city from under his nose. You'd think that at least Yormic would say something about it. They've been married the longest."

Before Finn could hear anything more, Logan had interlinked their arms and was pulling him ahead.

"What?"

"You're right, we need to find a way in."

Logan was heading in the same direction as the woman, but kept their pace leisurely enough to not raise suspicions. She headed towards a smaller door at the back of the court and the guards opened the door to let her in.

"And what's your plan?" Panic rose in Finn as Logan didn't slow down.

The guards closed the doors again. Finn looked around, desperately trying to understand what Logan was doing, his heart hammering wildly in his chest as he couldn't come up with anything that wouldn't get them caught.

"You'd be astonished how much you can get away with if you just do it with enough confidence," Logan said, leaning closer to Finn, then pulling away again to direct him to the right and accelerate his steps.

Finn had noticed the group of young men who were coming up beside them. He scanned their faces, seeing if he recognised any of them, wondering why Logan was heading their way. Then Logan slowed down so they'd be just a few steps behind the group and it hit Finn what he was trying to do. The closer they got to the door, the quicker their pace became, until there was barely any space between them and the other men. Finn's heart hammered wildly and he put all his willpower into not letting his panic show on his face. He didn't dare look around in case the guards thought him suspicious even though not being able to analyse their demeanours made the dread rising in him worse.

Then the guards opened the door for the group, presumably recognising the men, and Logan smiled and nodded at one of the guards as they entered the palace. Finn's mind was entirely numb, as if it had left his body. He didn't want to be present when everything inevitably fell apart. He counted every step they took, waiting for someone to yell after them, but nothing came. Logan slowed them down gradually so the group wouldn't notice them and soon they both found themselves alone in a side corridor, the hubbub of the upper floor audible in the distance.

"Have you lost your mind?" Finn hissed, pacing up and down, having to shake the feeling back into his hands.

"I'm happy that worked out," Logan huffed with an actual chuckle in his voice. "That could have gone *so* wrong."

"You are addicted to bad ideas — I can't explain it otherwise. You have a death wish and for some reason you want to drag me down with you. What were you thinking?!"

"Hey, I got us into the palace, didn't I?"

Finn stopped to glare at him but Logan's smile was radiant as if he'd never felt that alive before. He had to look away or he would have smiled too but he couldn't give Logan that satisfaction.

"And what now?" Finn asked, unable to stop pacing, his body feeling like it was made of a million angry ants. "Do you have another brilliant plan? Maybe something that involves a knife you can ram into my heart, or would that be too quick of a death for you?"

Logan laughed and leaned back against the wall, letting his head hang so that strands of his hair fell in front of his face.

"No, no, nothing like that." He leaned his head back against the wall and breathed in deeply to calm his laughter down. "You wanted to go up to the balconies, right? Then we do just that. The likelihood of someone questioning why we're here is so slim now that we're actually inside the building."

"But not nil."

Logan pushed himself away from the wall and stopped Finn in his tracks to hold his face in both hands.

"You just need to be a bit more confident, darling."

He patted Finn's cheeks twice, then grabbed his wrist and led them out of the corridor, not even looking whether anyone was heading their way or not. The palace's décor was kept quite simple — even though the lower half of the walls was decorated with an intricate mosaic of blue and green tiles, the upper half was plain white with no paintings or other art adorning any of the hallways. All the decoration for Tide-bringings had been kept to the outdoors, giving the insides of the palace a feeling as if no one lived in it.

The upper floor was much busier, with people hurrying from place to place, although it couldn't be compared to the inner court. Every time they passed someone, Finn held his breath, just waiting for the moment when someone would intercept them, but it never came. Logan led them onto one of the balconies but as they stepped onto it, the three people inhabiting it left.

"Great start," Logan murmured as he glanced after them.

He tried to lean forward to prop his elbows up on the banister but quickly changed his mind and turned his back to the court with a grimace.

"So," he started as he squinted and looked back at the door that led inside the palace. "Do we wait for someone to come to us or do we go out hunting?"

"This was your idea, shouldn't you already know the answer?"

Finn stayed a few steps away from the banister, afraid they might be too exposed to the crowd below. If the wrong person looked up, they could recognise Logan or Finn before either had the time to notice.

"Yeah, like I said, it's not as easy to find the right person to talk to up here. Ideally we listen in to what people are talking about, but it might look suspicious if we hop from balcony to balcony. Would make it too obvious that we're listening in on people's conversations. Do you recognise any of them? Maybe someone who'd know Silac?"

Finn looked around, scanning the faces of the people on the balconies closest to them.

"A few but I want to avoid them recognising me."

"I'm sure they already have."

"Yes but if I get too close, they'll feel obligated to talk to me and ask me why I'm here. We don't need that."

Logan sighed and let his head fall back.

"It could be a good conversation starter," Logan suggested.

"No, unless you have a valid reason for why I'm here and not in the archives?"

"You're making everything so complicated," Logan groaned and ran a hand over his face.

"It was your idea to come here," Finn muttered.

"Yes, you already said that," Logan snapped. "You could have just stayed at the inn, you know?"

"No, I couldn't."

They stayed silent for a while, looking in different directions. A tension had crept its way through Finn, locking his back and shoulders in place. He clenched his fists tightly, just waiting to see how Logan would react. That was what he liked least about meeting new people, not knowing how they would act in certain situations. He couldn't prepare his own response if he couldn't tell whether the other would get mad or sad or even violent. There were a million ways that Logan could react and all needed a different response from Finn.

"Listen," Logan said after a while, interrupting Finn's spiral. "I realise that this was a stupid plan — if you can even call it a plan — but that's just how I operate. Planning ahead just feels like my head will explode. There's too much to think about, too many unknowns, too much that can change once you get to a place. It feels like I'm trying to keep the entire universe in my mind and I really don't like that. I prefer reacting to what's right in front of me. So I don't really plan ahead, ever. And I'm good enough at reading people that it usually works out. But I know not everyone's like that. It does come with its risks if you don't have the right personality for it, I'm very well aware. I've just been doing it for so long that it comes naturally to me."

Finn didn't reply right away. He kept looking out at the crowd, letting his gaze wander over the architecture of the palace then up to the few clouds above them. He couldn't imagine a method of tackling things that was further from how he operated but hadn't people told him all his life that he was too rigid? Maybe he could try Logan's method, just for once, just to see how it would feel.

"The people downstairs were talking about a wedding," he stated, eyes still fixed on the sky. "How much do you know about that?"

"Wedding? Whose?" Logan turned to him and frowned.

"Zarkid. His third one, apparently."

Logan averted his gaze, his frown deepening as he bit down on his lips.

"I might have heard about it, but I don't really know anything about it."

"Yeah, me neither. If it's soon, we could use it as an excuse for why I'm here."

"Don't think it is, though. People in the city would be talking more about it if that were the case."

"You're probably right." Finn paused, trying to see if the wedding could still be used as a conversation opener. What do you know about Zarkid? Or his husbands?"

"Not much, honestly," Logan sighed. "He's related to someone from one of the royal families but I don't care enough to remember how. But I do know that his first husband is well-liked and everyone hates the second one. Maybe he'll hit the middle ground with this third one. What were their names again? The second's something Sitec, I think. Torec? Kyrec?"

Finn narrowed his eyes at the name. He felt like he had heard it somewhere before but couldn't place it. He mentally went through all the people he knew from the archives, then anyone important in the region. It took him a while until it clicked and the name associated itself with the Military Academy. Kyrec Sitec was the son of Sitec Jured, who in turn was the son of a high-ranking delegate from Napahrit. That meant Kyrec's uncle was Zawarec Jured, one of the generals in charge of the Military Academy in Vellashta.

"He might be related to Captain Silac," Finn said pensively. "Distantly."

"What?" Logan looked at him in utter confusion.

"Through the Zawarec family."

Logan's face made a journey from shock to disbelief until it found its way back to confusion.

"The fuckers who weaselled their way into every aspect of the Military Academy?"

Finn wasn't sure he would have expressed it quite like that, but Logan wasn't wrong.

"I don't remember exactly *how* Silac is related to them but I do remember people talking about it when he took over Hollowtooth's guard corps. Something about them helping him get the position because everyone thought that he shouldn't have been the one to become head of the guard. But I doubt those rumours are true. Silac doesn't seem to have a close enough relationship to the Zawarecs for it."

"I don't know," Logan replied, brows furrowed pensively. "From what I've heard, the Zawarecs are really power hungry. I wouldn't put it past them to put their distant cousins in charge of different cities in the region to keep it all under their control." He paused, then chuckled lightly. "Stars, it would be so stupid though after Silac's whole rant about his fate and not getting what he's owed."

It certainly wouldn't fit into the narrative Captain Silac was trying to project but he wouldn't be the first person to not recognise their own privileges. Finn wished they could be back in the archives. He knew exactly in which rooms he would find answers to the questions swirling in his mind. Silac had only taken over as head of the guards a few years ago. The official records of his appointment wouldn't yet be buried under hundreds of other documents.

"Do you think..." Logan started, then hesitated to continue, looking at Finn with worry.

Finn wasn't sure at first what Logan was trying to ask but then it hit him at once. If Silac were associated with the Crow and also with the Zawarecs, it wouldn't be much of a leap to think that the two were also connected to each other.

"I hope not," Finn muttered, afraid to even entertain the idea.

It was one thing if the captain of the guard in a city that was only known as a travel destination was working with a group willing to burn down entire towns for their fringe beliefs; it was something else if it was most of the higher-ranking members of a Military Academy.

A rhythmic clanking dragged them out of their conversation as a strange machine appeared at the entrance of the inner court. Instantly, the crowd quieted down, all turning towards the entrance. Large mechanical legs protruded from a comfortable seat on which an older man sat. They advanced slowly, like the legs of a spider, while a slim pipe behind the seat exhaled a plume of smoke high above the man's head. He looked serious, unsmiling as he manoeuvred his way through the parting crowd. With his left hand he steered the moving chair across the inner court, although Finn couldn't quite see how the mechanism worked.

"The lord of the castle," Logan whispered mockingly.

Viscount Zarkid had grown sombre in his older years, to the point where some people might call him unpleasant. He'd garnered a reputation for liking feasts and festivities held in his palace, but Finn doubted that was still the case. He barely greeted or even regarded the people surrounding him in his inner court and didn't exchange any words with the ones accompanying him.

Finn stopped breathing when he recognised *who* was accompanying Viscount Zarkid. How was she here? *Why* was she here? She had no reason to be in the South — she hated the region. She had insisted so, so often that she hated the South with her entire heart, that she never wanted to come back.

"I'm astonished he didn't also put these ridiculous ribbons all over his chair to match the occasion," Logan joked and turned to look at him, but Finn couldn't reciprocate the humour.

He hadn't seen her in years. It wasn't fair that she'd suddenly appeared so close to him without warning. If he'd at least known she would be in Baedan, he could have prepared for it, could have shielded his emotions from her. He needed to run away, to make sure she wouldn't notice him, make sure she couldn't break what he had so carefully reconstructed since she'd left.

"What?" Logan asked, slowly starting to mirror Finn's fear. He turned around to look at the court, scanning the crowd frantically. "Is Silac here? I don't see him. Is there someone else? The ones next to Zarkid?"

"My sister," Finn said past the knot in his throat.

"What?! Which one? The blond one? Fuck, she really looks like you. You never mentioned you had a sister before."

Finn's panic ebbed away as Viscount Zarkid and his entourage reached the other side of the inner court and disappeared into the building, but it was quickly replaced by a fear that his sister could pass their balcony at any moment. He stepped to the side so he could be hidden by the open door and tried to calm himself down. If Nara was here, it was to discuss something with Viscount Zarkid, not to be seen on a balcony.

"I don't see why I would have mentioned her before," Finn replied, eyes fixed on the Viscount's balcony just in case Nara would step out with him after all. "It has nothing to do with our search."

"I don't know, it seems like a pretty important thing to me."

Finn frowned, not seeing the connection between both things.

"You never mentioned any siblings either."

"Well, I have a brother, but that doesn't really matter now. Why are you terrified of your sister?"

"She's..." Finn paused, unsure how to put all his feelings about Nara into words. "She's a terrifying person."

"Care to elaborate?" Logan gestured impatiently for Finn to continue.

"Not really."

Logan breathed in deeply, then sighed and turned around, hands on his hips.

It didn't matter why Nara's presence filled him with so much fear as it had nothing to do with why they came to Hrevim. It was Finn's personal problem; the others didn't have to be burdened with it. He would snap out of it soon — he just needed some time. There was no reason that the others would ever have to confront her, so why would he bother telling them about it?

"Why is she here?" Logan finally asked.

"I don't know, it doesn't really make sense. She has no business with Zarkid. All of her work focuses on the North."

"All right. Listen, on any other day I would have suggested we go find out, but I think we already have enough on our plate. And also you look like you're afraid she'll kill you if she lays eyes on you, so do you just want to leave?"

Finn frowned, glancing at Logan for just a second.

"What happened to your plan?"

"Think long and hard about how much you want to stroll through this building while your sister is *somewhere* in it." Logan paused, both eyebrows raised, and gave Finn some actual time to think. "Now, would you like to leave this place?"

Finn's mouth ran dry at the thought of going from balcony to balcony to talk to people, all the while knowing that Nara was close by but never truly knowing where she was.

"I think that might be best," he replied. "I'm sorry we have to cut this short."

"Nah, don't worry about it." Logan waved him off. "We came here to solve problems, not create new ones. And to let you in on a little secret, I knew my plan was stupid, I mostly just wanted to get out of that stuffy room for a bit."

Chapter Twenty

Rena

As Rena and Rodrick left the library, something to Rena's right caught her eye and her head whipped up before she could think better of it. She thought she'd seen something orange, something fleeting, but as she scanned the street, she noticed that it was simply a stray dog — not too dissimilar to Vincent, just stockier and more orange — scurrying from one side of the road to the other in search of food.

"Rena?" Rodrick asked.

She shook her head, admonishing herself for seeing shadows where there were none. Between Silac, Deacon and the fox, her mind was too preoccupied with being followed.

"Sorry," she said and turned back around. "We can go. I just thought I saw something."

As they walked through the streets of Hrevim, the feeling that someone was observing her never quite left. Flashes of Deacon or Silac or just a random guard jumping out from behind a corner accompanied her as they found their way to the docks. She didn't dare look back, but even as they walked through winding side streets, it was as if a shadow loomed over her. The narrower the streets got, the more the feeling twisted into something sinister.

They hadn't been sure how to find Kalani, so had decided to find Asha instead. They walked past old, abandoned buildings from years past, fishers sorting their catch of the day, large ships anchored at the shore with workers swarming them like ants, until they reached the big hangars where these enormous vessels were being built. Rena's eyes darted from worker to worker but she wasn't even sure anymore what she was looking for. Was it the fox? Or Deacon? Or Silac? Why would any of them pretend to be a dock worker to get to her? It wouldn't even make any sense for the fox to have somehow transformed into a person, but no matter how much she tried to stay logical, she couldn't shake the dread running rampant in her mind.

They found Asha a short while later, sitting on a low stool, surrounded by a group of older men. In the middle of their circle, on another low stool, sat a bowl filled with small balls wrapped in vine leaves, still steaming hot.

"Asha!" Rena cried out as she ran up to her companion, throwing all caution to the wind.

"Rena?" Asha turned to her and looked at her in confusion before her eyes wandered over to Rodrick. "What are you doing here? Did something happen?"

"I'm sorry, I know we shouldn't be wandering around the city but we need to talk to you." She glanced over at the men besides Asha.

The one to Asha's left had clearly lived a life out at sea, his dark skin weathered by the salty winds. The other two looked a bit younger with lighter skin. One of them wore jewellery similar to Asha and her uncle's

— golden rings and chains framing his ears — but his clothing wasn't much different from the other two men's.

Asha glanced at Rena, her gaze serious, then looked back at Rodrick, as if she was trying to figure out what had happened from their demeanour.

"Sure," she said carefully and tried to get up but before she could stand, the man to her left put a hand on her knee.

He smiled widely at Rena and offered her one of the wrapped balls.

"Don't you want to sit and eat with us first?" he said and got up, gesturing for her to sit down on his stool. "It's not the time of day to be discussing serious matters."

Rena considered refusing the food but that felt too impolite and she knew that it would only result in an argument that would waste time.

"Thank you." She smiled back and accepted the ball of food the man was holding out to her. "But I'm terribly sorry, we don't have time to stay. It is very kind of you to offer but I could never accept your seat."

The man opened his mouth to insist but Rena cut him off.

"No, no, it's fine, I'm still young, I wouldn't dare take your seat."

"Maybe your companion then," the old man said and smiled at Rodrick.

Rodrick eyed the stool for a moment, clearly considering the offer, then shook his head.

"You are kind, but we do have something quite important to discuss with our friend."

Asha finally stood up, grabbing a handful of the leaf-covered balls, then bid the three men goodbye with a slight bow before turning to Rodrick and Rena.

"Let's go somewhere quieter," she told them and nodded towards some buildings to their right.

Asha led them to the backside of a hangar away from any prying eyes. A few meters away, a handful of workers were on break sitting on some crates in a circle, too engrossed in their conversation to notice anyone else. Paradoxically, what Asha had called *somewhere quieter* was anything but, as the noise of industry bled out from the hangars surrounding them, making Rena uncomfortable.

"What's going on?" Asha asked and Rena had to step closer to hear what she was saying.

Worry had finally reached Asha's eyes as she held out the leaf-covered balls to Rodrick. He happily unwrapped one to reveal a white-ish ball of fish flecked with red spices. Rena considered the one she was holding and unwrapped it, biting into it before responding to Asha. Between bites, she recounted the events of the morning. Asha's face went from confusion to concern to anger and back to confusion, as if she weren't truly certain what to settle on.

"That's why we told you to stay put," Asha said, more baffled than angry. "What happened to *you're gonna go straight to the library and back*?"

"I know, I know," Rena replied, a nervous energy coursing through her. "But they didn't exactly give me a lot of time to consider whether I should follow them or not. Maybe I shouldn't have run up to Jesper when I saw him in the entrance hall, then I could have observed them from afar, but I was just so happy to see him. And once that lady had talked to me and offered we go somewhere else, I was too afraid of losing

Jesper again to not go with them. I needed to know how he was doing! He really doesn't look well."

"And now you think Deacon's after you?" Asha asked, her expression turning sour.

"I don't know, maybe," Rena answered nervously. "It didn't seem like my answers satisfied him, but I don't know if that means he'll try to follow me to get to Logan. Since I left the tea shop, I've felt like someone was behind me, but that's probably just my nerves. I'm sure I would have noticed by now if someone was actually following me."

Asha glanced up and looked around, scanning the space around them, but besides the workers on their break, they were still alone.

"He's smart enough not to harm you," Asha replied, "but you're right that he might be following you to find Logan, or at least keeping an eye on you." She paused, her eyes still fixed on the horizon, then muttered under her breath. "For fuck's sake, what's he gotten himself into this time?"

She sighed and closed her eyes, before looking back at Rena and Rodrick.

"Deacon..." She stopped, considering how to phrase her thoughts. "He's a particular man. It's difficult to know how he'll react to things. Sometimes he'll forgive you for ratting him out to the guards, other times you knock over his drink and it's as if you'd stabbed his mother in the tit. But I'm sure Logan did everything in his power to royally piss Deacon off."

"Can't they just talk about it? Logan's probably making it worse by dragging it out. If you all know Deacon, it can't be that bad if they met up to talk, right?"

"Depends on what the fight's actually about," Asha said with a shrug. "From what I know, Ocassian already tried but both are too stubborn to admit fault."

"We should probably talk to Kalani about it," Rena muttered pensively. "She'll know what to do. And then we can think about how to save Jesper."

"She won't be happy that you didn't do what she told you to do," Asha said with one raised eyebrow. "And I doubt she'll like the idea of diverting our plans for someone she doesn't know."

"I don't want to divert our plans!" Rena corrected hastily. "I know we can't do both at once but maybe afterwards. Once Maya is safe we could also get Jesper away from the Historical Academy. He deserves better."

Before Asha could reply, Rena suddenly spun around, panic rushing through her as she thought she'd heard someone call her name. Her heart was beating frantically, the strange voice resonating at the back of her mind. She looked from one side to the other, then up at the roofs but nothing looked different from before. The feeling that she was being observed rushed back in full force, overwhelming her senses, and she was certain this was how deer felt when in the presence of wolves.

"Rena?" Asha asked, her shoulders square, unsure what had happened but ready for it nonetheless.

Rena wasn't even sure who to look out for. Was it Deacon or had Silac caught up to them? Had Inkra healed from her injury and was looking for revenge? Was the Historical Academy trying to silence her? But the voice hadn't sounded human, more like a whisper on the wind.

Had she panicked for nothing? The noise from the hangars was so loud, how could she have heard anyone calling for her?

"What is it, my child?" Rodrick looked around in concern, panic also rising in his voice.

She cursed herself for being so foolish, for causing her companions such panic when there was nothing at all to be worried about, but her heart refused to calm down, blood pulsing loudly in her ears.

As her gaze drifted back to Rodrick and Asha, something orange caught her eye and this time it wasn't just a stray dog. The fox was sitting calmly at the entrance of a small street behind the workers, staring right at her. Rena froze as if any movement would scare the fox away. The workers were paying it no mind as if they hadn't noticed it.

"Follow me," it said in an eerie voice that carried over the ocean wind.

Chapter Twenty-One

Rena

An ice-cold shudder ran down Rena's back as she realised, she hadn't just imagined the voice. The fox must have truly spoken to her. She didn't dare breathe, her eyes fixed on the animal as it slowly stood up, its tail waving calmly from side to side.

"Did you hear that?" Rena whispered, afraid that if she spoke too loudly, the fox would run away.

"Hear what?" Asha replied as her gaze followed Rena's, then she froze. "Is that... a fox?"

"The same one," Rena replied in a daze.

"The same one as what?" Rodrick looked at her in confusion.

"Come!" the fox commanded in its strange voice, then leapt up and disappeared into the small street.

Rena's body jerked forward as if it meant to follow, but Asha grabbed her arm, her fingers digging into Rena's flesh until it hurt.

"What is that?" she asked in a low voice.

Rena stopped despite every cell in her body screaming at her to follow the fox and even though Asha's grip shot pain up her arm, she didn't dare wrench herself free, afraid that if she wasn't held back, she'd simply run ahead.

"I've been seeing the same fox over and over again," she said, the words simply tumbling out of her. "It was in the Plains, and the archives, and the forest near Oceansthrow, and I even saw it when Captain Silac attacked us. It's been following me and I think it just spoke to me."

Her legs felt restless, her skin itching all over. If she didn't move soon, she'd lose the fox once more.

"I need to follow it," she pleaded, pulling against Asha's restraint but Asha's grip only tightened.

"It spoke to you?" Asha asked as if she couldn't wrap her mind around what was happening. "From that far away?"

"Yes!" Rena burst out but quickly lost her confidence. "I don't know. It told me to follow it. I need to know what it wants."

"Now, Rena, are you sure that you heard it?" Rodrick came to stand in front of her, blocking her view. "I've never known of a fox, or any other animal for that matter, capable of human speech. I think if such a thing existed, everyone would be aware of it, don't you think?" He chuckled lightly, as if the idea itself was too ridiculous to entertain. "I certainly didn't hear it speak just now. Did you, Asha?"

"No."

"I'm sorry to tell you this," he continued with great pity, "but you might simply be tired, Rena. Sometimes our mind plays tricks on us if we don't get enough sleep and then we can start believing that we hear sounds that were probably just the wind. And there must be a lot of foxes in big cities — they're opportunists after all, and it's much easier for them to live off humans' leftovers than it is to hunt. — I highly doubt that you saw the same animal twice, especially if you saw it in the Plains. Foxes don't typically travel that far."

It felt so belittling. She knew she was young and she knew she was tired from their journey but that didn't mean she was making it up! How had Rodrick experienced Silac's strange ability but couldn't believe her on this? After everything they'd been through, didn't he trust her?

"It *is* the same one!" Rena insisted. "I'm sure of it. And it isn't just the markings. It's the way it's staring at me. I've seen plenty of wild foxes in my life, but this isn't one of them! It doesn't act like one. I-It's like it's seeking me out, like it wants something from me, but I don't know what!"

The longer they waited, the more restless Rena became, as if something was pulling at her, and she didn't like that feeling at all. She'd never felt like this when she'd seen the fox before, but it was also the first time it had spoken to her.

It scared her, reminding her of what Silac's commands had felt like, even though it wasn't really the same. Silac's control had felt wrong. This feeling almost had a sweet undercurrent to it, like it was trying to tell her she'd be safe if she followed.

She turned to Asha and placed a hand on the other woman's grip.

"I need to follow it," she pleaded, tears in her eyes. "Please let me go."

"I don't know if that's the wisest use of our time," Rodrick said, but his voice barely reached Rena's ears. "We need to find Kalani, after all. Wasn't that why we had to leave the library so quickly?"

"Please," she whispered, only looking at Asha.

Asha stared back, deep concern clouding her dark eyes before she looked up and stared at the passage the fox had disappeared into. For a long time, she didn't say anything at all. A tightness formed around Rena's heart, the urge to slip her arm out of Asha's grasp and just run away rising, but then Asha nodded once and let go of Rena.

"Thank you," Rena whispered, relief flooding her, and it took all her force not to instantly rush after the fox.

She couldn't let Rodrick and Asha know about the feeling pulling at her. They certainly wouldn't let her follow the strange animal if they knew about it. She focused on her breathing, clasping her hands in front of her and digging her nails into the flesh of her palms so that the pain would overshadow this strange urge.

"But we have to be careful, you hear me?" Asha insisted, looking her deep in the eyes so that her message would sink in.

"I promise."

Rena whirled around and almost leapt forward but then stopped herself and forced her feet into a more regular stride. A part of her mind screamed that Rodrick was right, that she was just wasting what precious little time they had — after all, if they barely had time to consider saving Jesper, they certainly didn't have time to chase a fox through a maze-like city — but her body didn't leave her the choice. She simply had to. The fox had called to her and she was going to follow.

They walked past the dock workers on their lunch, murmuring a quick greeting in passing, before entering the narrow passage the fox had disappeared into. Rena craned her neck in the hopes she could still see a flash of orange but the road bent to the right a few meters ahead. She picked up her pace, dread rising in her that the fox might already be gone. She dashed around the corner and almost ran into a worker coming from the other side.

"Sorry," she muttered and was then promptly whirled around by an angry Asha.

"Didn't I say to be careful?" she hissed.

"Yes, I know, I'm sorry. I just don't want to lose its trail."

Heat rose to Rena's cheeks but luckily Asha only shook her head in disappointment and didn't say anything more. Rena forced her steps to stay in line with her companions', mentally cursing Rodrick for walking so slowly, then admonishing herself for the thought. She knew that Asha was right, that she couldn't simply run ahead without knowing where she was going, but that didn't mean Asha had to talk to her like a child. They would never catch up to the fox at this pace and then they'd have truly wasted their time for nothing.

The afternoon sun illuminated their way but the high buildings surrounding them cast the narrow street in shadows. The roads in this part of the city had clearly been built a long time ago, with carts having carved grooves into the stones underneath their feet over the centuries. The walls around them had once been white but had long since acquired a brown and green tint. The salt of the ocean still lay heavy on the air while the cacophony of the docks faded slowly into the background.

They walked for a bit, then turned another corner, to the left this time, only to see that the passage curved right again a few metres ahead. Rena stopped after the second corner, a flash of orange dashing away from her.

She leapt forward, her body moving before she could even consider waiting for her companions.

"Quickly!" she called out without looking back.

Luckily, no one told her to slow down this time. The fox disappeared between two buildings, into a passage that was barely wide enough for one person to fit through. Rena didn't wait, quickening her step so she wouldn't lose sight of it.

The fox was always just a few metres ahead even though it was much faster and nimbler than Rena, as if it waited for her after every corner. It was leading her away from the ocean and people, towards a part of town where each street looked just as nondescript as the other. She knew Asha was calling her name, could hear the faint echo of it, but stopping wasn't an option.

She didn't know where in Hrevim she was, or if she was even still in Hrevim. The walls around her grew higher, casting her path in shadows. In the back of her mind, she knew that something wasn't right, that there was no reason for a city to have been built like this, but if she stopped to reconsider her actions, she would surely lose the fox's trail.

Rena rounded another corner and was faced with a long and narrow street. The fox had disappeared but there weren't many options where it could have gone. The end of the street looked like a luminous dot, as if the dark passage led to a wide road that basked in sunlight. But first Rena needed to get to it. She ran ahead until the walls almost grazed her shoulders. A few metres further and she had to turn sideways to fit through the narrow space. The only sounds still accompanying her were her footsteps and her breathing, as if she were the only being around.

No busy market could be heard far in the distance, no ocean waves reached her, no wind rushed between these impossibly tall buildings.

She advanced quickly until she realised that she couldn't turn her head anymore. She paused, her eyes fixed on the dot of light in front of her that never seemed to get closer. She knew with certainty now that the fox had led her somewhere that wasn't truly Hrevim. Where she actually was, she couldn't even begin to imagine. She listened for her companions' footsteps, unable to turn her head to look for them, but all she could hear was her breathing and heartbeat.

All the heat vanished from her fingers, her lungs cramping as her chest couldn't expand. She pushed forward, the wall scraping against her skin.

She needed to get out.

Only a few more steps.

The end couldn't be far away anymore.

The light was bright, engulfing everything. The stucco of the walls dug into her back, her arms, her cheek. It ripped at her clothes and her skin but she had to keep going — there was no turning back.

Her steps got smaller and smaller; her hair got tangled in the rough surface of the walls.

Rena closed her eyes when her vision started to blur and with her last strength, she pushed ahead and stumbled to the ground.

She'd reached the end of the narrow passage. The glistening sunlight blinded her and only after blinking a few times could she see that she was in a new street, one that looked like it should — wide enough for two carts to pass through with houses to either side. She breathed heavily and looked up in astonishment. Across from her was an old tavern, with festive ribbons hung in front of its windows, but it wasn't open for business. The hubbub of the city had come back, with its faraway markets and seagulls and ship-building ruckus.

She took deep, desperate breaths, her lungs burning. She pressed her lips together, trying not to vomit, but her teeth didn't want to stop chattering. There was a small noise and her head whipped to the left.

A few houses down the street sat the fox, its shining orange eyes fixed on her.

Rena stared at it for a moment as she held her breath, then she slowly stood up, brushing the dirt from her dress. It faintly registered in her mind that her clothes weren't torn and that her skin felt unmarred, but she didn't want to take her eyes off the fox to confirm it. She took a careful step forward, afraid the fox would run away again, but it didn't budge.

"What do you want?"

"You have to hurry," the voice repeated even though the fox never opened its mouth.

It sounded like it was part of the wind, like it was coming from everywhere at once, and understanding it almost brought Rena to tears.

"Why?" she asked past the lump forming in her throat.

"Your time is running out," the strange voice told her.

"What?" Rena tried to wrap her mind around what the fox was saying but her head hurt just from listening to it. "What does that mean?"

The fox didn't reply right away, as if it was waiting for her to figure it out on her own. The longer the silence went on, the more outlandish the ideas popping into her mind became, although she kept circling back to the same conclusion.

"Is it about Maya? Is she in danger?"

"That's not for me to tell you."

Rena's confusion was quickly replaced by frustration. She'd run after the fox, lost her companions, and been taken to a strange reality, all just to be told something so vague.

"Why?" she demanded, unable to keep the anger from her voice.

"You'll have to figure it out on your own."

"Then what was all of this about?" she shouted. "Why did you make me chase you?! Why are you following me? Just to tell me that I have to hurry? I know that I have to hurry! But how is telling me that helpful at all when you can't even tell me why?! Is it about the Historical Academy? Or about Silac? Is it about Maya? If you can't tell me then why are you here?"

"I have my reasons."

She cried out in frustration but the fox barely moved.

"You're no help at all!" she burst out. "All you did was make me waste more time! And what was that weird street? What was the point of it? Why did I have to go through that just for you to tell me nothing at all?"

A knot tightened in her stomach, twisting until she couldn't breathe anymore. She couldn't understand it. There had to be a reason for the fox to seek her out besides telling her that her time was running out. She knew that already. She knew that if she didn't find Maya soon, something bad might happen to her. But she didn't know what. Why couldn't the fox simply tell her how to save her sister? Why did it insist on being so enigmatic?

Before she could say any more, someone grabbed her arm from behind and turned her around.

"Rena!" Asha shouted at her, only a few centimetres from her face. "Have you lost your mind?!"

Rena whirled back around, panicked, and saw that the fox had already vanished. A few metres ahead, an old church split the street and the fox could have disappeared to either side of it. Rena slipped out of Asha's grip and ran ahead, stopping when she reached the church, frantically looking from side to side, unable to decide which path was the right one. The church had been boarded up, its façade full of carved symbols and words. Rena dashed to the right, then thought better of it and headed left, but there was no sign of the fox.

"Rena!" Asha yelled, running after her. "I should have never agreed to this."

Asha grabbed her arm again, her fingers digging into Rena's flesh until it hurt.

"Why are you just running ahead?" she yelled. "You don't even know where you're going! Did your parents never warn you how dangerous cities can be?"

"Stop treating me like a child!" Rena yelled back, yanking hard to free her arm.

"Then stop acting like one!"

"Why don't you trust me? I know it's dangerous but you can't coddle me like an infant! How are we supposed to figure anything out if we're always too cautious to progress? Was I supposed to just let the fox escape?"

"Okay, fine," Asha spat out and let go of her arm before stepping back. "You want to be treated like an adult? Then don't come crawling back to me when things get messy."

"I'm not asking you to stop helping me," Rena said, the desperation constricting her throat and making it difficult to speak. "I just want your trust! I know that I can't do everything on my own, but that doesn't mean that I can't make my own decisions."

"Trust is earned," Asha replied through gritted teeth.

"And until then you're going to keep me locked up in a box so that I can never get hurt or lost, is that it?"

"Maybe I should."

Rena opened her mouth to argue but no words came to her. Her jaw was trembling, her eyes burning, and she had to look away, unable to withstand the fury in Asha's eyes. She saw Rodrick emerge from the narrow passage but he didn't struggle at all. In fact, the street looked just as wide as any other, even wide enough for a cart to pass through. Rena frowned and looked at the other side of the street. The tavern was right there, which meant it had to be the same passage she'd forced her way out of. She looked down at her dress, expecting it to be ripped, but besides some dirt around the hem, it looked untouched.

Asha sighed heavily then ran a hand over her short, tight curls.

"I'm sorry for yelling."

"I'm sorry I yelled back," Rena answered, exhaustion washing over her.

"Did you at least catch up to the fox?" Asha asked.

Rena nodded. "It spoke again."

"What did it say?"

"That I needed to hurry."

"That's it? So, all of this was for nothing?"

"No!" Rena insisted but she wasn't really sure about it herself. "It's probably trying to help us, we just don't understand it. I don't know. It's saved me before — I wouldn't have found my way back to Halvint without it — so I think we can trust it."

"Or it's playing tricks on you," Asha said, deadpan.

Rodrick had finally joined them, his white hair sticking to his forehead.

"Rena, I have to say," he wheezed between heavy breaths, "I'm a bit worried about you today."

A bitter taste formed at the back of Rena's throat.

"You don't have to be." She crossed her arms and looked out towards the other end of the street.

"This behaviour truly isn't like you," he continued, voice strained. "To chase a wild animal through the narrow streets of a city you barely know is extremely dangerous."

"So I've heard."

"And this talk of the fox speaking to you... Rena, I just can't condone it."

"Then don't," she snapped, "but don't tell me you wouldn't have done the same if you were in my shoes! The Crow has had Maya for over a week."

"We can't be sure of that. You—"

"Stop it! I'm well aware that she might be dead, but what's the point of dwelling on it? She'd still be dead in a week or month or year. But if she's alive, we have to hurry! We know nothing about what they're planning. Maybe they want to use her in one of those rituals you found. Maybe she's the last component they needed. What's the point of contemplating whether she is or isn't dead if it's only going to make us lose more time?!"

"I don't see what any of that has to do with the fox. Didn't we just waste time running after it?"

"It was trying to tell us something!" Heat rose to Rena's cheeks, partly rage and partly embarrassment that he might be right. "Maybe it led us here for a reason. We haven't even looked around yet!"

"Let it go, Rodrick," Asha said before he could argue further, her eyes still fixed on Rena. "I'm sure she's learned her lesson."

Rodrick opened his mouth to protest then thought better of it.

"If you say so," he relinquished.

"I would have done the same at your age, Rena." Asha's eyes grew softer — not so much that Rena could think her anger had vanished but enough to make it easier to meet her gaze. "I made my fair share of decisions I wouldn't recommend when I was looking for my brother, so I understand where you're coming from. But exactly because of that do I know how careful we have to be, okay? I'm not trying to be your enemy or parent or teacher; I'm simply trying to keep us all alive, and running ahead to follow some talking fox isn't exactly the safest of choices."

"I know." Rena pressed her nails into the palm of her hands, focusing on the pain so she wouldn't start crying. "I'm sorry."

Deep down she wanted to continue to argue, to yell at them that Maya had to be alive, that she couldn't keep on living if she couldn't have her sister in her life, but she forced all those feelings down one shaky breath at a time. She didn't feel like herself anymore. She had never felt so much rage and turmoil at once and she didn't know what to do with the feelings.

Asha turned away, scanning their surroundings.

"Let's get back to the main road," she said, nodding her head in the direction of the abandoned church. "I actually recognise this part of the city. Your fox didn't fuck us over completely, apparently."

Chapter Twenty-Two

Rena

Rena, Asha and Rodrick passed the old, decrepit church and emerged onto a wide road bustling with activity. In front of most buildings stood a decorated stall selling a myriad of foods, drinks and trinkets. No banners had been hung above their heads like the rest of the city, but the houses were still adorned in various blue, white and red fabrics as if every inhabitant had contributed their own. A thin line of gold had been added to the mix, waving around the other colours as if to tie them together, something Rena hadn't seen in the other districts.

The group stood at the end of the side street, huddled together so as not to lose each other in the crowd. Rena pressed her arm against Asha's side, her eyes growing wider as they scanned the street. Her astonishment at the festival in front of her soon dissipated her anger and all Rena was left with was a deep weariness in her bones. Asha kept her arm in front of Rena as she carefully looked around — to protect Rena or make sure she wouldn't run ahead again, Rena wasn't sure, but she welcomed the feeling of security it gave her.

After a while, Rena noticed two things: the stalls were giving away their wares for free — like she had seen happen in the city of Rancor

— and the majority of the stalls had some sort of mechanical apparatus on their table. Most of them looked old and rudimentary, ranging from turning plates displaying a variety of drinks to an undulating fish with red, flaking paint, but they were all more fantastical than anything Rena had seen in her life, even more so than the moving boxes in the library. A few of the bigger devices had thin plumes of smoke rising up above them, telling Rena that they worked on the same principle as Rodrick's old caravan or the moving boxes, but she couldn't tell from far away how any of the smaller ones worked. She had never seen such things before, and in Hrevim they were apparently so common that any small vendor could own one.

Was this what the fox had led them to? Was there something Rena should be looking out for? Something that would help them save Maya? Her eyes flitted from stall to stall, desperately trying to find a way any of these delightful gadgets could help them, but they all seemed to only have a decorative purpose. Then a question made her pause. Wasn't Tide-bringings still a few days away? Festivities weren't always celebrated on the same day from one province to the other, but Hrevim's other districts hadn't even finished decorating yet, so why was the festival in full swing here? Had the fox made Rena lose time? She couldn't tell if the tight passage she'd had to force herself through had been real or not — it had certainly felt real even if her dress and skin looked untouched — and if the fox could speak to her in her mind, who was to say that it couldn't also make her lose a week of her life?

"Isn't it too early for Tide-bringings?" Rena asked, her voice barely audible above the cacophony of the crowd.

"This isn't Tide-bringings," Asha replied with a strange bitterness to her voice.

"It isn't?"

"It's what existed before Tide-bringings. *Zaeuun*. The southern islands have been celebrating it for centuries. The mainland only stole it recently."

"I wouldn't call two hundred years *recently*," Rodrick chimed in with a chuckle.

Asha shot him a glance that quickly ended his laugh.

"Compared to the age of the dirt we're standing on, it is. And this travesty that the Royal Council has turned it into is even younger than that."

"Oh, no, no, no," Rodrick said, shaking his head vehemently. "That's not a nice way of phrasing it. Traditions change naturally with the people celebrating them."

"Only if it's change the Historical Academy approves of," Asha replied through gritted teeth.

"Wait!" Rena suddenly called out, pointing to the other side of the street. "Over there!"

Three people had just exited a house next to a stall selling intricately carved wooden fish, and one of them looked awfully familiar.

"See, I told you the fox was going to help us!"

"What did I tell you about drawing hasty conclusions?" Rodrick said.

Rena didn't dare yell Kalani's name, so she simply tried to catch the woman's gaze and waved frantically at her. Kalani frowned when she saw Rena, tilting her head as her expression grew increasingly puzzled.

She turned back to the two people beside her, spoke a quick word with them, then jogged across the street to join Rena and the others.

"What are you doing here?" she asked, looking at them all with concern.

"We were looking for you!" Rena answered, unable to contain her excitement that they'd finally found her.

"Why? Did something happen?" Kalani grew worried, automatically finding Asha's gaze for answers.

"Kind of, but we're all safe!" Rena replied before Asha could say anything. "Rodrick and I went to the library and then I ran into an old friend of my father's from Oceansthrow. He also survived the fire! I'm not the only one!"

"What?" Kalani looked back at her as if she wasn't following what Rena was saying.

"He looked pretty hurt, with burns on his face, and he couldn't walk well but I'm sure he'll survive it! He's in Hrevim with Deacon and a lady from the Historical Academy, which is a bit strange, but they said they're bringing him to a healer."

"With Deacon?" Kalani's voice rose as if that was the last person she would have ever considered showing up in a place like this.

"Yes, I don't really know why, I think he wanted to find me to find Logan. He seems quite upset about something Logan did. But Jesper, my father's friend, he doesn't know that the Crow set the fire! He still thinks it was all just an accident and I know we shouldn't tell random people about what we've found out but I had to tell him at least some of the truth."

Before she could say anything more, a hand grabbed her shoulder and jerked her back.

"Silac," Asha said under her breath and dragged Rena back into the street they'd come from.

Rena frantically scanned the space around them until her eyes landed on Silac, and her heart froze. He was standing with his back to them in front of the undulating fish, only the side of his face visible to Rena, but that was enough to see the look of disgust on his face and the faint traces of the yellow-green veins giving his complexion a sickly tint. Next to him stood another man in dire condition, someone Rena had barely thought about over the last few days. Michael — the acolyte who'd promised to show them where the Crow was keeping her sister — looked paler than she remembered, with dark shadows under his eyes, although whether it was from a lack of sleep or an injury, she couldn't tell.

"What do we do?" Rena kept her eyes on the part of the busy road she could still see, worrying her lower lip.

She held on tightly to Asha's arm, the memory of what Silac had done to them flooding back to her body.

"I know where we'll be safe," Asha whispered and led them back past the abandoned church.

They walked down the street with the tavern until they stopped at a small house. Its façade was a dull, greyish white with faded red window and door trims and a circular flower pattern carved into the door that resembled something Rena had seen in one of Rodrick's notebooks.

Asha knocked but didn't wait for an answer before walking in. She held the door open for the rest of them, her gaze fixed on the end of the road that led to the main street. Kalani followed her right in, but it took both Rena and Rodrick a second to overcome their reluctance to enter a stranger's house without invitation.

They stepped into a room that held a cast-iron stove and cooking utensils to the left and a large table with a dozen chairs of varying styles to the right. A short, older woman stood near the stove, staring at them in astonishment, absentmindedly stirring the large pot in front of her.

"Asha?" she said, astonished, then her face lit up. "Look at how much you've grown! I haven't seen you in so long."

She had dark brown skin and short, tightly curled white hair. She was dressed in an elegant tunic, with different layers of dark red and orange tightly fit around the chest and loose from the hips down. It looked quite similar to Asha's tunic, although the woman's had long sleeves. Thick-rimmed glasses adorned her nose even though they seemed too big for her slender face.

"You saw me five years ago. I haven't grown since then," Asha grumbled and walked over to the woman, gently taking her face in both hands and touching their foreheads together in greeting.

"Has it already been five years since Nura's funeral?" the older woman asked, putting a lid on the pot and wiping her hands on an old scrap of fabric. "Oh, how time flies. And who are your lovely friends? Did you come to introduce me to your new spouse?"

"I'd rather skin myself alive than get married," Asha said, then turned around and gestured between both parties. "Maniala, everyone. Everyone, Maniala. My aunt's cousin."

Before anyone could properly greet the older woman, Asha had already walked over to the table and sat down on one of the chairs.

Kalani walked over to Maniala and replicated Asha's greeting, softly murmuring something to her before joining Asha at the table.

Rena opted for a polite bow, not being familiar with the forehead greeting, but didn't join Asha at the table, knowing that her parents would have been horrified if she'd sat down at a stranger's table without being invited to first.

"Are you all hungry?" Maniala said with a wide smile. "You surely must be. Sit down, I'll bring you some stew. Asha, your cousin should arrive home soon too, he'll be delighted to see you again! It's been so long."

"I doubt it," Asha grumbled, "he never liked me in the first place."

As much as Rena tried to protest, there was no dissuading Maniala from feeding the whole group. Rena didn't actually feel all that hungry, not after the honey cake and the ball of fish, but the stew smelled delicious and she was curious to know what it tasted like. It was a hearty stew with roasted eel, olives and garlic, and it warmed Rena's heart right up. She couldn't fully relax, not knowing Silac was so close, but if she glanced around at her companions, she saw that she wasn't the only one on edge. Asha had a dark look on her face as she stared straight ahead at nothing, her fingers incessantly drumming on the table.

Rena tried to tell herself that it was unlikely that Silac had spotted them. He'd had his back to them and she hadn't noticed anyone following them into the side street; they were as safe in Maniala's home as they could be anywhere else in the city.

"We'll need to leave Hrevim soon if Silac has already found his way here," Kalani noted, more thinking aloud than addressing the group. "We could maybe sneak around for another day or two to avoid him, but it might be too risky." She paused, her expression not revealing much as she considered what to do next, before turning to look at Asha. "Did you find out anything useful?"

"Nothing concrete," Asha admitted with a grimace. "But I'm pretty sure I know who could tell us where they're hiding. I was just hoping we could avoid talking to them."

"I'm afraid to ask," Kalani said reluctantly. "Who?"

"Konrad."

"For fuck's sake, of course it's Konrad." Kalani squeezed her eyes shut and rubbed a hand over her face in frustration.

Rena had never heard that name before, but she could imagine what kind of person Konrad was if both Asha and Kalani reacted so negatively.

"Who's Konrad?" she asked carefully.

"The worst person you could ever meet in your life," Asha grumbled.

"Just some crook," Kalani added, waving her hand around dismissively. "We've had to throw him out of Rancor a few times. If I could choose, I'd never talk to him again, but he sadly knows a lot about all the strange stuff going on in our provinces so it's difficult to completely avoid him. I didn't know he was in Hrevim, though."

"Been here for a couple of years, apparently," Asha replied. "Specialises in blackmail now."

"Is there no one else?" Kalani groaned with unusual desperation in her voice. "He'll ask for the most outlandish thing as payment. I don't think he's given up on asking for your hand in marriage, Asha."

"Oh no!" Maniala interjected, appalled. "You shouldn't marry someone like that!"

"I don't want to marry anyone," Asha replied, as if the idea itself was repulsive to her. "What did you not understand about me rather skinning myself alive?"

"Maybe we could offer him something else," Kalani muttered, deep in thought. "We could tell him stuff about Rosiana. It would drive a wedge between our villages but she doesn't like us anyway."

"And who's Rosiana?" Rena whispered, leaning closer to Asha so as not to disturb Kalani's thinking process.

"Leader of another moving city up in the North of Baedan," Asha replied in the same whispered tone.

"If he's interested in blackmail that could satiate him enough," Kalani kept muttering, her eyes fixed on the bowl of stew in front of her.

"You would be shitting right on top of an already fragile relationship," Asha noted.

"Asha, language!" Maniala looked at Asha with a deeply upset frown, but Asha only rolled her eyes.

"But you think he would know where the Crow is?" Rena wondered, barely understanding the situation.

"Maybe." Kalani seemed unhappy with her answer. "Asha's right that he is the one most likely to know. Not the only one, surely, but we don't have time to find anyone else."

She stayed silent for a while, hands clasped together in front of her mouth as she stared unblinking at her stew.

"I'll have to think about it some more," she murmured, then sat up and crossed her arms. "Rena, what were you talking about before? Someone else survived the fire?"

As they ate the stew, Rena retold the events of the day, Kalani's expression growing more sombre with every word.

"And then she made us follow a fox through half the city," Asha said, rocking back in her chair.

"It definitely wasn't half the city," Rena mumbled into her drink.

"A fox?" Kalani asked curiously. "The one you saw after our encounter with Silac?"

"Yes! Exactly!"

It delighted Rena that Kalani had remembered the encounter even if she hadn't seen the fox herself. It finally felt like someone was taking her seriously.

"Apparently it spoke to her," Asha added in a tone somewhere between anger and jest.

Kalani looked at Asha curiously, then at Rena, her eyes narrowing in contemplation.

"What did it say?" she asked and Rena was astonished that there wasn't an ounce of judgement in her voice.

"That we needed to hurry."

"Hurry with what?"

"It didn't want to tell me."

Kalani hummed and looked at her stew pensively, spooning a bit of the liquid before letting it trickle down again.

"Certainly," Rodrick said carefully, "we can all agree that there are no such things as speaking foxes."

Kalani's eyes narrowed again before she looked up at him.

"There is so much in this world that you know nothing about, Rodrick, even with your fifty years of research."

"I can acknowledge that, but animals giving out cryptic messages?" Rodrick answered as if he couldn't believe she wasn't on his side.

Rena wasn't sure if she should also mention the ever-narrowing passage. She knew that Rodrick would only dismiss her again, but Kalani seemed open to the reality of the fox. She shifted uncomfortably in her seat, keeping an eye on Maniala who was at the other end of the room riffling through her cupboards for something more she could offer them. Only then did Rena notice a sort of bird in the corner of the room, a device similar to the fish she'd seen outside, just much smaller and older. It didn't have much of a distinct form and most of the colour had already faded away, but every few minutes it jerked into a new position in an imitation of life.

"Rodrick," Kalani said calmly, "I think your head would melt off your shoulders if you learned of all the things I've encountered before. What I'm not sure about, though, is whether the fox is a good or bad sign."

"It has helped me before!" Rena interjected. "When I was lost in the forest near Oceansthrow, it showed me the way out. And it led us to you today!"

"Or it led us to Silac," Asha pointed out.

Rena opened her mouth to protest but she had to admit that Asha was right. After all, they'd seen Silac only moments after finding Kalani. Their day could have gone very differently if Silac had been facing the other direction.

"It's just another piece of the puzzle we need to keep in mind," Kalani said before resuming eating her stew. "But let's circle back to the other thing you told me. Your father's friend is still alive? That sounds like good news, at least. Not too sure I can say the same about Deacon being here."

"Can't Logan simply speak to him?" Rena asked. "I'm sure the dispute could be resolved if they talked it through."

Kalani shrugged and waved her spoon around vaguely, an annoyed expression on her face.

"I don't know," she said as if she was already exasperated with the situation. "Logan doesn't always like to admit fault and Deacon isn't the calmest conversationalist either, especially not when he's angry."

"Is... Logan at fault?"

"Partially," Kalani admitted. "You'd have to ask him for details; I just know that they'd planned on getting some documents from some noble's house and it ended with Deacon in a cell for five days."

"Oh..."

Kalani sighed, then shifted in her seat.

"Logan claims he warned Deacon that his plan wouldn't work out, but who knows what truly happened. Neither of them is a friend of honesty. I'd love it if they could just brawl out their dispute, but we don't have the time for that, not if Silac's already here, and definitely not with Logan's injury."

"And do you think Ocassian could help my father's friend?" Rena asked shyly.

Kalani stopped and considered her question but the emotions on her face didn't reassure Rena.

"We'll have to see," she finally responded. "Not right away, I think. There's just too much going on and we don't know why the Historical Academy is so interested in him. We'll have to play our cards right.

Make sure we don't create more problems than we resolve. I say, if the Historical Academy is currently treating him well and helping him get back on his feet, we can leave him with them until we've dealt with the Crow. If the academy had wanted him gone you would have never found out that he'd survived, so in my opinion he's safe for now."

Kalani was probably right that Jesper was safe with the Historical Academy, but Rena really didn't like the fact that they were pretending that the fire had been an accident. Who knew what else they were telling him? The longer they left Jesper with the Academy, the higher the chance that they might turn him against her, especially if Rena was going against their wishes. It hit her that the fact she wouldn't show up to their meeting that evening could already be used to argue against her. Aldara could tell him all kinds of things about Rena and the bad influence of her companions and even if Jesper were to resist agreeing at first, how long would that last? He was tired and hurt and Aldara was the one to help him heal. That wasn't something he would be able to ignore.

"And afterwards?" Rena tried to keep the desperation out of her voice as best as possible, although she wasn't sure it was working.

"Once everything has calmed down, I'm sure Cass will be able to find him a new home," Kalani answered and smiled at her, trying to reassure her.

Maniala stepped closer, having found a tin box with candied fruit that she placed on the table next to all the other food.

"I really like your bird," Rena told her, desperately wanting to think of something else for even just one moment.

"Oh, that old thing?" Maniala said, looking back at the bird. "They're everywhere on Boerom."

"Boerom? Where's that?"

"The most western of the Grey Isles," Asha replied. "And they're not everywhere. Not anymore."

"Why not? They seem lovely. I'd be delighted to have one in my home."

Asha paused for a moment, then looked away, a heavy expression settling on her face.

Rena didn't know why the atmosphere in the room had suddenly shifted, but she instantly wished she could take her words back.

"They were outlawed after the takeover," Asha muttered.

"Oh... Why? They don't look like they can cause any harm."

"I don't know," Asha replied, annoyance seeping into her voice. "I'm sure they found some fitting justification. Too dangerous for children or something stupid like that. They don't quite like that we have our own way of living, especially not the new warden."

"Oluvad never signed off on any of these new rules," Maniala interjected, shaking her head in disagreement. "He's a good man! It's all this Royal Council meddling in our affairs."

"Oluvad also hasn't been the warden of the Grey Isles in over a decade, Maniala," Asha countered. "You can't tell me that you forgot that Dardec Prabec stole the isles from him."

"Stole?" Rena asked in shock.

"I'm quite certain that it was a voluntary abdication on Horec Oluvad's part," Rodrick interjected. "There's no reason to call it stealing."

"You can think whatever you want, old man," Asha grumbled and pushed her chair back.

She got up and stepped away from the table, walking to the door that led towards the rest of the house. Rena glanced at Rodrick, but he only met her eyes briefly, Asha's brusqueness clearly having wounded him. Maniala, ignoring the heaviness that lingered over them, started a pleasant conversation with Kalani, who indulged her politely.

Chapter Twenty-Three

Finn

Finn and Logan didn't talk much as they snuck their way out of the palace, nor did they talk on their way back to the inn or when they were back in their room. Finn could feel Logan's eyes on him, but the other man apparently had enough sense not to start a conversation. Finn wouldn't have responded anyway.

He replayed his sister's appearance in his mind over and over, analysing every second of it. How much she had changed; how much she had stayed the same. She'd cut her hair to above her shoulders but the way she carried herself hadn't changed since he'd last seen her — her confidence came a bit more natural this time around, but that was about it.

He couldn't wrap his mind around why Nara was in Hrevim but he didn't know about everything that was going on in the kingdom. Her appearance didn't have to be about him or connected to the Crow. It could be something as simple as the railway network Logan was obsessed with. Finn didn't quite know how Nara would fit into that picture either, but maybe their parents had asked her to act as a representative. There could be a million reasons for her visit that Finn simply didn't know anything about. Just because Silac had mentioned her in Oceansthrow didn't mean it actually had to be connected.

But all that reasoning didn't change anything about his unease. The fact of the matter was that Nara was in the same city as him for the first time in four years and Finn was terrified of her noticing him. He wasn't proud of the fact; he thought he'd grown out of that fear, had worked on rationalising their childhood to overcome these feelings, so why had the sight of her destabilised him so much?

Nara had never physically hurt him, at least not to a point where it would leave lasting marks. His fear came solely from her words. He was sure that if they were to have an actual fight, with swords or fists, he would win, but apparently she simply needed to be in the same room as him for him to crumble. He couldn't stand it that she still had so much power over him even years later.

The rest of their group came back not long after, looking just as nervous as he felt.

"What are you wearing?" Rena stared at both men in astonishment.

"I got something for everyone." Logan pushed himself up on the bed he was resting in and pointed to the pile of clothes.

Rena walked over to it with a deep frown and held the red dress up so she could look at it in full.

"Thank you," she said, more a question than a statement. "Why? From where?"

"From some shop," Logan answered and carefully lay back down, draping his arms over his face. His breathing was heavy and only his chest rose as he clearly tried to keep his stomach as still as possible.

"Is that why you were gone the whole morning?" Asha tapped him on the legs so he'd move them and let her sit.

"We stink," he grumbled. "If we can't take a bath then we can at least change our clothes."

"He's not wrong," Rena muttered and held the dress up to her body to see how it'd fit.

Kalani stood at the foot of Logan's bed, hands on her hips, looking at Logan as if she wanted to say something but was still debating with herself if it was worth it. Finn could guess what was going through her mind and he agreed that it was probably not worth starting a fight over, not with everything else going on. They had to trust that Logan knew what he was doing and wouldn't intentionally endanger them. Either that or tell him to go back to Vellashta, and Finn didn't see that happening anytime soon.

Kalani pursed her lips and turned around, briefly glancing at Finn.

"We saw Silac," she said.

Finn straightened and looked at her in concern, a cold shudder running down his back.

"Wait, what?" Logan shot back up, only a small grimace indicating that the movement had been too quick. "What do you mean? Where? Did he see you?"

"He didn't see us," Kalani interjected before Logan could ask any more questions. "At least I don't think he did."

"How is he already here?" Logan asked, a question that had surely been on everyone's mind.

"I don't know." Kalani crossed her arms, the tension in her shoulders revealing her unease. "Maybe we're just unlucky. Maybe Hrevim is just the most logical place to go. He knew we were going to Baedan and Hrevim is the biggest city close to the border. It's the best place to find out as much as possible about what's going on in the region — it's not absurd to think that it would be the first place we're heading. I'd hoped it would take him longer to get away from his obligations in Hollowtooth, but so be it. We can't change anything about the situation now. It just means we have to leave the city sooner than expected."

"Uhm..." Rena had sat down next to the dog and was absent-mindedly petting him. "I ran into another survivor from Oceansthrow. An old friend of my father's."

"What? That's amazing, Rena!"

A wide smile spread across Logan's face as he moved to sit on the edge of the bed. Rena mirrored his smile but only faintly, something else troubling her.

"He was with a lady from the Historical Academy... and Deacon."

Logan's smile froze, then vanished as he let his head fall forward.

"For fuck's sake."

"What the fuck did you do to him that he's hunting you down like this?" Asha leaned forward on her elbows so she could look at him past the curtain of his hair.

"Nothing!" Logan burst out. "I tried to clear things up with him but he's too stubborn to have a calm conversation. I don't get why he's still mad about it. As if he's got nothing else going on in his life."

"We really have other things to worry about at the moment," Kalani said as she rubbed her eyes. "Deacon will have to wait."

"He's not gonna let up," Asha noted, looking at Kalani, one eyebrow raised.

"It doesn't matter. We'll deal with it once we've gotten Rena's sister and ourselves to safety. We can't fix everything at once."

"Today's really just the day of running into people," Logan said and ran a hand through his hair. "We saw Finn's sister at the palace."

Heat rose through Finn at the mention of his sister. He hadn't told Logan not to tell the others about her so he really couldn't be mad at him, but he wished it could have stayed between the two of them. He wasn't quite sure why, maybe because he didn't want to complicate their situation any further, or maybe because he desperately wanted to forget about the encounter himself.

"Your sister?" Rena's face was full of wonder and excitement but quickly fell when she saw Finn's grim expression. She glanced over at Logan before turning back to him in concern. "Not good?"

Finn shook his head, unsure which words could explain Nara to the others without laying his entire childhood bare.

"She was with Zarkid," Logan said. "Looked like official business but we don't really know why."

"What were you doing at the palace in the first place?" Kalani eyed Logan suspiciously.

"Just gathering some information." Logan waved her off. "I didn't want to be the only one not doing anything productive. Finn thinks Silac is related to the Zawarecs running the Military Academy and therefore also to one of Zarkid's husbands."

"You're really allergic to resting, aren't you?" Asha asked, exasperation plainly written on her face. "I'm not dragging you back to safety a third time."

Kalani glanced over at Finn, a deep frown on her face, then her eyes looked down at the floor as if she was connecting dots in her mind but then she shook her head.

"We can't waste time on this. We need to get out of Hrevim as quickly as possible."

"Do we know where to go?" Logan asked.

"Not yet," Kalani sighed. "I really wish we had more time to find the right people to talk to but it looks like our only option is Konrad."

"Konrad?!" Logan stared at her in disbelief. "*The* Konrad? The absolute worst person that has ever walked this earth?"

"He'll know where they are," Asha replied, although it was clear that she wasn't happy about it. "The way we know him, he's probably even worked with them."

"We don't exactly have a million different people we could go to," Kalani said. "Especially not if we want to get out of here by tonight. And on that, we should stop wasting time and head out." She headed towards the door and Asha stood to follow her. "Hopefully we won't be gone for too long but you never know with that guy."

"Be careful," Rena called after them.

Kalani shot her a reassuring smile over her shoulder. "Don't worry, there's no way I'm letting Silac catch me a second time."

Chapter Twenty-Four

Rena

Kalani and Asha came back hours later with an approximate destination. Rena wondered what they'd given Konrad in return but she didn't dare ask. By the look on both women's faces, it wasn't anything good. She just hoped it wouldn't become a problem later.

They were out of the inn ten minutes later, mixing and matching the new clothes Logan had acquired with their old clothes so each would have something that would fit. Kalani led them through the smallest streets she could find even if it made their journey longer than needed, but Rena was grateful that it kept them away from the bigger masses of people. Her eyes darted around frantically, never stopping, fear creeping through her body the closer they got to the exit gates. They were so close to leaving Hrevim, but Silac could still be waiting for them at every turn.

In the back of her mind, she kept seeing the image of Jesper, broken and hurt, surrounded by the Historical Academy and Deacon. Her memory of Aldara twisted into something grotesque with every step — her smile turning vicious, her hands transforming into claws around Jesper's arm, her uniform suddenly blood red. She imagined scenarios where Aldara whispered lies into Jesper's ear, convincing him that Rena was the enemy. She didn't know if it would be worse to never see Jesper again or if the next time they met his heart was filled with hatred towards her. She felt like throwing up, her stomach twisting and turning at the thought that she could not save both her sister and her father's friend.

They emerged onto an open court just in front of a smaller side entrance to the city, mostly used by merchants from what it seemed. To their left and right, people led horse-drawn carriages past them or unloaded their goods. She quickened her pace to leave Rodrick and Vincent's side and stride up to Kalani at the front of their group, focusing solemnly on how close they were to rescuing Maya.

Kalani marched towards the stables on their right where several people were hitching horses to carts and wagons. Rena tried to assess which one of them was going to take them closer to the Crow but when her eyes landed on a lanky figure leaning against one of the stable's poles, her steps faltered.

"Well, well, well," Deacon called to them, a knowing smirk on his lips. "Who do we have here?"

"Oh for fuck's sake." Logan turned around as if he meant to walk away, then turned back around. "Not now, Deacon!"

Rena looked around to see if Aldara or Jesper were anywhere nearby but Deacon had apparently found them on his own. How had he known to wait for them here? They hadn't picked one of the bigger gates specifically to reduce the likelihood of getting spotted but maybe that was the logical choice that anyone would make. The city didn't have a million gates, after all, and even fewer faced the centre of the province. The rest must have just been luck.

"Thought you could just slip out without anyone noticing, did you?" Deacon pushed himself away from the pole and walked closer. "But no one slips past Deacon that easily."

"We don't have time for this," Kalani said in a tired voice as she kept walking.

"No, of course not, there's never time for *my* concerns but *he* gets away with everything in your books."

As Kalani reached Deacon, he circled her once, forcing her to stop.

"Whatever your problem is with Logan, take it up with Cass," she said, ignoring whatever he was trying to do and stepping around him.

She walked up to a girl hitching a black horse to a small, wooden cart, leaving Deacon with the rest of their group. His smile faltered for a moment as he sneered after her, then it returned in full force as he turned to Logan.

"Oh, I already did," he said, his beady eyes narrowing, "but our dear Sovereign Outcast plays favourites, like always. Total neutrality my ass. And I know exactly why you treat him so differently from the rest of us." He came to stand right in front of Logan, but Logan held his head high so he could look down upon the other man. "I know your dirty little secret," Deacon added in a sing-songy voice.

"Whatever the fuck you think you know," Logan replied, his voice calmer than his face looked, "I can guarantee that it isn't true."

"Oh, really? I know that you weren't born here in the South, or Hellar's Dip or wherever else you pretend to be from."

Deacon came closer and closer until there was no space between the two men, but Logan refused to back away. Rena looked at them in concern, glancing at her companions to see what should be done. Asha walked past both men to follow Kalani but Rodrick and Finn stopped with her. She didn't understand why Kalani and Asha weren't worried, why they seemed to want to ignore the situation, but both of them were familiar with Deacon, so they must know best how to deal with him.

"Yeah, I wouldn't consider my birthplace a big dark secret," Logan replied, annoyed.

"I know that your name isn't actually Logan," Deacon said in a low voice.

"No shit, most people can figure that out."

Rena glanced over at Logan. She hadn't imagined this conversation to go the way it was or to be happening out in the open. She felt like a million eyes were on them and they probably were. As much as the other people in the court pretended to carry on with whatever they were doing, it was impossible to ignore the fight unfolding just next to them. Rena wrapped her arms around herself as she scanned the roads leading back into the city. They were so close to leaving; why did Deacon have to intercept them now? Every second they stayed still increased the likelihood of Silac stumbling upon them and with the city's guards so close by, would they be able to escape? Rena didn't quite want to find out if the city guards also followed Silac's orders or if they wouldn't recognise his authority and she certainly didn't want to feel his control over her body a second time.

"I know who your father is," Deacon whispered, his eyes never leaving Logan.

"What do you want, Deacon?" Logan cried out, finally taking a step back. "You didn't come all this way to discuss my lineage with me."

"Maybe I did, considering all the other stuff I know."

"Deacon..." Logan started, then huffed, throwing his arms out to the side in exasperation.

Rena started to understand why no one seemed to much like talking to Deacon. She realised that he was trying to blackmail Logan into admitting something or other, but he was going at it in such a strange and clumsy way that she didn't really understand why he had followed them all the way to Hrevim.

Rena looked back at Kalani who wasn't paying them any heed and was instead helping the young girl ready the cart. Asha stood beside her, her eyes fixed on Deacon, the two burlap sacks with their belongings lying at her feet. Rena met her gaze and tried to gesture at her to intervene, but she simply shook her head no.

"You think I can't put two and two together?" Deacon snarled. "About the stupid documents you made me steal for you? About how I got thrown into jail because of those *totally unimportant, nobody's even gonna notice them gone* documents?"

Logan held his hands up apologetically.

"Listen, I'm sorry for that. I miscalculated, okay?"

"Miscalculated, my ass," Deacon spat, his anger finally boiling over. "Why didn't you do the job yourself, hmm?"

"I had other stuff to do!"

"Oh, of course! You just didn't want daddy to know you stole his stuff."

"You didn't steal the documents from my father!"

Both of their voices had now raised to a shouting match and the merchants had stopped pretending not to listen. Rena glanced over at the guards near the front who were watching Deacon and Logan like hawks. Asha was standing at the ready, holding in one hand the burlap sack in which they had stowed away her and Finn's swords. Rena wished she would interfere or that Kalani would say something. Certainly at least Kalani could defuse the situation, so why wasn't she trying to? The longer this confrontation lasted, the worse their chance was of leaving the city unnoticed.

"Logan," Rena tried, her voice shaky and unsure, but she was quickly overshadowed by another of Deacon's outbursts.

"No, I know, but they still belong to him! Or at least the stuff they talk about. All the ore being mined for the train. All the shit they're pulling with its construction. All the rumours about how they treat their workers. Daddy wouldn't like it if it all came to light, would he? Are you blackmailing him or helping him bury his shame?"

Logan's jaw was set tight, his eyes ablaze with fury as his hands clasped tightly into fists. The more Deacon said, the less Rena understood. She knew Logan had been researching the train network's construction but she'd never asked him what exactly had caught his interest. The woman they'd tied up in the Crow's hideout had also talked about the train, but she hadn't mentioned anything about bad working conditions, just that she wanted everyone to be able to use it equally.

"What do you want, Deacon?" Logan responded through gritted teeth.

"What I'm owed!" Deacon shouted. "You paid me a horse's crap for that job and now I have to fear for my life! I want more!"

"I don't have more!"

"Bullshit! Considering your *lineage*, you have a fuckton more!"

"The lineage you made up!"

Suddenly Kalani was right next to them again.

"Guys. Guys! Stop it!" She put herself between them so they were forced to back away from each other. "Deacon, I'll pay you your fair wage when we get back to Rancor! Money isn't worth the time you're making us waste with your petty bickering."

"Why are you protecting him?"

"I'm not! I just don't have the time for this idiotic argument right now."

"Do you know who he is?!"

Kalani came to stand right in front of Deacon so he could look at no one but her.

"I know more than you can ever dream of," she said calmly, and Rena had never heard her voice sound so menacing. "I also know who you are, *Deacon Hal'Vega*."

Deacon's face contorted in hatred as he stared at Kalani, red splotches forming on his skin.

"Now go back to Cass and wait for us to return," Kalani continued.

"I am not your dog," Deacon spat.

"Oh my stars, Deacon." Kalani stepped away and buried her face in her hands in exasperation, then looked back up at him. "Put your pride aside for one day. You will get your money!"

"If I don't, I can't promise that your little friend will stay safe for much longer," Deacon said, looking past Kalani to point a finger at Logan.

"What?" Logan stared at him in utter confusion. "Which friend? What the fuck are you talking about now?"

"She knows."

Without looking at her, he nodded in Rena's direction.

"What?" Rena asked in a daze until it clicked in her mind and her heart contorted. "Jesper? Why would he not be safe?"

"Oh come on, Deacon," Logan called out. "That's a low blow. The man was trapped in a fire a *week* ago. He doesn't even know me. Why would you pull *him* into this?"

"It's completely up to you if anything happens to him," Deacon said with a wicked smirk. "If I get my money, nothing has to happen at all."

"You don't even deserve that money!"

"Logan," Kalani called back to him as a warning.

"But he doesn't!" Logan cried out, gesturing wildly at the other man. "He's threatening me with something he just pulled out of his ass!"

"You just don't want to admit it!" Deacon yelled back.

Asha suddenly stepped forward, her sword glinting golden in the sunlight as it was held against Deacon's throat. In an instant, the guards had laid a hand on their own swords and were hurrying towards them. Rena's eyes widened as the guards approached, visions of their arrest flashing in front of her.

"Kalani told you to go back to Cass," Asha said, enunciating every word to punctuate her threat.

Deacon looked down at the sword and then his face slowly contorted into a grin.

"Always do as your masters tell you, right?" he muttered.

"Just shut up, you insufferable waste of skin."

Deacon lifted his hands in defeat and backed off. Asha sheathed her sword before the guards reached her and lifted her own hands, indicating that the fight was over.

"Apologies," Kalani told the guards with a small bow, then turned to her group. "We're leaving."

Rena's heart was hammering wildly in her chest as she followed Kalani to the cart. She could see in the guards' faces that they weren't quite sure what to do either. The situation had dissolved so quickly and no one had gotten hurt, so did they still have to intervene? In the end, one of the guards simply opted to shout a warning after them not to cause any further problems in the city but seeing as Rena and her companions were leaving, there wasn't much more they could do.

Chapter Twenty-Five

Rena

As the group sat on the floor of the wooden cart leaving Hrevim, Rena kept an eye on the vanishing city. Any time a rider exited the gate and rode towards them, her heart stopped. She was just waiting for *someone* to catch up to them — Silac or Deacon or Inkra or even Finn's sister — but, without fault, every rider passed them without incident. She wondered what Deacon's next move would be. She somehow doubted that Kalani's words had appeased him, and he certainly didn't seem like someone who would go back to Rancor and wait diligently for Kalani or Logan to come back to give him his money. Rena couldn't shake the feeling that it hadn't been the last time she would see the man. She just hoped he wouldn't run into Silac.

The sun was setting as the cart took them across the river to Hrevim's north. They drove past fields of barley and olive trees towards a small town called Paemehri. The monastery the Crow was hiding in was supposedly in the hills surrounding that village, although they didn't have a clear picture of where exactly. The girl who had helped Kalani prepare the cart was driving. Rena wondered who she was — had Kalani paid her to drive them or was she going to stay with them in Paemehri?

She certainly hadn't helped break the silence that had settled over the group since they'd left.

Rena was getting increasingly jittery the longer the ride took and the longer the silence persisted. She needed something to distract her mind from Silac and what the Crow might possibly be doing with her sister and all she came up with was revisiting their run-in with Deacon.

"What was Deacon talking about?" she asked Logan carefully, needing the silence to end. "About your father and the train's construction?"

Logan looked over at her, puzzled, as if he hadn't expected anyone to acknowledge his fight with Deacon. His assumption hadn't been completely wrong. Kalani had been staring at the landscape with her back turned to the others for most of the ride and Asha's jaw had been so tight that everyone could tell just how much willpower it was taking her not to yell at Logan. The other three glanced at each other occasionally, a question lingering between them whether they even had the right to say anything. Rena knew she was opening a can of worms that might further sour the atmosphere between them but it still seemed better than being left alone with her thoughts.

Logan opened his mouth, then closed it again. His eyes drifted away, one shoulder pulling up into a non-committal shrug, head shaking from side to side. Rena waited for anything more from him but he stayed quiet, avoiding her gaze, entirely different from the Logan she'd come to know. Rena clenched her teeth tight, wishing that *anyone* would say something.

Finn leaned forward, his legs crossed under him, a pensive look on his face.

"From what I've seen from documents in the archive," he started slowly, "the rail network's construction isn't advancing as smoothly as the North likes to pretend. But these documents aren't always easy to decipher and then there's all the rumours floating around. Not all of them are true, of course, but there's always a morsel of truth somewhere. The train line will run from Mak-Hemma's citadel in the east through Jodash and Menakala towards Mashod in the west. Some of it has already been built, leaving Mak-Hemma. I haven't seen how far they've come, though. And there's talk of connecting it to the Daishegian Empire but they'd have to find a way to get it over or through the mountain range north of Mashod. I don't think anything concrete has been decided yet. That would be... a tremendous undertaking. I'm not sure it would be worth it. Our relations with the Daishegian Empire aren't that great."

"Okay..." Rena replied, confused, unsure how most of this pertained to their current situation.

She'd heard of most of these places in passing from her history lessons, and there'd been a map of their kingdom in their school, but it hadn't been very detailed. Miss Kaari had always said it was a bit dated, so Rena hadn't bothered memorising it. She had trouble picturing what Finn was talking about, never having been to the North and never having seen the mountain ranges he'd mentioned.

"I've also heard that they're planning on building a bridge to the Kano-Raeki Federation in Jodash," Finn continued, ignoring all the confused looks. "There are places where the sea's quite narrow — shouldn't be too much of an issue to build a bridge that could carry a train. But they'll need to figure out how to run the train over bridges anyway if they want to get it to Mashod. It's quite clear that their main objective is to connect our kingdom to its neighbours and forgo maritime travel, for whatever reason. I doubt this train could ever become as interesting as our kingdom's shipbuilding tradition."

"As spectacular as maritime travel is," Rodrick interjected, the only other of their group who didn't seem baffled by Finn's speech, "it also takes quite a lot of time and depends a lot on weather conditions. This train would be able to complete the same journeys much faster and through any type of weather. And it would certainly benefit our kingdom's trade relations with our neighbours. It is no wonder we do not have a strong relationship with the Daishegian Empire if their representatives either have to travel the entire width of our kingdom by carriage or traverse the Federation to get to our capital. There is simply no easy way to get to Mak-Hemma by sea from the west.

"Granted, most of our relations have been with the East throughout our history, but we should not disregard any nation to the west of us. And I'm certain this train is not just being constructed to transport goods. It could also aid people to visit our wonderful home. I've heard that they're ramping up their cultural exchange efforts in the North to entice more people to visit us. Especially Jodash has been quite revolutionary in their approach to presenting our kingdom's gifts to our neighbours."

Before Finn could argue, Rena raised her hand to stop him.

"Thank you both for all this... information, but what does that have to do with what Deacon talked about?"

Finn frowned at her as if he didn't quite understand why she'd asked that, then his expression shifted into something more neutral.

"It's quite an ambitious project. Needs a lot of resources. Those resources have to come from somewhere and the North doesn't have a lot of mineral deposits."

"Okay..." she replied, frowning back at him, still not getting what he was trying to convey.

"So from what I know, most of the ore is being mined in Red Hill in the West. Some people claim it's unfair Red Hill is being mined bare for a train line that will never reach the province; others counter-argue that what benefits one part of the kingdom, benefits us all. There are also rumours about unsafe working conditions and people being underpaid. I can't talk much about that, though. I haven't been to Red Hill in a very long time and any of the documents I've seen about these working conditions haven't stood out to me as particularly dissimilar to any other work contracts for such a big project. But I must admit, I never looked into it in any detail. I'm not sure how Logan's family plays into this issue, though."

"Deacon's connecting dots that shouldn't be connected," Logan burst out, finally joining the conversation. "I just wanted to know what was up with this train stuff so I collected all kinds of information about it and I asked him to get some documents for me. People say someone's giving Red Hill's governor a shit ton of money to keep the iron flowing as fast as possible and I wanted to know who exactly that might be and now Deacon's somehow convinced that's my father."

"And it isn't?"

"No, of course it isn't!" He looked at Rena like she'd lost her mind. "You think I'd be sleeping in a tent if my father had enough money to build a whole train network?"

"It would have to be someone from nobility if those rumours are true," Finn replied, looking very carefully at Logan. "This is the Royal Council's project — they wouldn't let anyone they don't trust touch it, no matter how rich of a merchant they were."

"And they're only letting a very select group from the Royal Tinkering Institute work on it," Rodrick added.

"Exactly! And do I look like high nobility to you? Or smart enough to join that institute?"

"You're stupid and arrogant enough to be high nobility," Asha finally chimed in.

"Oh, shut up, Asha," Logan muttered, then sighed. He held his palms up to emphasise his words. "Listen, all I wanted was for Deacon to steal those documents so I could verify the identity of Red Hill's mysterious benefactor and maybe blackmail him, and potentially do a good deed while getting stinking rich."

"So noble of you. I can see how Deacon made those assumptions about your father."

Logan shot daggers at her, but Asha only grinned back, although it didn't quite reach her eyes.

"I don't know how Deacon came to that conclusion," Logan said carefully. "I'm not even sure he truly believes it himself. He probably just wants to intimidate me into giving him more money."

Kalani turned to look at Logan with an expression Rena had never seen before, and it made a cold shudder run down her back. All softness and kindness had left Kalani and were replaced with cold fury.

"You should have paid him his fair wage before sending him to do your dirty work. You can't always expect Cass to shovel you out of the mountains of shit you're creating on your own."

"I did pay him!" Logan called out in exasperation. "I paid him just as much as I've always done. All thefts come with a certain risk of getting caught. He knows that, you know that, we all know that! This one wasn't any more dangerous than any of the previous ones."

"Then you should have made sure the issue had been resolved before leaving."

Rena had known addressing the situation might bring everyone's resentment to light, but she hadn't expected it to be this harsh. She'd only known Kalani for a handful of days, but she'd not seemed the type to get angry like this. Rena couldn't tell if it was just the stress of their travels boiling over or if Logan had done things in the past that deserved the treatment.

"I tried!" Logan continued, his voice growing louder and shriller. "You brought me to him! We talked with Cass about the whole stupid situation. What more do you want me to do?"

"Was that when Rena and Rodrick went to get the letter from my uncle?" Asha asked. "Before we left for the archives? When you came back all twitchy and nervous and wanted to leave as quickly as possible? Didn't seem like you'd made sure the issue had been resolved."

"I—" His gaze darted from Asha to Kalani and back, a look of confusion and anguish on his face. "Why are you all so angry at me now? I'm sorry, okay? I made a mistake. I didn't know we were going to be gone for this long and how could I have predicted that Deacon would obsess over it to the point he'd be chasing me across half the kingdom?

It barely even makes sense, not for some money. I think he just... doesn't like me or something."

"Hard to imagine," Kalani replied dryly and turned around again.

Silence settled over them again, more oppressive than the one they'd been in before. Rena wasn't sure if asking Logan that question had been the right idea but, even if she didn't like it, a part of her was glad that it had distracted her from their other problems. She looked around at the others, everyone avoiding the others' gazes except for Rodrick who flashed her a small, apologetic smile when their eyes met. His expression changed, as if he'd just remembered something.

He turned to rummage through the inside pockets of his coat and pulled out a few folded-up pages.

"What's that?" Rena asked and leaned forward.

"I wanted to delve deeper into these documents at the library, but there was no time." He unfolded the pages, smoothing them down on the cart's floor. "Truth be told, I could have stayed there until the evening but, alas, our circumstances didn't allow it. There's so much more we can discover through texts. Between the documents mentioning reincarnation and those mentioning how to make someone become a god, I'm sure we can find out what the Crow is currently doing. It is truly fascinating all the things people can make themselves believe in."

Rena looked at the pages in horror, realising what he had done.

"You stole something from the library?" Logan said, a wide smile forming on his lips. "Didn't know you had it in you, old man."

"Oh no, no, I'll give them back!" Rodrick insisted as he riffled through the pages. "There was just no time to read it all in great detail before we had to leave the city. And I made sure I wasn't damaging any original manuscripts, only copies."

Rena could barely listen to his words from shock. She didn't know where he had gotten those pages from. All they had been allowed to touch at the library were bound books, so had he dared to rip these pages out? But how had he done that without the clerk noticing? The room had been so silent, even just turning a page had drawn attention.

She suddenly saw Rodrick in a completely new light, not sure what to think of him anymore. She would have never even dreamed of stealing pages out of a book, even if she'd been certain that they contained the answer to all their problems.

"I have a few theories but nothing concrete," Rodrick continued, oblivious to how everyone was looking at him. "It is difficult to tell what exactly the Crow is planning but I do believe they are working on something that resembles the practices in these old documents."

Rodrick explained how the old faith believed that a person never truly died but was instead reborn, a concept that still existed in some remote parts of the kingdom. It was very likely, according to him, that the Crow believed in this reincarnation and that was the reason for their actions. Rena wasn't too sure. She found the concept of a god dying strange but then again, she knew so little about these beings, it could very well be true. At least it fit with the other theories they'd already had over the last few days. How Maya fit into any of it, she wasn't quite sure.

She wished Rodrick had talked about something else, *anything* else. She was back in the spiral in her mind, imagining what the Crow was doing to her sister, how they would use Maya's body as a vessel for

Tavuu'Moda's spirit. She had the vision of seeing her sister again, but it wasn't her sister at all — it was someone else in her sister's body. A cold shudder ran through her and once more the cart seemed to be advancing at a snail's pace. She wanted to jump out and run ahead, comb through the hills until she'd found the monastery and just burst in before it was too late to save Maya. The fox had told her to hurry, after all.

They arrived in Paemehri after the sun had set. It was a strange town, if it could even be called that. Most of the buildings were huge, like the hangars in Hollowtooth and Hrevim. Rena doubted that anyone lived in those but then what were they used for? Was anything being built here or did they just exist for storage? She was too tired to think much of it and just let it be, having experienced too many strange things over the last two weeks to really care about it.

They booked a room in the only inn they could find and could only afford a room with three beds but they wouldn't be sleeping much anyway. Rena splashed some of the water in the basin on her face and then stood at the ready, waiting for them to head out on foot.

"You're staying here," Kalani said as she rummaged through one of their knapsacks for something edible. "Logan too."

"What?" Rena and Logan said in unison, both equally shocked and appalled.

"We're just scouting the area. We have to find the correct monastery first, which might take some time. There's no point in all of us trekking through the area, it would just make us easier to spot. And once we've located them, we're turning around. There's no point in getting too close without a proper plan."

"But that's not fair," Rena cried out, panic at having to stay behind rising in her.

"It really isn't," Logan echoed.

Kalani shot him an unamused glance, then looked down at his stomach and they all knew what she meant.

"And don't you dare say that you're fine," she added, turning her attention back to the knapsack as she pulled out a dinged-up apple.

"I'm staying here with you," Rodrick said, trying to assuage the situation. "It will be good for us to rest a bit, and someone has to stay for the dog anyway. We can take turns sleeping while one of us stands guard. Then we can also look out for whether someone was following us or not. That's also important, right?"

"But why can't I go?" Rena asked, ignoring Rodrick's proposition.

"Rena." Kalani turned to her, none of her usual warmth in her eyes. "Can you guarantee that you would be able to turn around once we've spotted the monastery?"

Rena opened her mouth but no words came out, knowing that anything but a *no* would be a lie.

"Exactly. And I'm not blaming you for it, I probably wouldn't be able to either if it were my sister, but that's why we can't take you along. We need to be careful and make sure no one notices us."

"Why do you even want to turn around?" Rena burst out, wanting to scream and thrash and tear at her skin. "Why find the monastery and then leave again? What kind of sense does that make?"

"Because we've all had a very exhausting day and you do not storm a building like that with no plan and no rest!"

"But what if it's too late when we come back tomorrow? What if tonight is the last chance we have to save Maya?"

"What if we storm the monastery and fail to rescue your sister and then the Crow leaves the region and we have to chase them across half the kingdom? Have you thought about that?"

Kalani stared at her, her jaw set tight, and Rena didn't know how to argue. She knew that Kalani was right. There was no chance that Rena would be able to head back to Paemehri once they'd found the monastery and that they were all too exhausted to fight. They knew nothing about the Crow's hideout, not even whether there were only ten acolytes hiding in it or a hundred. Would they be able to sneak into the monastery or was it heavily guarded? What would Rena do if they found themselves in front of a building they couldn't get into? To be so close to Maya with no way of getting to her... Wouldn't that be much worse than having to stay behind?

She sat down on one of the beds, defeated. After a few seconds, Kalani fished out two more apples and tossed one to Asha and one to Finn before the three of them headed out, leaving Rena, Logan and Rodrick in a tense silence.

Chapter Twenty-Six

Rena

Rena sat on one of the three beds, her gaze fixed on the lantern hung outside the inn that could be seen from their one dirty window. The fire flickered faintly behind the lantern's milky glass, burning its oranges and yellows into her eyes. She wrung her hands until her skin burned, then proceeded to dig her nails into her palms, then worried nervously at the ring and pendant around her neck. She heard the crackling of the lantern's fire but knew that was impossible, that such a faint sound would never travel through walls, not even if they were thin enough to let in all the cold from outside, but she could still hear it as if she were sitting next to a bonfire.

She squeezed her eyes shut and turned her head.

After a long silence Rodrick decided to step out with Vincent, citing that the dog needed to run around a bit. Logan was lying on the bed next to Rena's, arms folded beneath his head, eyes shut tight, a single bead of sweat running down the side of his face.

"Do you think they're doing okay?" Rena asked in a quiet voice.

"They're fine," Logan answered dismissively.

"You're not worried," she said, more a statement than a question.

"Worrying isn't gonna help anyone right now."

She was getting tired of him saying the word *fine*. It couldn't be helpful to ignore reality the way he was just to project a strong façade. Everyone knew he was hurt and everyone knew their search for the Crow was dangerous — what was the point of pretending none of it mattered?

"I don't think I can just switch it off like that," she muttered.

"Just think of something else." He gestured vaguely around, not getting up or even looking at her.

Rena stayed silent for a while and tried to think of other things but what else was there? Everything she had enjoyed during her life was gone or tainted. She couldn't think of baking without thinking of her parents; she couldn't think of Tide-bringings without thinking of her siblings; she couldn't think of Oceansthrow's school without seeing it in ruins in front of her.

"How?"

He sighed, then lifted his arms from his face and turned to look at her.

"What's your favourite thing to do during the summer?"

"My favourite thing to do?" Her lips formed a sorrowful smile as she thought back to days past. "I always liked swimming in the ocean. In the late afternoon, when the stones were still warm and the water was just the right temperature. When my parents wanted some time alone I'd take my siblings to the ocean. My friend Tala would join with her siblings, and sometimes my cousins would come, and we'd all swim together. We don't really have beaches near Oceansthrow, not like they have here or near Hollowtooth. It's a lot of cliffs and stones, but we'd know where the water's calmest and the ground hurts the least to walk on... But that's all over now."

She looked down at her lap, one hand coming to play absent-mindedly with her necklace. Thinking about it all still hurt so much, like her heart would cramp up into a tiny stone if she kept remembering all the people she'd loved and lost. She didn't know how she would ever be able to think back on her life before the fire without falling into a terrible sadness, but she hoped one day she'd know how to talk about it more freely. She desperately wanted to remember her family and friends, and some moments she could, but others felt like a wolf was clawing open her entire being and this was one of them.

"What did you like to do as a child?" she asked hastily, determined to think of something that wasn't her own life.

"Oh man, as a child?" He chuckled and looked up at the ceiling. "Tough question..." He paused for a moment, an unreadable expression on his face. "Mischief. Generally a lot of mischief. And once my brother was old enough, I'd teach him the mischief. But he was never as good as me, so he'd always get caught. He was a cute child, though — wouldn't actually get into trouble because of it, and he was loyal enough not to rat me out. Not a bad kid, all in all."

"What's his name?" A tired smile formed on her face.

He paused, his breathing heavy, and Rena wasn't sure this conversation was going to bring them to happier shores either.

"Vic," he replied quietly.

"Do you still see him sometimes?" Rena asked, knowing her questions wouldn't help to lift their mood, but she needed to know.

She knew so little about the people she'd been spending the last two weeks with — it didn't feel right. There was so much she wanted to ask them, so much she wanted to discover. She didn't know if they would stay together after they'd rescued Maya but she hoped they would. She couldn't imagine not spending all her time with them anymore.

"Nope," Logan said, letting the *p* pop. "Haven't seen him in almost a decade, probably."

"Why not?"

He hesitated, his head swaying from side to side as if he wasn't sure how to explain the situation.

"It's complicated," he finally admitted. "Family relations don't mesh well with this type of life if you weren't born into it."

"You weren't?"

"Not really." He grimaced in hesitation. "Not into this specific one. Cass and Rancor and all that. Not that my parents are the most upstanding citizens either."

This felt reminiscent of what Deacon had talked about. He'd mentioned that Logan pretended to be from Hellar's Dip, but she'd never heard him talk about it himself. She wasn't sure she'd ever heard of that town or city before which meant it was either extremely tiny or not in the South. But then again, Deacon had also mentioned Logan wasn't from the South. Rena had never gotten that impression anyway. He felt like a person who had been all over the kingdom, knowing a bit of something from everywhere. She hoped that one day he'd tell her all about it, even if not all of it would be the truth.

"Do you miss them?" she asked.

"My parents? Not even for a second."

"And your brother?"

"Sometimes." He hesitated again. Logan clearly didn't have good relations with his parents, but Rena could tell that he regretted the relationship he had with his brother. "But it's for the best... And I get why Deacon thinks my father has to be this big, dark secret, but he's just your garden-variety crook from the North. Nothing special about him. I just don't like talking about him cause the less I mention him, the less likely he is to find me. That's really all I want to avoid."

"That bad?" She winced.

"Yeah. Maybe. I don't know." He buried his face in his hands, then ran them through his hair, huffing out his frustration. "Like I said, it's been a decade. Not sure he's still thinking about me. In the beginning, when I first got away from him, I was a bit scared, didn't know what he'd do if he got to me, but... I haven't really been careful these last few years and I'm still alive so... who knows if he ever actually bothered to look for me."

Rena stayed silent for a while, observing the sadness in his eyes as he looked up at the ceiling. She couldn't really imagine what that felt like, to have a parent who might not care enough about you to want to reconnect, even if that parent wasn't a good person. As much as she could complain about her own parents for hours, they'd always loved her dearly. She knew she had been very lucky in that regard.

"I'm sorry," she murmured.

"Nah, don't worry." He waved her off. "I've got my own life now. Most days I don't think of him either."

She knew he was probably telling the truth but he couldn't fully hide that, deep down, it still bothered him.

"And your mother?" she asked carefully.

"I don't know." He sighed. "I was never great at figuring out what she thought, whether she could miss me or not. But she always preferred my brother anyway, so... probably doesn't need the unruly son back."

"I'm really sorry," she repeated, her eyes drifting to her hands in her lap.

"You don't have to be." He turned to look at her with a small smile, then looked up at the ceiling again, draping his arms over his eyes. "Life's just like that sometimes."

She let silence wash over them once more, only the faint noise from the tavern below breaking it.

She wished they could talk about happier times, that there was some subject that wouldn't hurt their hearts so much, but her thoughts kept going in circles trying to come up with anything. Even talking about the wonders of the library would bring them back to discussing Jesper and Deacon. She tried to think of her favourite animals, her favourite dishes, her favourite flowers, but all of it was tainted by what her family's favourites had been. She couldn't block them out and the more she tried to, the more they overshadowed the rest of her thoughts.

"I don't like that we have to sit here with nothing to do but wait," she said quietly, wringing her hands in her lap.

Her muscles were tense again, so tense that it made it hard to breathe.

"Yeah, not if we dive head-first into heartache with every subject we start," Logan responded, not lifting his arms off his face. "Next, you'll ask me about all my failed relationships... Maybe we can play a game instead." He carefully pushed himself up and turned to look at her, crossing his legs. "Wouldn't that be fun? Maybe... 'Round and round the council'? You know that one, right? One of us thinks of the next High Lord or Lady to die, how they met their *mysterious* end and which one of their siblings or cousins is responsible and the other one has to ask questions and figure out the conspiracy."

"I don't know if I'd be good at that game," she replied in a small voice. "I really don't know much about those families."

"Right, right, right." His face fell into a look of deep contemplation. "Something else then. 'The cat's donkey'? But we'd need to be at least three for that one. Maybe once Rodrick's back. Isn't there a game about the old gods, too? 'Faith unbound', something like that. I'm sure Rodrick knows all about it. He probably knows so many games if he's been travelling around the kingdom talking to people. What did he call himself? Scribe of the lands? Are games part of the lands?"

"What if," she blurted out but then lost her courage, the rest of her sentence barely audible, "we also go find the monastery?"

The smile fell from Logan's face and he looked at her with deep sorrow.

"Rena..."

"Just to make sure Kalani and the others aren't in trouble!" She pushed herself forward so she sat on the very edge of the bed. "I feel like I'm going to burst out of my skin waiting here, not knowing what's happening to them, not knowing where they are and what the Crow's planning or doing, not knowing if they're safe or hurting. Don't you feel awful sitting here, safe and secure, while any number of things could be happening to them?"

"And what do you want us to do about that?" he replied, his voice growing annoyed.

"I don't know!" She stood up, unable to keep the panicked energy rising in her from bursting out. "I'm sure there's something we could be doing. There's safety in numbers, right?"

"Not in this situation." Logan looked at her as if she'd lost her mind. "Not when there's probably like fifty or a hundred of them and six of us."

"But..." She paced around, her mind racing from one thought to another, trying to figure out how to best convince Logan. "At least we'd know what's happening. What if they're already dead? What if we wait until the morning and they don't come back and then it's noon and then evening and they're still not here? How long do we wait? And then what? We just go back to Cass and tell them Kalani's dead? We tell them we failed and let their wife die?"

"Rena, Kalani knows what she's doing. She isn't going to storm the monastery without telling us about it. They're just trying to figure out where the Crow's hiding so we can get to them in full force tomorrow. She'd never confront anyone without being one hundred per cent certain she has the upper hand."

"But what if something happens?" Rena asked, her voice rising with every word, panic overtaking her. "What if the Crow spots them and they get dragged into a fight?"

"I reiterate, what do you want *us* to do about that? You have no fighting experience and my stomach was ripped apart less than a week ago! I know I'm a phenomenal actor, but this shit hurts!"

"I don't know! Something!" She gestured around wildly, unable to stay in one spot. "I'm sure there's *something* we can do. Throw rocks or distract them or call for help. Not just sit here and do nothing while all our friends die. And who knows what they're doing to Maya? What they've already done to her! Empty her of who she is so they can put their god into her body. Make her someone she isn't. She's the only family I have left. Wouldn't you want to save your brother?"

"Don't," Logan simply replied, a warning to her.

Rena stopped and stared at him, terrified of her own self. She didn't know why she'd said that, why she'd tried to use what he had just told her against him. She didn't want to be this kind of person, didn't like what the last few days had turned her into, but the words didn't want to stop spilling from her lips now, as if she couldn't contain them in her mind anymore.

"Oh my stars, I'm sorry. I shouldn't have said that. I-I just... I can't stay here, Logan. I'm so sorry, but I just can't. And either you come with me or I go on my own and I really don't like forcing this choice on you but I can't stay here. At least if I tell you about it you'll know where I've gone and you don't panic thinking someone got to me. You can take your own decision whether you want to join me or not but I don't think you should, considering your injury, but also I'm terrified of going on my own and I wish I hadn't let Kalani convince me to stay here and I had just left with them. Why does Finn get to go and I don't?! I know Kalani's smart and she knows what's best for us but she doesn't realise what this feels like for me and who would I be if I stayed here, safe, and let everyone else get hurt again? So, yeah, I'm leaving, with or without you. I'm sorry."

"This is such a bad idea," he grumbled and rubbed at his eyes with the back of his hand.

"I'll be careful, I promise," she tried to reassure him. "I just can't live with the not knowing. I'm not going to engage with any of them! I know that I can't fight. You don't all have to remind me of it all the time."

"I'm not letting you leave on your own," he told her as if it were self-evident.

She wanted to run over and hug him but at the same time it scared her. She knew that it was a terrible idea, that they would never find the old monastery on their own, especially considering Logan's injuries, but staying in that room just wasn't an option anymore.

She wanted to throw up. There were too many emotions warring inside her and she couldn't figure out which one to listen to. She felt horrible for dragging Logan out of bed — she could plainly see, after all, how badly he was faring — but going out on her own terrified her even more.

"Thank you," she murmured.

"Yeah, yeah," he dismissed and stood up, pain contorting his face into a grimace for just an instant. "I was getting bored anyway."

"We should let Rodrick know where we're going," Rena said, guilt finally washing over her.

Half her mind was screaming at her to take back everything she'd just said, to stay put just as Kalani had told them — the rest of their group would be back at any moment, there was no reason for Logan and her to put themselves in harm's way — but the restless energy coursing through her made it impossible to sit back down.

"We really shouldn't," Logan replied. "He needs to stay here with the dog anyway. And he's got his ritual to investigate or whatever."

"He'll worry about where we've gone," Rena insisted.

"We can leave him a note. I'm sure he's got something to write with in one of the bags."

He walked over to their burlap sacks and kneeled before them.

"Do you think he'll be upset we left without him?"

"Rena." He looked up at her, exasperated. "You're one of us now. You lie and you manipulate and you weasel your way into getting what you want. You don't have to worry about others' opinions anymore."

"I am not one of *you*!" she cried out, knowing full well that he was right. "Whatever that means. I don't lie to my friends... if it isn't strictly necessary. And I don't manipulate anyone... Do I?"

"What do you think you just did?" He turned his attention back to the bags and fished Rodrick's journal out before rummaging further for something to write with.

"I—" she started, but then quickly lost courage.

"Rena, it's fine. I'm proud of you. You're finally learning something from me."

Logan pulled out a small tin box and opened it. Inside were several small pieces of coal and the strange stick Rodrick had used to take notes in Miller's Knee.

"Don't say that," she muttered, shame rising to her cheeks.

"You'll be the perfect thief in no time!" He looked up at her and winked before ripping an empty page out of Rodrick's notebook.

"No I won't!" Rena replied, upset at the suggestion.

"Don't worry, you can become an honest thief. You know, do a good deed while getting stinking rich and all that."

"That's not how it works! That's still bad. I don't want to *steal* from others!"

"You'll change your mind soon enough," he replied, amused that he'd gotten such a reaction out of her.

He placed the notebook and tin box back into the burlap sack and placed the note above it before he got up.

"Now come," he said, a wicked smile on his lips, "I'm sure there's a sword that's just waiting to be stolen somewhere in this hovel."

He didn't wait for her to reply and simply started walking backwards to the door before spinning around and exiting the room.

"Logan!" she cried after him.

Chapter Twenty-Seven

Rena

They did not, in fact, find a sword that was just waiting to be stolen, but they did find two kitchen knives that almost looked like daggers if you squinted at them from the right angle.

Rena wasn't sure what to do with the knife Logan had given her. She should have been used to holding it — she'd cooked enough meals in her life — but having taken it out of its usual environment, she'd somehow lost the ability to carry it naturally. She held it in front of her in both hands before remembering that her dress had pockets, but that turned out not to be a great solution either. It weighed her dress down unevenly, threatened to tear a hole in one of the only pieces of clothing she had left and banged against her leg as they snuck out of the town that was barely a town.

Rena's eyes shifted around nervously as they walked between these strange buildings that seemed more like warehouses than homes. None of them, besides the inn Rena and Logan had come from, had windows, and the further they got from the inn, the emptier the streets got. She almost hoped they'd run into Rodrick so they could tell him what they were up to after all, but luck wasn't on their side. Even when Rena strained her ears, she couldn't hear anyone else's presence, not even inside these strange buildings.

They walked out of town and into the surrounding hills until they couldn't see Paemehri anymore and only the moon guided them. Rena tried to scan the ground for any traces of footprints Kalani and the others might have left but she'd never tracked anything before, and learning a new skill was much harder by moonlight. She'd hoped they'd be able to see the monastery from far away, that a light would betray the Crow's whereabouts, but Rena and Logan had been walking for over an hour and still hadn't stumbled upon it. They'd seen lights in the distance once and had enthusiastically walked closer until they realised that the place the lights emanated from was much too big for an abandoned monastery and was, in all likelihood, simply a regular town.

"You know what I just thought of?" Logan asked after the both of them had spent a good while walking in silence.

Rena hummed in response, distracted by her aching feet.

"What if we don't find our way back to Paemehri?" he said nonchalantly as if that hadn't been the thought at the back of Rena's mind since they'd found that other town.

"Don't say that," she muttered.

"We've been walking for close to two hours now, probably, and we still haven't found anything."

"We'll find the monastery," she said, more to reassure herself.

"Sure. What if we don't?"

She sighed, unsure if her annoyance was more directed at him or herself. "Then we go back the way we came from."

"Do *you* remember where we came from?" He looked at her with one raised eyebrow.

"If we don't find it we just go back to the other town we saw and get back to Paemehri in the morning. Or we simply sleep out here somewhere. It's not that cold."

Something moved in the corner of Rena's eye and she automatically spun around but couldn't catch what it'd been. There probably were plenty of wild animals around them, maybe even dangerous ones; who knew if sleeping in the wild would be such a good idea? Rena slipped her hand into the pocket of her dress and wrapped it around the handle of the knife.

"Look," Logan replied, starting to get cranky, "I'm all for just storming out without a plan and letting luck decide where we're going — life would be horribly boring without spontaneity — but I wish luck would consider the fact that all the medicine's vanished from my body and walking isn't exactly the best activity for people with wounds across their bellies and I'm cold and I'm tired and walking really isn't that exciting."

"You're worse than Valerio when he was an infant," she muttered under her breath.

"When, exactly, do we admit that we have no idea what we're doing and we should simply head back?"

"I don't know either, Logan," she whined, turning back to look at him, "but we haven't been out here for that long. Have you never had to walk long distances before?"

"Sure, but not in the dark while I'm bleeding out."

"You're not bleeding out," she told him but then stopped when she saw something on the ground. "Wait!"

She ran forward and knelt down.

"Hoofmarks!" she called out in excitement.

Rena shot back up and frantically looked around, trying to find a logical explanation for why there would be a trail of hoofmarks in the wild. The trail was too narrow and well-trodden to have come from wild horses, and it was too broad to be from a single traveller. The path had been used more than once but not often enough to have become an actual road. They were too far away from any actual towns and no merchant would lead their horses over such rocky terrain for no good reason, so why were these tracks here?

Rena looked out over the distance, trying to determine in which direction they should follow the trail, when she saw something else. Orange fur glowing against the dark soil, brighter than should have been possible in the moonlight.

"Finally." The eerie voice appeared in her mind again as if carried by the wind.

She couldn't believe her eyes. Why here, of all places, had the fox decided to show up again? She would've been happy if she'd never seen it again. All it had achieved in Hrevim was to scare her more, make her panic faster. She still hadn't decided if the fox had led her through the city to find Kalani or be found by Silac, and she doubted the animal would give her a straight answer.

"Why are you here?" she called out to it, the anger rising in her. "What do you want?!"

"It is time," it simply said, as if nothing was the matter at all.

"Time for what?"

She was starting to hate it. She couldn't understand what it wanted from her, why it spoke in such vague phrases. She knew that they didn't have much time — she didn't need a bizarre fox to tell her about it in the middle of the night.

"Rena?" Logan walked up to her, a look of confusion on his face.

She whirled around to him and pointed at the fox.

"You see it, right? Tell me that you see it?!"

"The fox?" he asked, perplexed, his eyes wide as he looked at the animal. "Yeah, I see it."

"Do you hear it?! Can you also hear it talk? It speaks directly into your mind — I don't know how it does it."

"Yeah, yeah, I hear it..." He paused for a bit, simply staring at the fox, open-mouthed. "What is that?"

"I don't know!" Rena cried out, all her frustration with the animal bubbling to the surface. "It's everywhere! Everywhere I go, it shows up and just runs away! And now it's started talking and telling me to hurry up and I don't know what it wants!"

"Maybe my wound's worse than I thought," Logan mumbled, his eyes still transfixed on the animal that hadn't moved since it'd shown up. "I didn't think I had a fever but—"

"You don't! It's actually there!"

"Your time is running out," the voice said again, carried by a breeze that wasn't truly there.

"Why do you always have to be so mysterious?!" she called out to the fox, desperately wanting to get closer to it but afraid it would run away if she moved. "Why can't you just tell me what's going on? Are you helping me? Are you working with the Crow? What is this? What are you?!"

"I can show you the way," it said and stood up, still staring straight at her, its mouth never moving as it spoke.

"The way to what?! The monastery? Why can't you just say that? Why should I follow you when I'm not even sure where we're going?"

"Trust me."

It suddenly bounded up and turned around in the same motion before it simply ran away, never looking back to see if they would follow.

Rena's body lurched forward on its own, but she managed to stop herself, uncomfortable with the feeling the fox instilled in her. She watched it disappear into the darkness, a deep-down part of her crying out for her body to move, but she didn't want to repeat what had happened in Hrevim. She didn't trust the fox anymore, not as long as it refused to tell her the truth.

"Are we... going to follow it?" Logan asked hesitantly.

Rena stared at where the fox had disappeared and steeled herself.

"No," she said, determined. "I'm not going to reward this kind of behaviour. We can follow the hoofmarks on our own."

"Okay," Logan replied but she could see the nervousness in his posture and she was sure the same strange urge was coursing through him. "Left or right?"

Rena looked around but the night was too dark to see very far.

"Right," she finally said as it felt less like they would be heading back to Paemehri.

"So," Logan said, dragging the word out, "where the fox went?"

"Shut up," she muttered with a small smile on her lips and started walking again.

They walked for what felt like another hour. The further they got, the more Rena started to lose hope, started to think that maybe following the hoofmarks had been a bad idea and that she should have just gotten over her pride and followed the fox, but she couldn't think about all that for too long. She had to focus on the Crow and Kalani and her sister — trust in her own decisions. Simply going back to Paemehri wasn't an option anymore. It would feel too much like abandoning them all over again.

"Wait," Logan whispered as he grabbed her arm and stopped.

They could hear something far away, something very quiet that might have been an encampment. Rena slowly looked around, her entire body stiff, until she saw a faint light in the distance to their right.

"Is that... it?" she whispered, her heart in her throat.

"I really hope so," Logan responded.

Even though she couldn't see it yet, her nerves started to unravel. She couldn't believe they had finally reached it, that she was only a few steps away from her sister.

"Okay," Rena replied in a shaky voice. "Let's get closer."

They approached slowly, glancing in every direction to make sure they were alone. More lights joined the one they'd seen as they got closer but not enough to signal they'd found another city. Whatever they were advancing towards, it was on top of a hill, partly carved into the rock, with partially collapsed stone walls covered in lichen.

They were coming up to the structure from the side, making it hard to see if anyone was standing guard at the entrance. Out of caution, they snuck closer as quietly as possible until they saw that hundreds of the same crudely carved bird figurines Rena had found in Oceansthrow were hanging from the walls. Rena's heart skipped a beat at the sight of them, the memories of the fire flooding back instantly.

Logan kept a hand on her arm as they reached the old monastery, careful not to alarm any potential guards. They stopped to listen and scan the area, hoping they could find any signs of Kalani or the others. It was impossible to know if they had found their way here or if they had potentially already headed back to Paemehri— maybe they had even dared to enter the monastery. Some activity could be heard from inside the building, indicating that it was indeed occupied, although the noise was so faint that it didn't tell Rena and Logan much.

They stepped forward a bit until Logan stopped her and dropped low, nodding in the direction of a person leaning against the monastery's stone wall where Rena supposed the entrance gate had to be. They observed the person for a bit, but there was no indication that Logan and Rena had been spotted. Indeed, the person barely moved at all, making Rena wonder if they had maybe nodded off.

She glanced over at Logan, asking him without words what they should do next. He looked hesitant, just as she felt. Both of them knew that the smart choice would be to head back before anyone noticed their presence but they'd discovered so little of use, it would feel like a waste of time if they turned around. And Kalani had been right — of course Rena couldn't leave without making sure her sister was inside and unharmed.

She glanced over at the building and the surrounding hills, wondering how they could possibly sneak their way into the monastery.

"Come this way."

Rena's head spun around to the fox that was sitting on a stone to their right, eyes glowing in the dark as it stared at her.

Chapter Twenty-Eight

Rena

Rena stared at the fox, both of them unmoving. She wanted to argue, to tell it she didn't want to follow until she knew what it wanted, but it was becoming increasingly difficult to resist its strange pull. She stepped forward, involuntarily, then tensed her body so she wouldn't walk any further.

"Rena," Logan said, an air of distress to his voice, "I don't think I like your fox very much. Something feels wrong."

"I know," she replied in a shaky voice, not taking her gaze off the fox's glowing eyes.

"Almost like when Silac did his trick," Logan murmured, his body swaying next to hers.

She grabbed his arm to make sure he wouldn't follow the fox but her grip soon loosened. The fox's pull felt warm, safe, as if nothing bad would happen to them if they followed, and maybe it really wouldn't. Last time, the fox had brought her exactly where she wanted to go, even if it had been through strange means. Who knows when they would have found Kalani if it hadn't been for the fox? Captain Silac had been right there when Kalani had exited that house; if Rena hadn't called her over to the other side of the street, would he have noticed her? Would he have captured her again? How could she mistrust it, if it had helped her so often?

"Please bring me to Kalani again," she whispered and stepped forward.

The fox stood up slowly and turned around. For once, it didn't run away, but simply jumped off its stone and walked away at a pace Rena could easily follow.

"You think it knows where to go?" Logan asked, his hand coming to lightly grab Rena's arm after she had let go of his.

Even with his grip on her, he didn't stop her and they slowly followed the fox, too entranced by it to really pay attention to their surroundings.

"Yeah," she replied, breathy, and found herself truly believing it.

The fox led them through the dark, past one of the crumbling walls until they reached a crack in it. The wall had split right in the middle of Tavuu'Moda's symbol, the same one they'd seen in Miller's Knee and Oceansthrow. The symbol had clearly been carved into the wall a long time ago as moss had formed in the grooves of the triangle. Back in the day, it must have been almost Rena's size, but now the lower triangle was missing and the dot in the middle was barely more than a speck. Fresher symbols had been carved all around it, much smaller and much less precise, as if someone had carved it over and over by hand.

The fox slipped through the crack and Logan right after, letting go of her as if he barely remembered she was there. Rena approached the crack but then her body lurched back, the memories of the shrinking passage in Hrevim flooding back. She stared at the crack, at the darkness beyond it where the moon couldn't reach, and she could feel the walls closing in on her again, could feel her lungs struggle to breathe.

"Logan?" she called out, her voice barely above a whisper but she didn't dare speak louder.

She waited for him to reply, strained her ears to hear his footsteps, but all she could hear was a strange murmur from far away.

The fox's warmth was still pulling at her, telling her to follow it through the crack, that nothing bad would happen to her, so she closed her eyes and squeezed herself through. She opened her eyes and breathed in deeply on the other side. Her eyes needed a moment to adjust but she wasn't in complete darkness. She appeared to be in a small, empty room, and a faint trickle of light came in from an open door in front of her. She paused to listen if anyone was close by, but couldn't hear anything besides the hum she'd already heard outside. She slowly advanced, holding her hands out to not trip over anything in the dark.

She recoiled as she reached the entrance but soon noticed that the motionless figure standing in the corridor was just Logan.

"Where did it go?" she whispered and turned to look down both directions.

"I..." Logan looked at her in confusion as if he'd just woken up. "I don't know."

The strange pull was gone and Rena could feel the cold of the night settle on her skin again.

"I really don't like this fox," Logan muttered, a strange look of fear on his face, one Rena hadn't seen on him even after their encounter with Silac.

She wrapped her arms tightly around herself, her eyes still wandering from side to side as if she hoped the fox would come back for them. They were in a sparsely decorated hallway that looked down upon an inner court. Rena carefully stepped forward and finally saw where the faint light was coming from. At the other end of the monastery, where the building had been carved into the rock of the hill, was a giant bonfire. A shudder ran down her back, her muscles instantly tensing up as she saw the fire, and her body automatically turned away from it. Without thinking, she headed back into the room they'd come from, pushing her forehead into the cold stone until she was surrounded by darkness, but the fire had etched itself into her vision. Her breathing came in too shallow and too fast, making her head dizzy. She planted her palms against the wall, letting the cold run through her arms and ground her.

"Rena?" Logan asked quietly, staying a few steps away from her.

"I'm okay," she said feebly as her breathing calmed down. "I just hadn't expected to see such a big fire."

"Yeah, no, of course. Nobody can blame you for not liking that sight anymore."

She slowly pushed herself away from the wall and took a few shaky breaths before turning around. She stepped out of the room again but didn't get close to the banister, letting Logan describe the scene to her instead.

"I can't see much but I think there are a handful of people around the fire. Not that many though."

"What are they doing?"

"I don't know... They're sitting around the fire? Or maybe kneeling. Hard to tell from far away."

He paused for a moment, frowning at the scene in front of them. The break in his description gave them a chance to hear the hum they'd noticed outside. It was loud enough to make out human voices but not loud enough to understand the words.

"Are they... chanting?" Logan wondered, baffled.

The hum was monotonous, repetitive, and Logan probably wasn't far off the truth with his guess.

"The ritual," Rena whispered absent-mindedly.

Something strange twisted in her belly, pulling at her heart and lungs, as her mind imagined the million things that could be happening near that bonfire, the million things the Crow could be doing to her sister.

Logan looked at her as if he didn't quite understand what she was talking about, mouthing the words back at her.

"What Rodrick was talking about," she replied, but her mouth was too dry to explain further.

She still couldn't wrap her mind around all the theories Rodrick had tried to explain to them. It felt too strange, too surreal, but then nothing in the last two weeks had felt normal. She wanted to run through the entire monastery until she found her sister but she knew how stupid that would be. Now wasn't the time to let her feelings get the better of her, not when she was so close to saving Maya. No matter how much the fox's warning weighed on her, she needed to stay calm.

Logan stepped back from the banister and looked to the right and left, trying to determine which way they should go, then nodded to the right.

"Let's be careful, okay? We don't know how many of these freaks are here."

Rena nodded and took a deep breath to regain control of her body.

They walked down the corridor, careful not to let their steps make too much noise. Rena wondered how many people inhabited this building. It had to be more than just the ones around the fire, but she had kind of expected the entire monastery to be brimming with acolytes. She remembered the tracks she'd seen near Oceansthrow before stumbling upon the fire, how she'd thought an army had ridden through their region. All this time, she'd assumed that the Crow had to be massive, that even if not all of them were staying in this monastery, there at least had to be a hundred people, but she couldn't feel the presence of any of them.

She knew that it partially had to do with it being the middle of the night. The part of the monastery they'd found themselves in looked decrepit and probably uncomfortable to live in, but she couldn't even hear any footsteps coming closer which meant no guard was patrolling the corridors. Most rooms they passed were empty, with no doors in the doorframes, dust and lichen having taken over the stone floors. Maybe the Crow simply hadn't anticipated that anyone might enter the building from the crack the fox had shown them — they might not even be aware of it — and had therefore not bothered with securing that area of the building.

They rounded a corner, following the corridor along the inner court. They were getting closer to the bonfire and slowly Rena could feel its heat. She still couldn't make out what the people were chanting, but it seemed to be a short sentence, something soft they murmured over and over again. She wasn't sure it was in any language she understood. In all likelihood it was something in Mohrishim, the language inscribed on the bird figurine, but she doubted her short session at the library had been enough to comprehend what they were saying.

On the other side of the monastery, in the dark shadows beyond the inner court, stood three figures. Rena froze, afraid they'd been spotted, until her eyes had adjusted to the dark. It took Rena no time at all to recognise Kalani and even though there were several metres between them, Rena could still see how her eyes grew wide in shock that quickly turned into anger. Rena tried to smile but it was a pitiful one.

"She is gonna rip our heads off when she gets to us," Logan whispered from the corner of his mouth, waving weakly at Kalani.

"She will understand," Rena whispered back but she didn't really believe it herself.

To either side of Kalani stood Asha and Finn, both with looks of confusion, although Asha looked angrier.

Kalani gestured to the side, her movements quick and harsh, and Rena understood that she wanted them to meet up somewhere safer. If she understood the monastery's layout correctly, the corridor they were in was one piece that wrapped around the inner court so it would be easy for the two groups to meet in the middle.

"At least we know they're safe and sound, right?" Logan said as he turned back around.

They found their way back in front of the empty room the fox had led them through with an angry Kalani hurrying towards them from the other side.

"What are you doing here?" she hissed as she got to them.

Logan stepped back and pointed towards Rena and she couldn't believe that he would rat her out that quickly.

"I was worried," she pleaded, forcing herself to look into Kalani's furious eyes. "I felt like I was suffocating just waiting in that room!"

"You didn't try to stop her?" Asha asked Logan in a hushed voice as she walked up beside Kalani.

"I couldn't have even if I'd tried to," he replied, his hands up in defence. "She would have left with or without me!"

"I really don't understand what got into you, Rena," Kalani said, looking at her in bewilderment.

"It was never fair of you to demand I stay behind! You don't know what it felt like — I was about to burst out of my skin!"

"You couldn't have waited just a few hours for us to get back?!"

"No!" she burst out, louder than she'd intended. She froze, waiting to hear if anyone had noticed them, then continued, quieter. "I can't stand the thought of not knowing if you all are safe or not! And knowing that we're so close to Maya and not going to look for her?! That's torture, Kalani. The fox told me we needed to hurry and I know not everyone agrees that we should listen to it but what if it's right? What if we come back tomorrow and it's too late? What if right now is the last moment we have to save Maya?"

Kalani stared at her, her jaw clenching as if she wanted to reply, but then she whirled around and ran a hand over her face.

"For fuck's sake," she muttered into her hands and turned back around. "This was such a stupid and dangerous decision." She paused, the fury in her eyes slowly dying down. "But I get it. I can't pretend I wouldn't have done the same."

"How is your injury?" Finn asked Logan, the only one of the three where concern had replaced his confusion. "I thought we'd agreed that you should rest."

A look of surprise washed over Logan, quickly replaced with a bold grin.

"At least someone cares about me," he said, one hand running through his hair. "But I'm fine, there's really nothing to worry about."

"You were complaining the whole way here," Rena muttered.

"Then maybe you shouldn't have dragged an injured man along with you," Kalani told her and instantly the heat of shame rose up Rena's chest and face.

"Where's Rodrick?" Asha demanded. "Please tell me you didn't bring an old man and dog with you to this."

"Still in Paemehri," Rena replied.

"At least one of you morons has some sense."

"Have you found Maya?" Rena asked carefully, strangely afraid of what Kalani might answer.

"No, but that wasn't our priority." Kalani crossed her arms and looked out at the inner court. "We first need to figure out how many people are here and what they're doing."

"It seems calm," Rena said.

Kalani stayed quiet for a while, then replied pensively, "We can't know that until we've explored the entire building. Most of them are probably sleeping in the rooms below."

"Michael also mentioned that they had more than one base," Asha noted.

"Yes but if they are doing the ritual here, shouldn't this be the main base?" Rena asked.

"You think the bonfire is part of some ritual?"

"What else could it be? If they're keeping Maya here and they've got all those figurines hanging everywhere and they're chanting, it does feel like it's all part of a ritual, even if we don't really know what they're trying to do."

"Rena..." Asha started, clearly unsure how to continue her sentence. "There is always the possibility that Maya isn't here."

"But the fox led us here!"

"You saw the fox again?" Kalani turned to look at Rena in shock.

"Yeah, just now." Rena gestured back to the room they'd come from. "It showed us a safe way in."

"It's a fucking weird animal," Logan said, remembering the encounter with some unease. "The way it can speak right into your mind."

"What?" Finn asked, a terrified look on his face.

"And it's almost like Silac's controlling thing but different. Less forceful. Makes you think you want to do what it tells you."

"That's not possible," Finn replied, his voice barely over a whisper, trying to wrap his mind around something that shouldn't exist.

"Fucking dangerous is what I'd call it," Asha muttered.

"It led us back to you," Rena said sheepishly even though she didn't completely disagree with Asha.

"We can talk about this fox another time," Kalani said, her gaze back on the inner court. "The longer we stay here, the likelier they are to find us."

Chapter Twenty-Nine

Rena

The others reluctantly agreed to search the premises further. They all knew what a mess Rena would be if she had to leave without seeing a sign of her sister's location and well-being. Rena had had to promise that she'd let Kalani decide when it was time to head back. She could admit that all of them getting caught — or killed — was a worse outcome than having to turn back and try again in the morning, no matter how horrifying the thought of leaving her sister behind was to her.

They silently walked down the corridor in the direction of the bonfire, stopping every once in a while to listen whether they were still alone. The corridor they were in was at least two storeys higher than the inner court, which gave them the perfect view of the fire with minimal risk of being spotted. Rena counted about six people but the fire was concealing at least three more from her view. They were hunched over something, a repetitive motion accompanying the words they were chanting.

She carefully stepped forward until she was at the banister. The people seemed to be carving something and she had the suspicion that it was the same bird figurines she'd seen in Oceansthrow, the same ones that were hanging in droves outside the monastery. She vaguely remembered Rodrick mentioning something about carving as an act of prayer, as if the act of doing it over and over again would reinforce whatever they were praying for.

As one of the acolytes finished their carving, they held the bird up high for a moment, then tossed it into the bonfire. Only then did Rena notice that the base of the fire was filled with these birds. Ash spilt out below it, as if the fire had been going for a very long time, and Rena wondered how many of these figurines had been carved and thrown into the fire for it to roar so high.

She suddenly caught a whiff of the fire and she gagged, instantly having to whirl around or she might have puked. She could feel the taste of it at the back of her throat, like the day of the fire when she'd had to approach Oceansthrow and the air had been a torture to breathe.

"Everything all right?" Asha's hand came to rest lightly against Rena's elbow.

Rena nodded, her breathing coming in shakily. She squeezed her eyes shut and forced herself to take deep breaths before she turned around again.

"What does your sister look like?" Logan asked, his gaze wandering over the scene below, his eyebrows slightly knit together in concern.

"She's fifteen," Rena said in a trembling voice, "a bit shorter than me, with hair that looks like mine, just cut short below her chin, but our faces look quite similar."

"I don't think I see her down there," he muttered as he craned his neck.

"I didn't see her either."

"I think it's more likely she's being held in one of the rooms below," Kalani said in a quiet voice. "Probably one that is guarded."

They moved carefully as a group, making sure their steps made as little noise as possible, and took the stairs down. As they reached the floor below, they started hearing footsteps and Kalani signalled for their group to stop until she was satisfied that the one patrolling the corridors was far away. They continued on while crouching, aware that the architecture of the place would make it easy for someone to see them from the other side of the court. Kalani peeked around the corner and waved at the others to advance as a door a few metres away opened. Kalani grabbed Asha's trouser leg and yanked her back, then whirled around and pressed her back against the wall. They all stayed perfectly silent, not even daring to breathe, waiting to hear in which direction the footsteps would go. Rena found it difficult to hear them above the hammering of her heart. She counted the seconds that passed, terrified of what they might have to do if the acolyte saw them, but after she'd reached a hundred and no one had spotted them yet, she relaxed. She could feel the collective relief run through her companions as their shoulders untensed one by one.

Kalani waited a few more heartbeats before she gestured for them to advance once more. They headed down to the ground floor, not having noticed any acolytes guarding any doors on the first floor. Rena barely dared to breathe as they snuck through the old monastery. The closer they got to the bonfire, the brighter the corridors were lit, which made it incredibly daunting to advance. It felt like anyone could spot them from metres away if they only turned around at the right time and the thought of it made Rena nauseous.

Kalani stopped them again at the foot of the stairs and peeked around the corner before turning to Asha and nodding once. Rena's heart skipped a beat. Had they finally found the right room? Asha's hand wrapped around her sword and she stepped away from their group, any noise she made overshadowed by the chanting near the bonfire. Only a few pillars and the open court separated them from the fire, but Rena desperately tried not to look at it. Her eyes drifted up to the bird figurines hanging from the banisters all around the court and she started counting them to prevent herself from rushing after Asha. They were so close to rescuing Maya; she couldn't ruin it by letting her concern for her sister get the better of her.

A muffled hit, a strangled cry, then nothing. Kalani stepped out from behind the corner, signalling for the others to follow her slowly. An acolyte lay unconscious on the floor, Asha crouching in front of them. Rena rushed past Kalani on tiptoes and pressed her ear against the door, then leaned down to look through the keyhole.

The room beyond wasn't fully dark as a soft glow illuminated it — probably from a candle — but all Rena could see beyond the keyhole was the stone wall and the edge of a bed. She tried to look through the hole from different angles, but the room didn't want to reveal itself to her. She stood back up, placing a hand on the door handle, then looked back at Kalani for approval. Kalani looked worried — her glance flicking between the acolyte on the floor, the banisters above them and the bonfire that was much too close — but then still nodded for Rena to open it.

Rena placed her second hand on the space between door and frame, and pushed down on the handle as slowly as she could. When the handle was fully down, she carefully pulled the door but then felt the strain against the bolt.

She sighed and turned back around to her companions, shaking her head in disappointment. Asha rummaged through the acolyte's uniform until she located a key, which she threw to Rena, who caught it between both hands.

Rena breathed in deeply and turned around, sliding the key into the lock as quietly as she could. She turned it, wincing at the loud *thock* the bolt made as it unlatched. She pushed the handle down again and this time the door opened.

She'd never opened a door so slowly in her life, but she desperately wanted to avoid it creaking. She could feel everyone's eyes on her and their tension multiplied hers. Rena's heart hammered wildly in her chest as the door opened wide enough for her to peek inside, but then it dropped. She frowned, a deep confusion settling over her. In the bed to her right lay a person who could not be Maya. The light that illuminated the room, the one Rena had assumed to be a candle, emanated from a person. At first, Rena tried to find the object the person had to be holding that could create such a light — something like what they'd encountered in the archives or in Hrevim — but the more she looked at the body, the more it seemed like a fire was dancing under their skin.

She stepped into the room as if in a daze, transfixed by the person in front of her.

"What?" Logan muttered as he entered the room behind her, just as confused.

The rest slowly spilt into the room, dumbfounded, staring at the glowing person who didn't seem conscious enough to have noticed their entry.

"Rena?" a small voice asked from behind them.

Chapter Thirty

Rena

Rena whirled around. In a corner behind her sat a small figure, legs pulled close to the body. It took Rena's mind a second to recognise who it was, but then she leapt forward, falling to her knees as she reached her sister.

"Oh my stars, Maya!" she cried out, her hands sliding around her sister's face, turning it from side to side to inspect it. "How are you? Are you hurt? What did they do to you? Did they treat you right? Did they feed you?"

She kissed her sister all over, not waiting for Maya to reply, so relieved that she was alive, that the Crow hadn't done anything bad to her. No strange green veins ran over her face, nothing had replaced her beautiful eyes, no burn marks poked out from beneath her clothes. The fox had been right to urge her along. Who knew how long Maya would have stayed unharmed like this?

"Stop," Maya mumbled, trying to pull her face away from Rena's attack. "I'm fine! Rena, let go!"

"I will never let go of you ever again," Rena affirmed between kisses.

"Please," Maya said between giggles, dragging out the word, and it was the best sound Rena had ever heard.

Rena gave her another dozen kisses, then pulled away to look at her. "What happened to you? Did they hurt you?"

Maya shook her head and unfolded her legs, putting her hands over Rena's to free herself.

"Too much happened. I'll have to tell you later. It would take too long." She stopped and looked over at Rena's companions, who were all staring at her in various stages of disbelief. "Who are they?"

A wide smile spread over Rena's face. She felt so thankful to all of them that they'd helped her get her sister back. She would need to take the time to thank them thoroughly.

"They're my friends," she told her sister, full of pride. "They helped me find you."

Warmth spread all through Rena's body, all the joy that had been drained from her in the past two weeks flooding back as if a dam had broken. She wanted to hug Maya and never let go, to grab her hand and tie them together so nothing could separate them ever again.

Kalani stepped forward, crouched next to them and held a hand out to Maya in greeting.

"Hello, Maya. My name's Kalani. We're here to free you."

Maya looked at her with wide, suspicious eyes, then looked over at the other three, observing them carefully for a while, then down at Kalani's hand before she decided to shake it.

"Okay. Then let's go."

Rena backed off and got up, giving Maya enough room to stand up. The Crow had dressed her in the same clothes they wore — dark red tights under black trousers with a loose, white shirt — and an unreasonable rage overtook Rena. She wanted to rip the uniform off Maya's body and burn it, but she would have to endure the sight until they were back in Paemehri and she could give Maya back her dress.

Beyond the clothes, Maya didn't look in bad shape. Her hair was unruffled and her face and hands were dirty but she didn't seem wounded. Even when Rena observed her getting up and stepping into the middle of the room, she was relieved to see that Maya did everything with ease.

"You're all here for me?" Maya asked sceptically as she eyed Rena's companions.

"Pretty much, yeah," Logan replied, then gestured vaguely at the open door. "And for whatever the hell's going on out there."

As if Logan's comment had dragged her out of a trance, Asha stepped out and dragged the unconscious guard into the room, closed the door behind her to lean against it, and turned to Kalani.

"Should we keep going or head out? We still have no idea what they're trying to do here."

Kalani turned to Maya, her expression growing serious.

"Did they take anyone else from Oceansthrow?"

"Yeah, but I haven't seen them since we got here," Maya replied.

"Who did they take?" Rena asked.

"Túlio and Luisa."

"They're so young," Rena muttered.

Mixed feelings rushed through Rena. She hadn't really considered that the Crow might have taken more children but the thought of it horrified her. Why did the Crow need these children? What were they planning? Was it truly to implant their god into the children's bodies?

Rena didn't want to continue that thought spiral. She had to focus on what was right in front of her, on the fact that she could finally hold Maya's hand again.

"We'll have to come back for them later," Kalani said but it was clear to see that she wasn't very happy with the decision.

It was, sadly, also very clear to everyone that they might not be able to come back for the other two children. Once the Crow noticed that Maya was gone, they would probably move location. Rena ignored the panic trying to spread through her and only focused on her sister. Once they found their way back out of the monastery, they would need to search for a place where they could be safe. She hoped Cass would let them stay in the city of Rancor, at least for a little while.

"So... what's up with this guy?" Logan pointed to the glowing figure on the bed, pulling everyone out of their gloom.

A strange shadow fell over Maya's face, a mix of pain and anguish. Rena wanted to tear the whole place down because of it, rip reality and time apart so whatever her sister had gone through would never actually happen. If the fox could play around with reality, why couldn't she?

"He's..." Maya clearly struggled to express what was going through her mind. "... strange. I don't know how to explain it."

"Is he... alive?" Rena looked the body up and down.

"Yeah, I think so. At least he moves around sometimes."

"Why did they lock you in here with him?" Logan asked.

"I don't know," Maya replied, her eyebrows drawing together in concern. "They're trying to do something but they didn't explain it to me. I'm supposed to get used to his presence, for some reason. They treated him like the highest royalty but, honestly, he's just a jerk."

If the Crow treated this person like royalty, that could only mean one thing. It was strange knowing that she was in the presence of a god, or at least the Crow's vision of one. In any case, he didn't look much like a god, even with the light emanating from him. She had imagined Tavuu'Moda to be grander, to instil fear in her or at least awe, not to be an unconscious body struggling to breathe being consumed by a fire in his chest. She almost pitied him. Had he chosen this existence or had the Crow forced it upon him? It was hard to tell. It could very well be that he had never chosen to be reborn.

As they all stared at the body, the rasping suddenly got louder and the glow intensified. With a jerky motion, the body sat up and turned to look at them, a red-and-orange light shining out of his eyes, blinding them.

Before Rena could truly grasp what was going on, Maya had grabbed her wrist and was running towards the door. Asha jumped out of their way and Maya ripped the door open with no regard for the noise it might make. She darted out and headed right, not caring whether there were any acolytes waiting for them or not.

"Which way out?" she called over her shoulder to Rena.

"The stairs! Go up the stairs!"

The chanting from the bonfire got quieter but never disappeared. Maya ran up the stairs three steps at a time until they'd reached the second floor. Doors flung open from the corridors around them and Rena thanked the stars that the fox had shown them a way out so far away from any human being.

Asha dashed past them, Kalani close behind. Rena looked back and was relieved to see that Logan and Finn were not far behind. Distant shouting accompanied them as they raced through the upper corridor and they were halfway to their exit when Logan cursed and stumbled forward. He held one hand to his stomach, the other on the banister to hold himself up.

"Logan!" Rena called out, turning around to help him, never letting go of her sister's hand.

"Go!" he shouted back, gesturing for her to keep running, but his face was contorted in pain.

She could see in horror how a red stain spread over his shirt, but Maya didn't give her the opportunity to stay with him. Instead, Finn ran up to Logan, wrapping one arm around him, and pulled him up. He dragged him ahead, Logan stumbling along, not able to mask the pain on his face anymore.

A red glow appeared behind them, growing ever brighter until Rena could see the figure approach. He was limping but somehow that was enough to keep up with them. There was no time to wonder about that as a group of acolytes ran up to them from the other side, trying to cut off their way out.

Rena's hand slipped into her dress pocket, pulling out the knife Logan had given her in Paemehri and held it so tight that her fingers hurt. Asha and Kalani had stopped a few metres ahead, Asha's golden sword glinting in the light of the torches as she swung it at the on-coming crowd. Maya soon came to a stop, dashing from side to side to see if she could slip past the fight, but the corridor was simply too small. Five people had come their way and drawn various weapons — from daggers to wooden poles to shovels. They hardly looked ready for a fight but that didn't matter. They attacked erratically, Asha barely managing to block their attacks and control the cramped space they were in. Kalani managed to wrestle a wooden pole out of its owner's hands and pushed them back, but that only freed up space for the next attacker to approach.

Rena turned around, ready to run back where they'd come from. More people had caught up to them from behind, blocking their path. Finn drew his rapier to fend them off, letting Logan hold himself up against the wall. He held on to his own knife as if he might join the fight, but only stared at the oncoming acolytes with wide eyes.

Maya tried to drag Rena into one of the empty rooms to get away from the action, but Rena stopped her, realising right away that they'd be stuck in there with no way out. Instead, she tried to run past Asha and Kalani in hopes of reaching the crack in the wall, swinging her knife frantically at anybody in front of her. They dashed back and forth, desperate to find a gap they could slip through. The glowing body was waiting for them right behind Finn and Rena wanted to turn around once more, her mind racing trying to find a solution that simply wasn't there, but, to her dismay, Maya managed to slip out of her grasp and bolted ahead, hitting the body with her shoulders before he could even realise they were coming his way.

"Come!" she shouted at Rena as the body tumbled back, dropping to the floor to save himself from falling over the banister.

There was no time for Rena to really think about what her sister had done. Maya was too fast for her; she'd always been the fastest in the family, and Rena struggled desperately to catch up to her. She looked back at her companions, dismayed at the thought of leaving them behind, but she knew that Maya wasn't going to stop no matter what and she couldn't let her escape on her own.

Someone rounded the corner in front of them and it took Rena a moment to realise who it was. Then she recognised Inkra's wild brown hair, her furious green eyes, the scar running over her nose and under her left eye. As much as Rena had thought of the woman in the last few days, she hadn't actually expected to run into her then and there.

"You little disrespectful brat," Inkra said through gritted teeth, rage and hatred blazing in her eyes. "We should have you hanged for the way you dare treat the *Vöshirem*."

Maya dropped low and tried to dash past Inkra, barely giving her time to finish her sentence, but Inkra was faster and grabbed Maya's shirt, stopping her movement instantly so that she fell backwards. A blinding rage overtook Rena and with a roar she had never emitted before, she swung the knife at Inkra. The woman instinctively raised her free arm to protect herself and the knife slid through her clothing into her flesh. She cried out and almost stumbled to the ground as Maya tried to slip past her again. Rena didn't give her much time to adjust her stance and swung the knife at her a second time, her movements wide and uncontrolled, the rage exacerbating her ignorance of correct fighting techniques. She managed to cut the other's hand but Inkra ignored her injuries and slapped the knife out of Rena's grasp, her fist swinging around to hit her in the temple before Rena had the time to regain her stance.

Rena stumbled back, her vision momentarily going bright and blurry and it took her a moment to be able to breathe again.

"You think you can just steal what is rightfully mine?" a voice rasped behind her.

Rena turned around, the glowing body approaching slowly, the one Inkra had called *Vöshirem*, the one Rena was convinced was the current iteration of Tavuu'Moda. She stared into his eyes, the sight making her stop instantly. It was as if an inferno danced behind his eyes, as if it held the memories of Oceansthrow's and all the other towns' destruction.

Maya cried out, a fight that Rena was not privy to playing out behind her back, but she simply could not look away. The fire came ever closer but no matter how terrified Rena was, she couldn't take her eyes off it.

"I will not let you be the end of me." His voice was like the crackling of fire, like bones popping and wood snapping.

"Rena!" her sister called out behind her. "Don't look at him!"

"Shut up," Inkra said with a strain to her voice then Maya cried out again.

Something got dragged away behind Rena, but she simply couldn't move. She couldn't blink, couldn't breathe — the only thing that still existed was the terrible fire in front of her.

Chapter Thirty-One

Rena

A hand grabbed Rena's arm and pulled her away from the ever-approaching fire, and she finally snapped out of her haze.

"Where's your sister?" Logan yelled over the cacophony of the fight.

Rena whirled around in circles, panic overtaking her. Maya had been right next to her just a second ago; how could she have vanished? How could Rena have let her disappear?

"Inkra took her," Rena yelled back, petrified as the memory flooded back.

The glowing body had also disappeared. One moment it had been there, the next it was gone, as if it had never existed at all. There was no time to reflect on that, however. She needed to find her sister, fast.

"Downstairs!" she told Logan with determination, then looked down at his shirt in horror. "You're bleeding!"

"Doesn't matter now," he said and pulled her along as he ran after Inkra.

Rena looked back to where Kalani, Asha and Finn were still fending off the masses of acolytes. Her eyes met Asha, her own terror reflected in the other woman's gaze.

Logan led her down the stairs quicker than was safe as footsteps ran after them, but Rena had to focus too much on her own movement to check whether it was friend or foe. As they reached the inner court the chanting that had almost died out before got louder and more intense. Six acolytes knelt before the flames carving furiously into their figurines, the same effigies that were hanging into the court from the banisters. The intertwined triangles had been carved into every stone on the floor, the bonfire's ashes lodged into the grooves.

"Where are they?" Logan cried out as they reached the fire.

"I don't know," Rena stammered, her head whipping around in every direction, only seeing her sister once they'd run to the other side of the court.

Inkra was standing behind Maya, holding her arms tight, as Tavuu'Moda placed a hand on Maya's face. She was thrashing around, whipping her head from side to side, but the glowing body gripped her tightly, his hand enveloping her. He stepped backwards into the fire, the ash crackling under his feet. Inkra advanced with him, making sure he wouldn't lose his grip on Rena's sister. The flames licked up his legs, filling the space between him and Maya, until both their bodies glowed.

Rena cried out and rushed ahead, letting go of Logan, who was slowing down, his breathing laboured as he fell down to one knee. She tackled Inkra with all her might but it wasn't enough to make the woman lose her footing. It gave Maya, however, the opportunity to lean back against her restraints and drive her feet into Tavuu'Moda's chest, making him lose his grip and fall backwards into the fire.

"No!" Inkra yelled in distress, letting go of Maya to lunge forward.

She grabbed a hold of Tavuu'Moda's foot and dragging him out of the fire. The flames latched onto her hair and clothes but it was as if she didn't notice; it was only once her god was out of the fire that she flailed around to extinguish the flames. Tavuu'Moda tried to push himself back up but the fire was eating away at his skin, the light in his chest glowing brighter as if it was trying to burst out.

"Get her," he rasped, one arm reaching towards Maya.

Inkra whirled around, a wild rage in her eyes. Rena rushed to her sister, helping her up before Inkra could reach them. Maya had strange markings on her face, as if she'd been burned where Tavuu'Moda's fingertips had touched her.

"What did he do to you?" Rena cried out, taking her sister's head in her hands to look at the burn marks, horrified at the sight.

"I'm fine!" Maya yelled back and wriggled out of Rena's grasp.

She grabbed her sister's arm before dashing away from Inkra.

Finn

Finn had made sure no one could chase Logan and Rena downstairs as they ran after Maya. It didn't feel right to abandon Kalani and Asha on the second floor, but they were perfectly capable of keeping the acolytes at bay and the other two would need his help more. He reached the inner court as Logan was scrambling to get back up and Rena and her sister were running away from Inkra. Finn darted forth as Inkra got a hold of the back of Maya's shirt and was trying to pull her back to the bonfire. He lunged forward, unable to calculate his movement precisely so that his rapier only grazed the top of the woman's ear. It was enough to destabilise her and with a second flick of his wrist, he swung his rapier up, making Inkra lean back to avoid the tip of the blade. Rena pulled her sister forward, ripping her out of Inkra's grip as the woman stumbled backwards, unable to keep her balance.

"Rena!" someone called out from the other end of the court, and they all whirled around to see Rodrick ride in through the half-open entrance gate, Vincent right at his side. Next to Rodrick rode a second man, someone Finn had never seen before.

"Oh my stars, what happened?" the second man called out and slid off the horse. He didn't land right and tumbled to the ground but quickly pushed himself back up, ignoring everyone to run ahead towards the glowing body. "*Vöshirem,* what happened?"

"Michael?" Inkra called out in disbelief as the man ran up to their god and knelt before the crumbling body at the edge of the fire.

"Rena, are you all right?" Rodrick exclaimed as he slid off his horse.

"Why was Michael with you?" Rena asked as she ran up to him, looking back at the man who'd accompanied her friend in bewilderment.

"I'll explain later."

Rodrick looked up, his eyes meeting Finn's before looking over at Logan.

"I've got him," Finn called out, waving for the others to get out.

He turned back to the injured man and slid an arm around his waist. Blood was dripping down Logan's body, leaving a trail on the floor as they hobbled towards the exit.

From either side, acolytes rushed into the court. Finn counted a small dozen, a handful less than had been on the second floor. The commotion made the horses nervous, and it didn't take long for them to flee the monastery. Finn cursed under his breath. Horseback would have been the fastest way to get Logan back to Paemehri. Without it, Finn dreaded how long it would take them to get him the healing he needed.

Finn looked back, rapier at the ready to push any attackers back, but then he saw a flash of of gold at the base of the stairs. Asha had followed the acolytes down and was keeping them from reaching the rest of their group. Finn supposed Kalani couldn't be far behind. Rodrick came up to them and slid under Logan's other arm, the two girls far ahead weaving a path towards the exit. The dog circled them, then ran ahead, darting from companion to companion to make sure they were all accounted for.

"What are you doing, you useless cunt?" Inkra screamed at the one who'd accompanied Rodrick. "Go catch the girls! We have to finish the transference."

"This isn't right, Inkra!" Michael said, his voice full of desperation.

Inkra roared and turned her attention back to Rena and Maya. Before she could leap ahead, Finn slid out from Logan's grasp, trusting Rodrick to hold him up, and darted in front of her, rapier at the ready. Inkra didn't let it stop her as she rammed into him with full force. He toppled to the floor, the impact knocking his blade out of his hand.

He tried to scramble back to his feet but Inkra kicked him in the chest, pushing him closer to the fire, the impact pushing all the air out of his lungs.

Inkra turned her furious gaze back towards the girls but then Michael came to stand in front of her.

"I said this isn't right!" he insisted. "It was never meant to happen like this. None of this has been right for a long time. We've lost our way, Inkra!"

"Get out of my fucking way," she growled, pushing him to the side, but he held on to her arm.

"Look at the *Vöshirem*," he pleaded. "This is not what the transference is supposed to look like. You should never have rushed it."

"You fucking traitor," Inkra screamed and punched him in the jaw with all her might.

Michael tumbled back, losing his grip on her, but the argument had given Finn enough time to regain his footing and jump at Inkra from behind. They tumbled to the ground, squirming around in the bonfire's ashes, tearing at hair and clothes and skin.

Rena

A broad-shouldered acolyte put himself in Maya's path, but she swiftly slid underneath his arms, never letting go of Rena's hand. Everything was happening too fast for Rena to process or even register how her body was moving. She simply had to trust her sister and hope luck was on their side. Someone caught Maya's arm and, without really thinking about it, Rena punched them in the throat. Pain shot up her entire arm but the impact had been enough for the acolyte to choke and let go of Maya.

"You can't escape," Tavuu'Moda said in his deep voice, the sound carrying over like a far-away fire, barely audible above the cacophony of the fight.

Maya faltered and tripped over her own feet, tumbling clumsily to the ground.

"I will always exist," Tavuu'Moda continued, the voice coming from everywhere and nowhere. "You cannot stop it."

Maya looked back, a look of absolute terror on her face, the bonfire reflecting bright orange in her eyes. Rena couldn't stand the sight of it. She put herself between her sister and the bonfire, blocking the reflection in her eyes, and pulled her up with all her strength.

Two more horses dashed past them, rearing up as they reached the centre of the court. Rena ignored them, her entire focus on the old metal gates at the end of the inner court. She dragged her sister up, holding on tightly to her wrist, and started running again.

"Get back here!" Silac's voice echoed over the court.

Rena looked back in shock, only then realising that he had been one of the riders who had passed them. That horrible energy flooded her body again and she changed direction without wanting to, heading back towards the fire.

Rena fought the feeling with all her might as panic settled over her. She tried to turn her body but all she managed to do was twist her head to look back at Maya in fear. She needed to move her shoulders. If at least she could twist her body, she might be able to destabilise her core and make herself fall to the ground. She wouldn't be able to forgive herself if she led Maya back to the bonfire and into Tavuu'Moda's arms.

"Bring me your sister," Silac called to her, his horse rearing up.

The green veins shot across his face and down his throat, overtaking most of his skin. His coat was ripped apart at his sleeve and revealed a bloody bitemark on his left forearm, the veins reaching the edge of the wound.

Rena's grasp tightened on her sister's hand as her vision focused in on Silac, everything else drowning in a blur.

"Rena, what are you doing?" Maya cried out, pulling desperately at her sister. "You're hurting me!"

Rena pushed against the feeling until it felt like her body was about to rip apart. If she strained any more, she might break her own bones, but that would be worth it. Through pain, she managed to move her eyes to the right, trying to see where her other companions were.

Logan had found a rock on the floor and was throwing it at Silac, but his aim was off and it landed short. Rodrick stood a few feet behind, paralysed with fear. Rena wanted to cry out to him, to beg him for help, but her throat was so tight she could barely breathe. Logan hobbled forward, faster than he should have been able to, and that finally dragged Rodrick out of his stupor. He ran past Logan and gestured for the injured man to slow down but before either of them could reach Silac, the captain turned his attention on them.

"Stop!" he yelled. "Lie on the ground."

The veins pulsed erratically over his skin, covering even his hands, as a trickle of blood ran out of his nose and past his mouth into his beard. Rodrick fought the command for a few more steps, then fell to his knees. Besides him, Vincent stood close to his master, snarling and barking at Silac, jumping back and forth as if too afraid to get close to the man.

The second command was enough to break Rena out of her own, as if Silac had given her a choice to follow either one. She let herself drop to the floor, pushing her fingers open, her knuckles popping with pain, freeing Maya's hand. She wanted to yell at her sister to run away, to forget about her and her companions and just get herself to safety, but she hadn't regained control of her voice yet. Maya tried to pull her up, yelling words that barely made it to Rena's ears.

Silac wiped the blood on his face away with a trembling hand. His eyes were bloodshot, more red than white, and his pupils were so small that they were barely visible. He looked over to the bonfire, searching for something until his gaze landed on the decaying form of Tavuu'Moda and his eyes widened in disgust and bewilderment.

He turned back to Rena and opened his mouth, about to give another command, when Vincent jumped up and bit him where his sleeve had already been torn. Silac cried out, the dog not letting go no matter how much the captain flailed around in pain. The attack was enough to scare his horse, which reared up again, the weight of the dog dragging Silac to the ground. He landed on his shoulder and the impact made Vincent lose his grip on the captain's arm, but it didn't take long for the dog to jump at him a second time.

The attack was enough for Silac to lose his concentration and Rena snapped out of his command, scrambling back to her feet to return to Maya.

Finn

Finn had managed to free himself from Inkra when he noticed Silac's presence. He faintly heard what he was yelling at Rena but Inkra didn't give him the possibility to go help anyone. She grabbed his leg as he tried to run away, making him trip to the ground. She lunged at him, but Finn rolled away in time and he pushed her away with his feet, destabilising her.

A horse rode up to them and someone jumped off only a few metres away.

"Don't you fucking dare touch him!" the person yelled and kicked Inkra, hitting her straight in the head, making the woman fly back.

Finn scrambled backwards, his body instinctively trying to get away from that voice.

"Nara?"

He felt like he was hallucinating. It simply made no sense that his sister was standing in front of him, her eyes filled with disgust as she looked down upon him.

"What?" He breathed the words out, unable to form coherent thoughts. "Why are you here?"

"Because of you, moron." She stepped towards him with determination and grabbed at him but just at that moment, Inkra swiped at Nara's coat to pull her down.

Nara stepped to the side, avoiding Inkra's grip, and unsheathed her rapier. Inkra pushed herself back up on her feet, blood running down her nose, a crazed look on her face as she pulled her knife out and lunged at Nara. The fight was messy and quick, a flow of swipes and grabs and strikes that never really hit anything until Nara managed to hit Inkra just under the eye with the pommel of her rapier. Inkra fell backwards, collapsing on the floor, and curled in on herself in pain.

Nara turned back to Finn, her expression wilder than before.

"It was an order," Nara told him with disdain. "Don't start believing I'm here out of the goodness of my heart. If it were up to me, I'd let these savages tear you apart."

An acolyte lunged at her from behind but Nara stepped out of the way and, in one swift motion, pierced her rapier through their throat, the attacker's motion driving their body all the way to the hilt of the sword. Nara used the momentum to let the acolyte collapse to the floor and slide her blade out of the wound, swinging the rapier once to shake the blood off.

"Why are you staring like that? Get up. You've made me waste enough time."

She stepped closer to Finn and pulled him up to his feet, her grip so tight that it hurt through layers of clothing. He wanted to react, to fight her, to free himself from her, but between the heat, the exhaustion, and the surprise of her appearance, it felt like he had lost control over his body.

"You're so fucking useless," Nara muttered and even then Finn said nothing.

His muscles were rigid as he stood up, his hands balled into tight fists. He desperately screamed at his body to do something and not just let her drag him away, but he was still stuck on the question of why she was there in the first place. Why had she arrived at the monastery with

Silac? What connection did she have to these people? None of it made sense.

From the side, Logan swung at her with his fist and hit her square in the jaw. He had put so much force into the punch that he stumbled to the ground, taking Finn's sister with him, her rapier skittering away. She cursed at him, fumbling to get back up and get to her blade but Logan whirled around and tripped her up, Nara hitting the floor hard. Logan attempted to push himself back up but slipped, clearly having run out of energy. Nara tried to rush back to her rapier but Finn got to it first and slid it to the other side of the court.

She screamed, trying to lunge at her brother. One of the acolytes got in between them, although it was clear on their faces that they weren't even sure who they should be fighting. Nara swivelled the acolyte around until they had their back to the bonfire, then kicked them into the flames. Finn didn't take the time to look at the horrifying scene, instead rushing to help Logan up. His sister turned back to face them but Logan had picked up Finn's rapier and swung it up just in time to graze the front of her shirt and cut into her chin.

From the corner of his eye, Finn noticed the glowing body kneeling next to Inkra, the fire having burst out of his skin and melted his body. Parts of him fell to the ground in disgusting dollops, leaving behind blood and exposed flesh. He leaned down and helped Inkra up, smearing her with blood and gore, before pulling her towards the fire.

A scream to his left pulled Finn's attention to flames that had spread to the lichen and vines covering the stones of the monastery, climbing up the walls until they leapt onto the figurines dangling from the banisters.

The place erupted in chaos, people running in every direction, the fire spreading over every surface it could get a grip on. Finn pulled Logan up, dragging him away from the fire and Nara. The flames of the bonfire roared impossibly high, spreading further and further as if they were trying to swallow everything.

Nara wiped the blood off her chin, her furious gaze darting between Finn, Logan and her rapier on the other side of the court. Before she could move, Asha ran into her, shoulder first, and pushed her to the ground. Nara slid over the floor, getting dangerously close to the fire.

Finn turned around, knowing there was no time to waste. He couldn't worry about his sister anymore, he needed all his focus to be on getting Logan out of there alive. Nara would find a way out on her own. She always did; it was impossible for those flames to destroy her. Rena and her sister were almost at the exit, expertly evading any last attackers who were still trying to catch them. Most of the acolytes, however, were either trying to escape the burning monastery themselves or darting back to the fire — to help their doomed god or Inkra or keep the fire from spreading further, he couldn't say.

Asha caught up to them as they reached the gates, just in time to catch Logan's collapsing body. Finn didn't hesitate to pull his shirt over his head and rip it apart. They bound it around Logan's waist as best as they could, then hoisted him up on Asha's back. A half dozen horses darted past them, an acolyte running after the animals, yelling to make them flee the chaos.

Finn, Asha and Logan regrouped with the others outside the monastery. Kalani and Vincent were keeping the last attackers from reaching them; Kalani with the pole she'd confiscated from an acolyte while Vincent only had to growl at them, Silac's blood still smeared around his muzzle.

Chapter Thirty-Two

Rena

The group started the long track back to Paemehri, the burning monastery illuminating their path, eyes focused behind them to make sure no one would follow them. They stumbled their way back to Paemehri with great effort. Logan's condition grew more dire with every step but there wasn't much they could do about it. Rena tried not to think of it, tried only to focus on not collapsing herself. She wasn't sure what their plan was, but she trusted Kalani or Asha to know what to do.

They reached Paemehri and tried to enter the inn to gather their belongings, but the innkeeper had locked up for the night. They found the window to the room they'd rented and smashed it open, hoisting Rena up to retrieve their bags.

"We can't walk all the way to Hrevim," Asha hissed as they stood in the shadows next to the inn, waiting to see if they'd woken anyone up. "None of us have any energy left and Logan's bleeding out."

"I know," Kalani answered, driving the palms of her shaky hands into her eyes.

"There was a merchant's cart in the shed," Rodrick pointed out. "If we steal it, it could bring us to Hrevim before the sun rises. As long as one of the horses listens to us."

A dim light appeared in the window they'd smashed.

They stood still, holding their breaths. Someone leaned out of the window and looked around. They paused, listening to the night, but all that could be heard was the wind. After a few minutes, the figure retreated and the companions waited to hear the door creak open and shut again.

Asha moved out of the shadows, gesturing for the others to follow her. She led them to the shed and piled them all into one corner. They all pressed together and stood still as someone exited the inn with a lantern and looked around, before inspecting the window from the outside and rounding the corner of the building.

Asha held a hand to her lips as she backed out of the corner and they snuck further into the shed. As Rodrick had mentioned, a rudimentary cart stood next to the tied-up, sleeping horses. A few barrels had been placed on the cart but the rest of the space was big enough for them to travel on, even if it wouldn't be comfortable. Kalani approached the horses carefully, studying which one would be most agreeable to them, then untied a sturdy, dark brown gelding that responded calmly to her touch. They manoeuvred the cart out of the shed as quietly as possible and after some bribing with food they'd found in the shed, Rodrick managed to hitch the cart to the horse. They laid Logan flat in the middle of the cart and sat around him between the barrels while Rodrick and Kalani sat up front.

The horse wasn't a fast one, but it was the best solution they had. It would have been entirely impossible for them to find their way back to Hrevim or the city of Rancor on foot. Rena finally dared to look at Logan. His clothes were dark from blood and Rena was thankful that the moon didn't reveal their actual colour. She wished they had some water with them to clean Logan's wound. The quicker they could act, the better Logan would fare, but with the prospect of riding a few hours back to Hrevim and then finding their way to Rancor, she didn't know how he would survive. Tears blurred her vision as she pushed his shirt up, instructing Maya to pull the tin of remaining ointment and all other shirts out of their burlap sack to bandage the wound as best as they could. The skin of his stomach was covered in blood and she wiped most of it away but more flowed out of the open gash. She pressed the flesh together as she bandaged it, knowing that nothing she did would guarantee his survival.

"I know people in Hrevim," Kalani said in a tired voice, leaning her head to the side so those behind her could hear. "They'll be able to get us to Rancor as quickly as possible."

"We can stay with Maniala until Logan's better," Asha mentioned.

"No, I don't want to pull her into this. We can't guarantee we won't be followed, especially if Finn's sister's after us."

"I told you he was bad luck." Asha stared at Finn, anger burning bright in her eyes.

"Not now, Asha," Kalani said but there was no fire behind her words. "We can deal with everything once we're home. Cass will know what to do. We probably won't be able to stay in Rancor for long, not if we want to keep everyone in camp safe." She turned to look ahead, then continued in a quieter voice, "I just don't know where to go yet."

Rena leaned back against the wall of the cart, pressing her shoulder against her sister's, her trembling hands covered in blood. She still saw the flames dance in front of her eyes, how Tavuu'Moda had burned from the inside out, how his eyes had shown her Oceansthrow's inferno again. She dared a glance at Maya, at the burn marks on her temple. She didn't seem any different besides those marks, but Rena couldn't get the image out of her mind, remembering how Tavuu'Moda and Inkra had tried to drag her into the fire, how she thought she'd seen the same glow in her sister's chest that the god had had.

Maya leaned her head against her sister's shoulder and Rena rested her cheek on top, quietly looking at the darkness surrounding them, vowing to get her sister as far away from this place as possible.

DO YOU WANT TO HELP DETERMINE HOW THE STORY CONTINUES?

A Searing Faith is based on the award-winning, interactive audio drama *The Heart Pyre*, meaning that fans can help shape Rena's story. If you want to participate in determining how the adventure continues, follow *The Heart Pyre* on social media for updates, visit **www.theheartpyre.com**. Not a fan of audio dramas? The transcripts of each episode will be posted to the website, so you can also read along and help determine the story while reading.

You can listen to *The Heart Pyre* on every platform where you find podcasts, visit **https://theheartpyre.buzzsprout.com/share** to find it on your favourite platform, and listen to the bonus content.

ACKNOWLEDGMENTS

First of all, I wanted to thank Mona May for the amazing cover. It is always a delight to work with you and I cannot wait to see what we'll come up with for the rest of the series.

Then a big thank you to my editors, Maria Tureaud and Rachel from Bard & Butter. Without your hard work this book would not be half as good as it ended up being. Your commentary is invaluable to my evolution as a writer.

To all my friends at the Science Fiction and Fantasy Society Luxembourg, thank you for championing my work and being the best community you could ask for. Finding a local community is one of the best things that has happened to me. Life wouldn't be half as fun or meaningful without you.

Thank you to Jean and Keren for being my writing partners (even if there's fairly little writing getting done during our weekly meetings).

To my partner, Thierry, my parents and my family, thank you for always believing in me and being my number one fans. Thank you for being my most effective PR strategy and being better at marketing than I could ever be. So many people would never have heard of my books if you didn't spread the word for me. Your support is the main reason I keep going.

And most of all, thank you to the audio drama community and anyone who listened to The Heart Pyre on their podcatcher and helped determine how the story progresses. This book would quite literally not exist without you.

About the Author

Audrey Martin is a writer, con organiser and librarian from Luxembourg. She has a Master's in English Linguistics and a Bachelor's in 3D animation, which she definitely totally still has use for. She loves stories in all forms, be it books, video games, audio dramas, old folk tales, or anything else you can think of. As a writer, Audrey likes writing about the weird and the dark, about injustices and about how we can retain our hope until the end, about regular people who got thrust into unusual situations and about the hubris of humankind. She occasionally writes short stories which you can find on her website www.audreymartinbooks.com.

Find her on twitter and Bluesky **@audreywrites** and on Instagram and Tumblr**@audreywritesfantasy**

www.ingramcontent.com/pod-product-compliance
Lightning Source LLC
La Vergne TN
LVHW100510110826
845146LV00002B/585
9789998797260